SL BEAUMONT

The Carlswick Affair

For Mum

Contents

Prologue

T he clock in the old tower chimed eight times and fell silent. The neoclassical building was in darkness, except for a pool of light emanating from a single lamp burning in the curator's office.

A loud pounding on the front doors echoed through the stillness of the night. Karl Hoffman was startled and jumped up from his desk. Who could it be at this hour?

The pounding sounded again, louder and this time accompanied by shouting: "By order of the Führer, open up!"

"I'm coming," muttered Hoffman as he hurried down a sweeping staircase to the foyer. The moon shone in through the large picture windows, bathing the foyer in an eerie light. The normally benign marble statues standing in a semi-circle facing the doors, now cast menacing shadows. Hoffman, a short, slightly overweight, balding man in his mid-forties, shuddered and felt his heart racing as he began the process of unlocking the bolts and lifting the heavy metal bar from across the massive wooden doors. Inserting a large metal key in the lock, he had barely finished turning it when the doors

1

were pushed open with such force that he was sent sprawling backwards across the marble floor.

Heavily armed soldiers filed into the foyer and stood to attention as an officer strode in and stood over him.

"Hoffman?" he sneered. He cut an imposing figure in his Nazi uniform. He was over six foot tall, with cropped blond hair protruding from under his peaked cap.

"Yes," Hoffman replied, the icy hand of fear clutching at his throat. Having your name known by a Nazi officer was never a good thing.

The officer thrust a piece of paper towards him. "I have orders to gather all the remaining Degenerate Art that is in your possession."

Hoffman scrambled to his feet, sweat beading on his forehead. "Now? At this hour?" he asked.

"Are you questioning an order from our Führer?" the officer shouted as he began to peel off his black leather gloves.

Hoffman held up his hands and took a step backwards eyeing the soldiers' rifles uneasily. He, like many Germans, had heard the rumours of people who disagreed with a request from Hitler, disappearing, never to be seen again. "No. No – of course not. I am just surprised not to have been given more notice. I have no staff here at this hour to assist."

"This is why I have brought my men." The officer smiled a cold, cruel smile. "Now, where are they?" he demanded.

Hoffman ran a hand through his thinning grey hair and took a deep breath to steady his nerves. "Follow me." *What would they want with the art and why suddenly at this time of night?* he wondered.

He led the soldiers down a winding staircase into the depths of the gallery to a large basement room. He paused, unlocking the door.

"Now, which pieces do you require?" He glanced at the document he had been given by the officer. It didn't specify, it just stated all Degenerate Art still being held at the Nationalgalerie.

"All," the officer said sharply.

Hoffman stood up straight at the officer's tone. He wanted to know where the soldiers were taking the artworks, but he was too afraid to ask. A few years earlier, Hitler had labelled all types of modern artistic expression as Degenerate Art, and called any artist who did not have Aryan blood a degenerate. Hitler's decree of June 1937 had given Goebbels authority to ransack all of the German museums. Along with works by German artists, his team had also scooped up pieces by painters such as Picasso and van Gogh.

"The items in this room are all by lesser known artists and have little value on the international market," Hoffman said indicating the hundreds of paintings stacked on their ends in rows along the walls. Shelving at the back of the room contained many books and row upon row of bronze and terracotta statues and sculptures, stacked there only because they had been created by Jewish artists.

A wave of nausea passed over him. He recalled the Degenerate Art Exhibition he had seen in Munich in late 1937 where 650 paintings, sculptures, books and prints had been gathered from German museums and were displayed in a way that made a mockery of them. Hitler had called the artists 'incompetents, cheats and madmen' and over two million visitors had flocked to see the exhibition that Hitler said showed qualities of 'racial impurity, mental disease and weakness of character.'

Hoffman prayed that this wasn't about to happen again. He, like many in the art world, had been horrified to see works by artists such as Chagall, Klee and Mondrian treated in such a dismissive manner. But they had been powerless to stop the exhibition, which had been the brainchild of Hitler himself.

The officer signalled to his men, who pushed past Hoffman into the room and began gathering the paintings and marching back up the stairs to the foyer.

"Careful," Hoffman couldn't help but call after them, his curator's hackles raised at seeing artistic treasures so roughly treated.

The officer gave a nasty laugh. "Oh, you needn't worry about that."

The first of the soldiers returned to the room, carrying out more paintings and sculptures. In no time the room was empty.

The officer turned to Hoffman. "Are there any more?"

"Only those being prepared for auction," Hoffman lied.

The officer studied him. "Very well," he said, and turned on his heel and marched back up the stairs. Hoffman let out a shaky breath and looked sadly into the empty room before closing the door and following the officer.

"Excuse me?" he called. He couldn't help himself. He had to know. "What are you going to do with them? Is there to be another Degenerate Art exhibition?"

The officer paused at the top of the winding staircase and looked down at Hoffman with scorn and laughed. "Come, my friend, you will see."

It was then that Hoffman smelled smoke. He ran up the stairs past the officer, whose laughter echoed through the silent gallery. He pushed open the massive doors leading onto the front steps. There on the gently sloping grass frontage, the Berlin Fire Brigade had started a large bonfire and soldiers and firemen were tossing the paintings and books from the gallery's basement room onto it. Hoffman gave a cry and sank to his knees, watching in disbelief and horror as hundreds of works of art were systematically destroyed.

Chapter 1

London, August

Stephanie Cooper hauled two large suitcases out of the black cab and deposited them on the footpath. The taxi driver remained seated behind the wheel, no offer of assistance forthcoming.

Well, there goes your tip, Stephanie thought, paying him the exact amount owing for the journey. The cab pulled away, the driver muttering something about bloody tourists.

Stephanie smiled to herself. That may have been true on her previous visits to London, but she was no longer just a tourist, now she was a bona fide resident, due to start studying for her degree at Oxford in October.

Turning, she gazed across at the National Gallery, which dominated one side of Trafalgar Square. With a smile she remembered attending an exhibition with her father a couple of years earlier. Her love of Impressionism had begun that day. *I must make time to visit the Gallery again before uni starts,* she thought.

Stephanie pulled the retractable handle out of each suitcase, and adjusting the strap of her bag across her body, started walking into Charing Cross Station, wheeling the heavy suitcases behind her. Her father had offered to drive her down to Carlswick at the weekend, but Stephanie was keen to get settled into her grandmother's house, so she had decided to take the train. She might as well get used to being independent.

The light streamed onto the station concourse from the magnificent arched glass roof that joined the brick entrance of the underground to the platforms for the overland trains.

After purchasing her ticket at the electronic ticket booth, she stopped beneath the large overhead arrivals and departures board and located the platform that her train was to depart from and slowly made her way towards it. She paused briefly at a coffee stand, but just couldn't work out how she could balance a coffee cup and manage her bags at the same time. Coffee was one of the things she really missed about home. Londoners, for all their cosmopolitan ways, still seemed to be focused on tea. *God only knows what Carlswick will be like*, she thought. *I might have to start drinking the stuff.*

The train was already at the platform, its doors open ready for passengers. Bypassing the first class carriages, she stopped at the next empty one. She glanced around to make sure that it was safe to leave one of her suitcases on the platform for a moment, while she lifted the other one onto the train. A guy around her age caught her attention as he sauntered down the platform towards her, guitar case slung over his shoulder. He looked vaguely familiar. He was very attractive – tall, with messy dark hair, tight black jeans and a Beatles t-shirt. She was puzzling over where she had seen him before, when he looked up and locked eyes with her.

Caught staring, she blushed and busied herself retracting the first suitcase's handle and struggled onto the train.

"Here, can I help you?" a deep, slightly husky voice asked behind her.

When she looked around, the guy had stopped. She automatically started to say, no thank you. But looking back at her were gorgeous green eyes, framed by unfairly long black eyelashes, and the words died on her lips. Deciding it would be churlish to refuse his help, she instead replied, "Sure, why not. That would be great, eh."

He easily lifted the second bag, and placed it beside her first one in the carriage. Together they pushed the two suitcases into the empty luggage rack.

"Thank you," she smiled at him, as she took a seat in the row nearest the door.

"No problem," he smiled back at her, holding her gaze. "Going on holiday?" he asked swinging his guitar off his shoulder and sitting down opposite her.

"No. Moving. Temporarily, at least," she replied.

"Anywhere nice?" the cute guitar player asked.

"I'm going to stay with my grandmother for a couple of months before uni starts. She lives in a little village called Carlswick," Stephanie replied, before remembering that this was London, and she shouldn't be chatting to strangers as openly as this – even good looking, helpful ones. She silently admonished herself and looked down at her hands.

"I know Carlswick very well," the guy replied.

"You do?" she asked, looking up.

"Yeah, I live there," he said with a grin. "I'm James," he added, introducing himself.

"Stephanie," she replied. "You know, you look familiar. I haven't been there in a while, but maybe I've seen you in the village."

"No, I don't think so. I'd remember meeting you, trust me," James replied flirtatiously.

Stephanie inclined her head slightly and smiled shyly, acknowledging the compliment.

"And you are Australian, right?" James caught his bottom lip with his teeth and frowned slightly as he guessed.

Stephanie dragged her eyes away from his mouth and instead pulled a face at him.

"God, I got that wrong, didn't I?" James grimaced. "New Zealand?"

"Yeah, I'm a Kiwi," Stephanie confirmed.

"Would I be digging myself an even deeper hole if I said Australians and New Zealanders are very similar?" James teased.

"Similar? New Zealand wasn't settled by convicts, we have a superior rugby team, friendlier people, bigger mountains and better ice cream," Stephanie said with mock seriousness.

"And more sheep than people, if I remember correctly," James added.

Stephanie rolled her eyes and laughed. She glanced at his guitar. "You play?" she asked. *God, shoot me now! Stupid question. Of course he plays, he wouldn't be carrying it around if he didn't,* she thought, mentally kicking herself.

James gave a slight chuckle, "Yeah, you could say that. I'm in a band."

"That's cool. I might have to come and see you play," she said. One thing Stephanie loved was live music and it didn't matter how big or small the band, she could watch and listen for hours. And with eye candy like James playing, even better.

The train gave a jerk as the doors closed and it slowly pulled out of the station. Stephanie looked out of the window and watched the buildings start to rush by as the train gathered speed. She gave a sigh and settled back happily in her seat. Her adventure was beginning.

She studied James as he, too, looked out of the window. From the artfully messy hair, to the sexy grin and easy laugh, he was gorgeous. Stephanie suddenly wished she had worn something a little nicer than skinny jeans and a little tank top.

As though he sensed her scrutiny, he turned his head and locked eyes with her again. Her breath caught in her throat. *Wow. Now say something witty and entertaining*, she told herself.

"So what do you do other than play in a band?" she asked. *Not witty or entertaining, but it would have to do.*

James gazed at her for a moment, a slight frown on his face and then broke into a relaxed smile. "Nothing much. Gap year, I suppose you could call it. A long gap year," he said.

The journey passed quickly as they relaxed and chatted, mainly about music – Stephanie explaining about the small New Zealand music scene and James discovering that her musical taste ranged from The Beatles to Snow Patrol and Muse.

"You must find London strange after growing up in New Zealand," James commented.

"I've been to London a lot. My father lives there and I visit him a couple of times a year. But I seem to discover something new about it each time. It's my favourite city in world," she explained, as the driver came over the intercom announcing that Carlswick was the next station.

James nodded in agreement. "I love it too. I saw Key City play at the Roundhouse last night. It's so great to have all that live music just on the doorstep," he said.

He stood and slung his guitar back over his shoulder, and

held out his hand to her.

"This is our stop," he said. She took his hand and jumped up, their legs brushing in the enclosed space. They stood holding hands and gazing at one another for several long seconds. Stephanie knew that she should say something, but she didn't want to break the moment.

"Would you like to catch up for a coffee sometime?" James asked finally, as the train eased into the station. She released her hand from his and reached into the luggage rack for her suitcases and wheeled them towards the doors. James followed her and took one.

"Yeah, I'd like that," she smiled shyly at him and held onto a pole with her free hand to maintain her balance, as the train eased to a stop.

James pulled his mobile phone from his pocket and nudged her shoulder with his. "So, what's your number, then?"

She gave it to him and he keyed it into his phone. The doors opened and they stepped off, pulling the suitcases down behind them onto the platform. James continued wheeling one as they walked through the station to the car park.

"I'd offer you a lift, except, I just don't think all your bags would fit," he grinned, waving his hand in the direction of a row of motorbikes and scooters.

"That's okay. I'm getting a cab," she said, smiling at the driver who jumped out and started loading her suitcases in the boot. She turned towards James. "It was nice to meet you," she said quietly.

"Likewise, Stephanie," James said, his eyes roaming her face. "See ya." He turned and sauntered off towards the row of motorbikes. Stephanie gave her grandmother's address to the driver and climbed into the backseat of the cab. She watched out of the window as James pulled away on a Vespa.

She smiled and crossed her fingers that he would call, soon.

Chapter 2

S tephanie's grandmother, Ellie Cooper, lived in a six-bedroom, two-storeyed, red brick Georgian manor house called Wakefield House, on the outskirts of the village of Carlswick. Stephanie had always loved visiting the house as a little girl. It had been in the family since the First World War and it was where her grandmother had been born.

The front door was flung wide open before the taxi had even come to a halt. Stephanie leapt out and greeted her grandmother with a warm hug and kiss on her cheek.

"I am so pleased that you decided to come down early. I have been so looking forward to seeing you," Ellie said, smiling. She was an elegant woman in her eighties, immaculately groomed, with soft white hair pushed off her face and curling gently at the nape of her neck.

Stephanie paid and thanked the taxi driver and pulled her bags up the front steps and into the house.

"Now, I have put you in the blue room with the little bathroom at the top of the staircase. I hope that's alright?" Ellie asked.

"That'll be perfect, Grandma," Stephanie said smiling. She paused at the bottom of the stairs and studied the pictures of various ancestors and family members which hung there. As a little girl, they had meant very little to her, but now with her burgeoning interest in history, she looked at them through new eyes. *Wow,* she thought, *some of these are really old. I wonder how far back my family history goes?* Making a mental note to study the photos further, she began lugging her suitcases up the stairs.

Stephanie wasn't due in Oxford until October, which meant that she had two whole months of summer to enjoy. And enjoy it, she intended to do. She had worked hard for the previous six months juggling two jobs to save as much money as she possibly could, and now she needed a holiday, before the real work began.

A couple of hours later, a quiet knock on her bedroom door offered Stephanie a welcome reprieve from an afternoon of unpacking. Her bedroom looked like a clothes bomb had detonated.

A tall, gangly boy with short dark hair and glasses slipping down his nose stuck his head around the door and grinned at her.

Stephanie stood up, smoothing down the short vintage dress that she had changed into, and smiled back at the face of her old childhood friend. "Michael Morgan, how are ya?"

"My God. How did the airline allow you to bring so much stuff?" he exclaimed, looking around the room. Suitcases lay open with their contents spilling out, stacks of books sat haphazardly on the desk by the window, and a large pile of shoes at the entrance to the small walk-in wardrobe looked about ready to collapse.

"I didn't bring it all this time," she said a little defensively. "I left quite a lot of things at Dad's house in London when I went back to New Zealand in February and he brought them down here." Although, she had to admit, she had been rather surprised at just how much stuff she had accumulated.

Michael shook his head in disbelief. "Hey, your grandmother thought you might like a break from all of this, and I just have to take someone for a drive in the MG. I've finally got it running again," he said excitedly. Michael's pride and joy was a 1956 MG Roadster which he and his father had spent several years restoring.

"Great idea, I could do with a break. Give me a sec, eh?" Stephanie replied. She disappeared into her bathroom to fix her hair and makeup, leaving Michael looking through a box of books, which had just been delivered.

"You really are into this history stuff, aren't you, Steph?" he called.

Stephanie stuck her head back around the doorframe, lipstick in hand. "Yeah. They're all suggested pre-reading for my course." She nodded towards the box.

Coming out of the bathroom, she rummaged through the shoe pile, selected a pair of purple wedges and slipped her feet into them. She grabbed a small bag off the desk and throwing the long strap over her head and across her body, said, "Let's go." She followed him down the stairs to the front door.

"Actually it will be nice to get out and see Carlswick again," she said. "It's been a while." She hadn't spent a lot of time in the village at all over the last two or three years, preferring to stay at her father's house in London, when visiting England.

"Wow. This looks amazing," Stephanie said as she ran her hand lightly over the highly polished bonnet of the sky blue MG. The spokes of the chrome wire wheels shone in the sunlight. Michael beamed proudly and proceeded to wax lyrical on the quality of the engine and the original parts that

15

they had managed to source.

Stephanie's eyes must have glazed over, because he stopped talking after a couple of minutes and grinned sheepishly, pushing his glasses back up his nose, "Sorry, I'm boring you."

Stephanie laughed. "Not at all," she said. "Although you lost me at the bit about carburettors. I didn't realise that you had become such a car guy."

"I am assuming that is a compliment and not some sort of backhanded Kiwi insult?" he replied uncertainly.

"It's a compliment, mate. Now let's go for a ride," she said, opening the passenger door. "Ooh, hang on – I need to get something." She ran back into the house and up the stairs to her room and returned carrying a scarf. "The last time I rode in a convertible, I didn't tie my hair up and I ended up looking like a scarecrow when we stopped," she said laughing, as she slid into the passenger seat. She pulled her mane of straight dark hair into a high ponytail and tied the scarf around her head, securing it in a knot at the back of her neck.

Michael hit the accelerator, and they sped down the drive-way, waving to her grandmother, who was sitting on the terrace, enjoying the late afternoon sun.

Stephanie grinned as they raced along the lane towards the village. Michael's family were neighbours of her grand-mother's and he had been Stephanie's childhood playmate when she had visited each year. Apart from her best friend Anna, who lived in London, Stephanie didn't have a lot of friends in the UK, so she was delighted that he still wanted to hang out.

Carlswick had originally been a fishing village, with a bustling harbour, until the estuary had silted up. Now the sea was ten km away, but the pretty little village had survived thanks to the local farming community and in recent years the many lawyers, stockbrokers and successful musicians who had decided to make the area their home. The village comprised quaint stone buildings, which tumbled their way down either side of the hill to a green village square nestled at the bottom of the valley.

Michael slowed upon entering the village's main street. Without warning, he spun the car around and brought it to a screeching stop in front of an old pub. Stephanie had to grab the door to stop being thrown around. "Whoa," she shrieked, laughing. "A bit of warning next time."

Michael's entrance had the desired effect and no sooner had he turned the engine off, than a voice called, "Hey, Mikey."

Stephanie turned her head in the direction of the voice. In the car park beside the pub, a group of girls were sitting at an outdoor table chatting to three guys, who were unloading amps, guitars and drums from a beat up Combie van. The shorter of the guys waved and started walking towards them.

"Looks like you're about to meet the local rock gods – The Fury," Michael said, as they got out of the car. "Y'know, they played all the summer music festivals and are on the cusp of the big time according to those in the know."

Stephanie had heard of them. She'd also seen them play in London in January. Her friends in New Zealand would be so jealous to know that she was actually about to meet them. Removing her headscarf and throwing it on the seat, she quickly composed herself; she certainly didn't want to appear star-struck. *They're probably completely full of themselves anyway, especially with an entourage hanging on their every movement*, she thought, glancing towards the group of girls.

Michael came around to her side of the car. "I designed

their official website," he whispered proudly.

Stephanie looked at him in surprise. The guy, who Stephanie now recognised as the band's drummer, reached them, before she could respond. His blond hair was styled so that it stood straight up all over his head and he peered out over his small round sunglasses. "Hey, Mike – nice car. Who's ya friend?" he asked, turning his attention to Stephanie.

"Hey. This is Stephanie," mumbled Michael, slightly put out that he was more interested in Stephanie than in the MG.

"Hi," Stephanie said looking him straight in the eye, as she arranged her features into an expression of confusion. "And you are?"

"I, ah, I'm Jack," he stuttered, obviously used to being recognised. He ran his hands through his blond spikes and straightened his shoulders, stretching himself in a way that reminded Stephanie of a cat who had just woken from a long nap.

She smiled to herself. "G'day, Jack," she said. "Mike, I just need to pick up a couple of things from the newsagent. I won't be long," she said, indicating, with a flick of her head, to the shop three doors down.

He nodded. Stephanie turned and started walking along the footpath. She could feel herself being watched and glanced sideways, where the other two guys were leaning nonchalantly against the van, taking a break. One had short dark, dreadlocks and dark skin. He had a couple of the girls looking up at him admiringly, hanging on his every word. Stephanie's eyes met those of the other guy. James. He held her gaze steadily and gave her a half smile, before turning and lifting another drum out of the van and carrying it in the side door of the pub.

No. How did I not recognise him on the train? Stephanie thought, pulling her gaze away and trying desperately to ignore the blush rising up her face. *He must think I am such an idiot.*

There was a crowd of people around Michael's car when she came back from the newsagent several minutes later.

James separated from the group as she approached.

"Hello again, Stephanie," he said.

"Hello again, James," she blushed.

"So you know Mike?" he asked quietly, holding her gaze.

"Yeah, we go way back," she replied, self-consciously chewing on her bottom lip. *Should I say something about not recognising him earlier?* she wondered.

"Huh. It's strange that we've never met before, then. I've known him for years too," James mused. "What's your surname?"

"Cooper," Stephanie replied.

The smile disappeared and his face fell. "Not a Wakefield Cooper?" he asked.

"One and the same," Stephanie answered, studying him. Now that she knew who he was, she could see why he carried himself the way he did. *Typical wannabe rock star – oozing confidence,* she thought.

James sighed and his expression darkened. "So you don't know that we're not supposed to have anything to do with one another, then? My family hates yours."

"Really?" Stephanie was surprised at the sudden change in the conversation. "Why? Did we win more prizes than you at the Royal County Show or something, eh?"

"Ha. That's funny," he said, the smile returning. "No, there's some old feud. The Knoxes have had nothing to do with your

19

family for years."

Before Stephanie could ask him to elaborate, a pretty girl wrapped her arms around James's waist and kissed him on the cheek. She glanced at Stephanie, giving her the kind of once over that girls everywhere recognise – assessment of a threat.

"Victoria. This is Stephanie. She's from New Zealand," James introduced them, not taking his eyes off Stephanie.

Stephanie smiled and said hi, as Victoria muttered, "well I guess that explains the outfit."

Jeez, what have I done to deserve that? Stephanie thought, surprised and a little annoyed. Her next words flew out of her mouth before she could censor them. "Well, I guess London fashion hasn't reached the country, yet."

Victoria gave her a dirty look and tossing her long copper tresses, turned her back to talk to another girl who had joined them.

James raised his eyebrows at the catty exchange. He went to speak, and then stopped, looking as though he were waging an internal battle. "My band is playing at the pub here on Friday night – you should come," he said, finally, almost reluctantly.

Stephanie shrugged. She'd suspected on the train that he was too good to be true. *Of course, there would be a girlfriend hanging off his arm*, she thought, disappointed. "Maybe. Are you any good?" she teased. Although she knew The Fury weren't just good, they were great.

James's mouth dropped open in surprise, but before he could answer, Michael called to her that they had to go.

She grinned at James's expression, as she jumped into the passenger seat of the MG, hanging on for dear life as Michael roared off down the street.

Chapter 3

S tephanie woke early the next day. She rolled over in her big, comfy bed and looked into the smiling eyes of her adorable four-year-old half-brother, laughing back at her from a photo on her bedside table. She felt her heart give a painful squeeze. Toby. She missed him already.

Stephanie's parents had met in London in the early 1990s, when her mother Marie, had been on what New Zealanders called their OE – Overseas Experience. It was almost a rite of passage for many young Kiwis to come to the UK after finishing school or university and spend two or three years working, partying and travelling. Marie had been no exception, until she met Max at the law firm where they both worked. Following a whirlwind romance, Marie discovered that she was pregnant and returned to New Zealand. Max followed and although they tried to make a go of family life, New Zealand was just too small for the ambitious and driven Max. After three years and much heartache, he returned to London, alone.

It was testament to the obvious affection that Marie and Max had for one another, that they put their differences aside to ensure that Max remained a strong presence in Stephanie's life. And so, twice a year, she and Marie would return to the

UK, to enable Stephanie to spend time with her father. When her mother remarried and Toby was born, Stephanie began travelling on her own.

It was during these visits that she got to know her English cousins, particularly Matt, who was just a year older. Max and Stephanie would often holiday with Matt's family when she was younger. Matt's passion was rugby. He captained his school team and had just completed his first year at Oxford, playing for the university. It would be good to have him around. She made a mental note to call him later, but first she had to call Toby.

Checking the time, Stephanie determined that it would be early evening in New Zealand. She could hopefully catch him before his bedtime. Grabbing her iPad, she sat up in bed and put a video call through on Skype.

By late morning, she had her room in order. She sighed and sat down on the small sofa in the corner by the window. The beginnings of a dull headache threatened and she massaged her temples. Fresh air and coffee – that's what she needed.

"Grandma, I'm just popping into the village – do you need anything?" she offered, passing the sitting room where her grandmother was getting ready for her weekly bridge game.

"No thanks, dear," she called.

Earlier, her grandmother had pressed a set of car keys into Stephanie's hand.

"My car is yours to use while you are here, darling. I am not allowed to drive it anymore, more's the pity. Eyesight, apparently," she said with a disgusted shake of her head. "Michael's given it a tune-up, so you should be good to go."

Stephanie skipped around to the garage and heaved open the wooden doors. An old purple, two-door Fiat 500 was parked waiting for her.

"Yes," she breathed excitedly, "I've always loved this car." She slipped into the driver's seat and adjusted the rear view mirror to her height and admired the black leather seats.

She had noticed a new café across the road from the pub, when she was out with Michael the previous day, so that would be her first stop.

Stephanie heard the café before she saw it. Situated on the main street, it looked as though two old buildings had been knocked into one. It had bi-fold windows pushed wide open at the front and rock music blaring from inside. Stephanie smiled to herself – *I bet the old locals love that.*

She pulled into the car park to the right of the building and walked around to the front entrance.

A loud roar coming down the street took her attention and she watched as the same Combie van she had seen the previous day pulled into the pub car park opposite the coffee shop, smoke billowing in its wake. She suppressed a smirk. *I would have thought up and coming rock stars would be able to afford better transport,* she thought, amused. James opened the front passenger door and jumping down, ran his hands through his hair, causing his t-shirt to ride up exposing a hint of what looked to be very toned abs.

Stephanie stood rooted to the spot, appreciating the display. James looked around as though sensing he was being watched, and caught her eye, just as someone roughly brushed past her knocking her shoulder. Taken by surprise, Stephanie dropped her car keys and turned to see who had bumped into her. Victoria strutted past, take-out coffee cup in hand. "Close your mouth, he's way out of your league," she murmured nastily. Stephanie stooped to pick up her keys and watched as Victoria crossed the road to where James was standing.

Rise above it, Stephanie, she told herself, swallowing the retort which had formed on her lips. Shaking her head at Victoria's retreating back, she turned and walked through the open double doors, into the café.

The café's modern interior completely contrasted with the traditional exterior. The walls were painted white and about ten square tables each with four chairs were scattered throughout the space. Along the two side walls were black leather sofas with lower wooden coffee tables and matching small leather armchairs. A long wooden counter ran along the entire back wall with black and chrome bar stools dotted along. The whole room smelled of freshly ground coffee mingled with fresh paint. The exposed wooden floorboards had been polished until they shone.

Stephanie instantly felt transported back home. *Now, I just hope the coffee is good.* A small drum kit was set up in the front corner by one of the windows on a square red paisley rug. Beside it rested several guitars.

Ooh, thought Stephanie, *live music too – this just gets better.*

A young guy was working flat out behind the counter making coffee, whilst keeping up a steady banter with his customers – all teenagers.

He had long curly, sandy-coloured hair and when he looked up Stephanie recognised him as The Fury's bass player. *Huh, they're everywhere,* she thought.

She joined the queue at the counter and watched him working for a few minutes. The guy was clearly swamped, but very relaxed and good natured about it, which seemed to rub off on his customers, none of whom appeared to be getting impatient.

He looked up. "Sorry, love, will be with ya soon," he said.

Stephanie grinned back. "No problem – are you on your own?"

"Yeah – I haven't long opened and I think I slightly underestimated demand," he said laughing.

Stephanie stood up from the bar stool that she had propped herself against.

"Can I help? I can clear tables, maybe?" she asked, looking around at the tables, several of which were covered with used cups and plates.

He looked at her for a moment, assessing whether she was serious, and then smiled gratefully.

"That would be fantastic. I just haven't managed to even get to the tables, since I opened. Come around and get an apron – on that hook there." He indicated behind him, with a toss of his head. Stephanie walked around the end of the counter and helped herself to a brand new black apron with THE CAFÉ written in white lettering across the front.

"I'm Stephanie," she said, introducing herself to him as she pulled the apron over her head and crossed the ties behind her back, securing them in a bow at the front.

He took one hand off the milk steamer and shook her hand. "Andy." The girls at the counter were busy chatting and took no notice of her.

Stephanie was busy for the next half hour clearing tables, taking orders and laughing and joking with Andy. The atmosphere in the café was laid back. The music which had seemed loud from outside was at a level which still allowed conversation. Andy fostered the relaxed mood, greeting his customers by name more often than not.

"Thanks," he said to her when they had a pause between

customers. "You don't want a job, do ya?"

"No," Stephanie replied, shaking her head.

"I'm serious – you've obviously worked in a café before," he said.

"No I haven't – just spent way too much time drinking coffee in them," she replied.

The conversation ended there for the time being as they got busy again. About half an hour later, Stephanie looked up to find Michael and a friend, waiting to be served.

"Steph – you do realise that you're on the wrong side of the counter?" Michael teased.

She laughed.

"You must be Stephanie – we used to play together when you came to visit your grandmother," said Michael's friend, a short, chunky girl with a kind face and a big smile. "You probably don't remember me, I'm Mary."

"Of course, hi, Mary." Stephanie smiled, but she had no recollection of the girl.

"So are you really working here?" Michael asked.

"I'm trying to convince her," Andy said. "Whadda ya think?"

Michael grinned. "So long as she doesn't do a haka and scare off all your customers, I guess it'll be okay."

Andy cracked up laughing.

"Yeah, yeah, amuse yourselves." Stephanie couldn't help, but grin.

"Well, I think it's lovely to have someone from 'down under' living in Carlswick," Mary offered kindly.

"Thank you, Mary. I knew I liked you," Stephanie replied, pulling a face at Michael.

She took their order and said she'd bring it over to them.

Andy had gone to clear the tables, so Stephanie decided to

make her friends' drinks. Andy's machine didn't look a lot different to the one her father had at the house in London – just bigger. She worked quickly to grind the beans and steam the milk, and in no time had the two coffees made. Satisfied, she stepped back to admire her creations.

"So when can you start?" Andy asked. He was standing at the dishwasher with another load of dirty cups.

"Andy – I am only here for a couple of months until uni starts. Here – these are for Michael and Mary," she replied.

Andy delivered them and returned to start loading the dishwasher, his face thoughtful.

"Okay – a couple of months will give me the breathing space I need to get on my feet with running this place. You can pick your hours and days – but I'm doing live music, poetry and comedy on Sunday nights. It'll be a lotta fun. And I will need a barista who can handle themselves – because I expect it will be the hottest gig in town. Why don't you start then?" he said enthusiastically.

"Well…." Stephanie hesitated. Maybe earning a few pounds would keep her from dipping into her savings too much before she started uni, and the afternoon with Andy had been fun. Working at the coffee shop might be a good way to get out of the house and get to know a few more people too, especially if this was to be her base in the holidays. *Maybe I will fit in around here, after all*, she thought hopefully, after the uncertain start with James and Victoria.

"I can't pay you much more than the minimum wage – but you can have free coffee," Andy said, pouncing on her hesitation.

"Well now, that settles it – deal," she smiled, making a snap decision.

"Well, this is all very cosy," said a husky voice. Stephanie whirled around. James was standing at the counter with an odd expression on his face. "Do you know who you just employed, Andy?"

Stephanie frowned, confused by his attitude.

Andy shook his head and looked at her, his eyebrows raised questioningly.

"Stephanie, ah, Cooper," she said hesitantly.

"What – a Wakefield House Cooper?" Andy asked and grinned when she nodded in affirmation. "The enemy," he said with a knowing nod at James.

"I'm sorry, am I missing something here?" Stephanie said, looking from one to the other.

"From ancient grudge break to new mutiny," Andy quoted Shakespeare.

Realisation dawned on her and she looked at James. "Really? You were serious yesterday, eh?"

James shrugged nonchalantly. "History has shown that your family are liars and troublemakers."

Ouch. Stephanie was visibly shocked at his rudeness.

"Dude, what can we get ya?" Andy asked, quickly changing the subject.

"Latte please? Double shot," James replied.

He propped himself up on a bar stool and watched Stephanie as she busied herself tidying and wiping down the counter top and emptying the first dishwasher which had finished washing. She kept her head down, feeling very self-conscious under his scrutiny. Andy watched the interaction between the two with interest.

Stephanie looked at her watch – it was four-thirty. Where had the afternoon gone?

"Andy, I'm gonna have to go shortly," she said.

"Sure, darlin'. Let me make you a coffee first – you never got one in the end, did you?" he replied.

"Has he had you working all day?" James asked sipping his latte. "You're a rogue," he grinned at Andy, shaking his head in disbelief. Andy had the reputation for being able to talk anyone into doing anything for him – girls especially. Andy merely inclined his head and shrugged.

"*Society produces rogues, and education makes one rogue cleverer than another,*" he replied quoting Oscar Wilde dramatically.

Stephanie rolled her eyes and smiled, as she hung up her apron and waited while Andy made her latte.

"Back home, we have something called a flat white, which is like a cross between a latte and a cappuccino. I'll make you one next time, see what ya think," she said to Andy.

Andy looked up, interested. "I've heard of that. If I like it, we could add it to the board," he said.

Stephanie nodded and took her cup. "Thanks. So I'll see you on Sunday at seven?" she said.

"Perfect," he replied.

James snapped his head up and looked questioningly at Andy, as Stephanie walked over to join Michael and Mary on one of the sofas.

"Are you taking her out on Sunday?" he asked as soon as Stephanie was out of earshot, his voice cold.

"I'd love to say yes, just to wind you up," Andy laughed, "but sadly no – she'll be working here then."

James let out the breath he had been holding and visibly relaxed.

"Intention declared then, dude?" Andy asked, his eyebrows raised.

"Nah," said James dismissively, scowling. "She's a Wakefield. Grandpa won't be happy to hear that there is another one in town."

Chapter 4

The following afternoon, Stephanie was lying in the sun in her grandmother's garden reading one of her new history texts, *The Histories* by Tacitus. Her mind kept drifting back to the previous day – to James and his comments about the feud between their families. *He actually seemed to buy into the whole idea, which is weird given that a feud seems such an outdated concept.* She decided to ask her grandmother about it.

Her mobile chimed, announcing an incoming text.

She rolled over and picked it up off the edge of the rug, waving her hand lazily at a bee that was buzzing about the flowerbeds. She flopped on her back and tapped the screen to open the message.

Wanna see The Fury tonight? Pick you up 7:30. Matt

Stephanie smiled and text back: *Love 2. Ok if Michael comes?*

No probs, was the reply.

A little while later, Stephanie gathered her things and wandered inside. She paused on the stairs studying the photographs.

"Oh, there you are dear," her grandmother said, walking out of the kitchen. "Did Matthew get hold of you?"

"Yes, thanks, Grandma. I'm going to see a band with him

tonight," Stephanie replied, her attention being captured by an old black and white photo of two men and two women laughing. "I have been meaning to ask you, who are these people?" she asked.

Ellie came to join her on the stairs, putting her hand on the banister and leaning against it slightly. "That's me with my brother David and sister Sophie, just before the war," she said. "And the other man is Edward Knox."

"Knox?" Stephanie asked. "I think I met his grandson yesterday."

Ellie looked stricken. "That would be his great-nephew, not grandson." She clutched the banister.

"Grandma, are you okay?" Stephanie asked alarmed, reaching for her.

"We have *nothing* to do with that family, Stephanie." Her voice rang out stronger than Stephanie had ever heard it.

Stephanie opened and closed her mouth. *So this was 'the feud' in action – James was right.*

"Grandma," she began.

"I know it may seem old-fashioned to you, but if it weren't for them, my darling sister, Sophie, would still be alive." Ellie's strength of a moment earlier seemed to have deserted her, and she closed her eyes for a moment.

"Really, Grandma? What happened?" Stephanie asked wide eyed, shocked.

"Well, it's a long story, but she died in a car accident in 1940. It was all very suspicious," Ellie replied, a faraway look in her eye.

Stephanie opened her mouth to ask another question, when the doorbell buzzed. Sighing slightly, Ellie released the banister and walked over to open the front door. A lady of her age stood there. "I don't suppose you have the kettle on, Ellie?" she asked.

"Of course," Ellie said opening the door wider and letting her friend into the hall.

Stephanie smiled at them both, suppressing her annoyance that the story had been interrupted. *What could she mean that her sister would still be alive? Was Edward Knox a murderer?* She looked back at the faces smiling back at her from the photo – *I wonder what secrets you hold?* she thought, vowing to find out more, as she wandered upstairs to her room.

* * *

Later that evening, as the sky darkened, Stephanie pushed open the door of The Smugglers Inn. Matt, his girlfriend Fiona and Michael followed her through. Matt nudged Stephanie. "You can legally drink here this time, Steph," he teased. She stuck her tongue out at him. Matt was tall and solid, with short cropped blond hair. Typical rugby player build, with a nose that looked to have been broken on more than one occasion. It somehow gave his face character. "Come on, little cousin, come and meet some of the guys."

The half-timbered building was one of the oldest in the village, proudly displaying a sign which read 'since 1550' above its low Tudor doorway. Above the windows at the front, a dozen hanging baskets, overflowing with colourful flowers, swayed gently. Inside, the front room was a traditional old style English pub, with wood panelling and busy patterned carpets and a long wooden bar along one wall with a food serving hatch on opposite side. Through a large archway at the back of the room a modern extension had been added, with a stage at the far end was hung with red velvet curtains. Tables and chairs were clustered throughout. The carpet ended about ten metres before the stage and in its place a wooden dance floor stretched across the width of the room.

The lights were dim and the tables were full of groups of people, none older than about thirty. The area in front of the bar was crowded with people standing around talking and laughing. The stage, which was lit with coloured lights, had a drum kit on a raised platform towards the back, a keyboard on one side and three microphones across the front. A mixing desk stood off to one side with two racks each holding five different guitars. The whole setup looked very professional.

Not what you'd expect from a country pub, thought Stephanie, her excitement rising. *I think I am going to like spending my holidays here.* From around the age of fifteen, whenever she was visiting London, Stephanie and Anna had gone to as many concerts and music festivals as they were allowed.

"Hey, you're quiet," Matt boomed. "Wanna drink?"

"Yeah, just taking it all in." she said. "Let me buy you one, since you drove me, eh?"

"Okay. Just a diet coke for me. Pre-season training," he explained, pulling a face. "Fi will have white wine," he added, smiling at his girlfriend who was already deep in conversation with several people sitting at a nearby table.

"Coming right up. Michael?" She raised her eyebrows, silently asking him the same question.

"I'll come with you," he said.

Stephanie and Michael pushed their way to the bar, excusing themselves around people who were standing drinking and chatting. The bar staff were busy working the crowd, but it took Stephanie less than a minute to attract attention.

"What can I get you?" The young barman gave Stephanie a flirty smile.

Stephanie and Michael gave their orders and showed their IDs to the barman.

"Geez, you got served, like, twenty minutes quicker than I would've," Michael complained pushing his glasses up his nose. "It is so unfair that the less attractive amongst us get ignored," he complained dramatically.

Stephanie laughed. "I don't think it's attractiveness, just assertiveness. Catch their eye and don't let it go and they feel compelled to serve you."

"Who are you trying to bewitch now?" said a voice on the other side of her.

Stephanie spun around. James was at her shoulder looking every inch a rock star in fitted black jeans, tight black t-shirt and denim jacket. His dark fringe was pushed back off his forehead with hair product and his eyes were amused, as he smiled down at her. She was speechless for once.

"Glad you could make it, Stephanie," he said.

"Yeah, looking forward to hearing the 'local band'. I do hope I won't be disappointed," she replied cheekily, recovering her composure somewhat.

James grinned at her teasing understatement and said, "Well, we'll just have to blow you away then, won't we? See you after the gig? We're having a small get together at the café."

"Maybe," she said indifferently, but underneath she felt her blood racing. *So much for having nothing to do with me,* she thought.

The barman placed Michael's bottle of Heineken in front of them and Stephanie turned to pay for the drinks. When she turned back, James was gone. She and Michael wound their way back to where they had left Matthew, balancing their drinks carefully.

She handed Matthew his coke and he introduced her around his group of rugby mates and their girlfriends. Everyone was really friendly, although she had to correct them when they assumed that she was Australian.

"Love your shoes," a girl named Felicity commented, smiling and looking down at Stephanie's three-inch denim wedges, which put her on eye level with most of the guys in their group.

"Thanks," Stephanie replied. "Shoes are a bit of an obsession, I'm afraid." Whilst shoes really had become something of a passion of Stephanie's, she had learned fairly young that the way to direct people's attention away from a spotty face and round tummy, was by having something gorgeous or unusual on your feet. And now that the acne and puppy fat were, mostly, a thing of the past, she still had a wardrobe full of great shoes.

A loud guitar chord cut across the room and the lights immediately dimmed further. The stage was plunged momentarily into darkness and suddenly the room was alive with a wall of sound and flashing lights as the band launched unannounced into their first song.

Stephanie watched mesmerised as the lead singer strutted his stuff across the stage. *Boy, does he own it,* she thought. By contrast, Andy was a laid back figure holding it all together with a tight bass track, his eyes roving the crowd. Her attention was inevitably drawn to James on lead guitar. His hair now flopped over his forehead as he concentrated on a guitar riff and flicked back as he launched into the fast strumming of the chorus and stepped forward to the microphone to harmonise with Liam. *Wow, he is really hot,*

Stephanie thought, blushing as she watched him.

The rest of the set continued at the same frenetic pace. Dave's dreadlocks bounced as he danced and played the keyboard. During a couple of songs he broke away from his position and joined Liam at the front of the stage, performing a fast and furious rap. Jack was a demon behind the drums, beating out frantic fills and occasionally tossing a stick into the crowd. Stephanie danced with Michael, Matt, Fiona and others in their group.

The band took a break after a long first set and James sought her out, beer in one hand, G&T in the other. His hair was wet with sweat and pushed back up on top of his head making him seem even taller. He offered her the G&T.

"Thought you might need a top up, after all that dancing," he murmured.

"Thanks," Stephanie said smiling at him. So he'd not only noticed her dancing but he had taken note of what she was ordering at the bar earlier!

"So – what's your verdict?" he asked, looking down at her with a half-smile on his face. He was down to just the t-shirt and jeans, and she could see the hard curve of muscle on his upper arms. His t-shirt had the words *Guitarists do it better* emblazoned across the front.

"Actually, not bad for a village band," Stephanie replied, pretending to be thoughtful. "You might even go places, eh. Rye for instance," she said, naming a town near theirs.

James threw back his head and laughed. "You're unbelievable," he said. "I'm used to a little more respect than this."

She laughed. "Respect? *Really*, old man?"

He opened his mouth to retort, but was interrupted by Jack beating out a march on the drums.

"That's my cue. See ya." He turned and made his way back towards the stage. Only he didn't have to push through the crowd, it somehow magically parted for him. Stephanie watched him walk away. When she turned back to Matt's group, she found a number of them looking at her open mouthed.

"What?" she said quietly to Michael. "Do I have something on my face?" She put her hand self-consciously to her cheek.

"No one talks to the *wonderful* James Knox like that, Steph," Matt said sarcastically. "You do know that they are The Fury, not just some garage band?"

"Yeah, of course. I was just having a bit of fun. He knew that I was kidding….I think." Stephanie looked up at the stage where James had slung a guitar across his body and winked at her.

Oh yeah, he knew, liked it and came back for more, she thought, her heart racing a little.

She glanced around the bar. Victoria was standing off to one side with a group of older guys and several of her look-alike girlfriends. She looked over at Stephanie as if she were something that she had trodden in.

Stephanie sighed. *Oh great, I should have known you'd be here.*

The second set was even more energetic than the first, with James and Liam leaping and jumping and Dave performing somersaults and cartwheels across the stage. After the gig ended, the crowds began to disperse, some still singing the band's final number enthusiastically as they left the pub. Stephanie watched James rack his guitar and look over to her. He held her gaze with such intensity that she blushed and looked away.

Matt had one arm around Fiona and threw his other arm

around Stephanie's shoulders and turned her away from the direction of the stage, shooting a dirty look over his shoulder at James as he did.

James swore under his breath and took a step towards them, but was intercepted by Victoria, who took his hand and said loudly, "Where to now, baby?"

Stephanie turned at her voice and saw them standing close together, James's hand in Victoria's. She dropped her eyes, her face hot. *How could you be so stupid to think that he would be seriously interested in you?* she angrily told herself. *She did say that he is way out of your league.* She allowed herself to be propelled to the door by Matt, with Michael trailing along behind.

James pulled his hand out of Victoria's, having just caught the look that flashed across Stephanie's face as she turned away. He started after them, but Victoria grabbed his arm stopping him, "Now, now, Jamie. Don't go getting all hot over her. She's a Wakefield and you know what we think of them," she said.

James shook his head with a look of distain. "For God's sake, Vic, that's ancient history," he said.

"Try telling that to your grandfather or your brother for that matter." She nodded towards the door, where James's brother Alex stood laughing with a group of people.

"Whatever, Vickie," he said, emphasising the nickname that he knew she hated. He pulled his arm out of her grasp and strode towards the door. Victoria stood with her hands on her hips glaring at his retreating back.

Matt was holding the back passenger door of his car open for Stephanie, when James caught up with them in the car park.

"Hey, are you guys coming to the café?" he asked, trying to catch Stephanie's eye. She kept her head down. She felt really stupid for letting herself so publicly flirt with him, when everyone else obviously knew he was with Victoria.

"I don't think so, Knox." Matt slammed his door and started the car and backed out of his parking space, looking protectively at Stephanie in the rear view mirror who was staring at her hands.

James sucked in a curse and, lip curled, stomped back inside to pack up his gear.

Chapter 5

Stephanie woke the next morning with her father delivering her a cup of coffee.

"Hey, sleepyhead. Late night?"

Stephanie groaned and sat up, accepting the coffee gratefully. "Went to see a band at the pub," she replied sleepily, running her hand through her sleep tousled hair.

"Now, why doesn't that surprise me?" Max smiled indulgently at his daughter. Max Cooper was a handsome forty-something, with slightly greying dark hair, who had the confident air of a successful man. Rather than his usual business attire, today he was wearing jeans and an open-necked pale blue shirt. He looked very relaxed.

"I've come down from London for lunch and I'm told we need some fresh bread. Why don't you get up and come for a drive with me into the village? Give us a chance to catch up," he suggested.

Half an hour later, Stephanie and Max drove down the long driveway of Wakefield House and turned into the lane leading into Carlswick. It was a bright, sunny late summer morning, with clear blue skies dotted with the occasional white fluffy cloud. The lane, lined on either side by hedgerows, sloped gently down towards the village.

Stephanie and her father chatted easily. Gone were the days when she felt a slight resentment towards him for abandoning her. Whilst Max had always been part of Stephanie's life, the distance between England and New Zealand meant that their relationship had developed into more that of a big brother and little sister, than of a parent and child. However, it was obvious that Max was now feeling the responsibility of having his only child, albeit an eighteen-year-old one, living near. Stephanie sincerely hoped that he wouldn't start trying to 'parent' her, just when she hoped to have a more adult relationship with him.

"Let's park at the top end by the church and walk down to the bakery," Max suggested. "It's been quite a while since I've had a stroll through the old village."

"I'm sure not much has changed in the last hundred years or so since you were a kid, Dad," Stephanie replied cheekily.

Max feigned hurt feelings by clutching his chest. Stephanie laughed and hooked her arm through his. "You must show me this new café that you are working at," he said.

They returned to the car a while later, still chatting and laughing, carrying two loaves of warm fresh bread, as the doors of the church swung open and the congregation poured out, organ music heralding their departure.

The church looked as old as the village itself. Nestled on the side of the hill, its austere grey brickwork was augmented by the wildflowers that grew all around it in a riot of colour.

Stephanie felt her father bristle beside her. She glanced at him and followed the line of his narrowed gaze.

There on a trajectory to intercept them was a very upright elderly gentleman with a shock of white hair and at his side a much younger tall, dark-haired man with sunglasses shading his eyes.

"Cooper," the older man spat disdainfully, coming to a stop in front of them.

"Oh God. The tone of the village has just been lowered," his companion added in a condescending tone.

"With you still living here, I didn't realise it could go any lower," Max retorted, his voice tightly controlled.

The elderly man glared at Max and shook his head. They pushed roughly between Max and Stephanie.

"Who was that, Dad?" Stephanie whispered, her eyes wide as she watched them getting into a silver Mercedes and drive away.

Max's gaze followed the retreating vehicle, a frown marring his features. "No one that you need to concern yourself with. Come on, let's get home," he said in a tone that very definitely signalled the end of the conversation.

* * *

Stephanie deliberated over her 'work' outfit on Sunday night. She still hadn't quite worked out what passed for casual among the teens of Carlswick and she didn't want to appear overdressed. Dark blue jeans and a black V-necked t-shirt looked simple enough. Satisfied, she pulled on a pair of purple peep-toe ankle boots. She scraped her hair back into a high ponytail and applied a small amount of makeup – mascara, eyeliner and lipstick. She stared closely at herself in the mirror searching her skin for any early signs of a break out. All clear for now.

Her grandmother had been bemused when she announced that she had a job.

"But didn't you work hard all year to earn money in New Zealand?" she had enquired.

"It's more about meeting people than earning money, Grandma," Stephanie explained.

"Yes – but does one really need a job to do that?" Ellie had shaken her head in one of those 'not in my day' shakes.

Stephanie pulled into the café's car park at ten to seven, and walked around to the front entrance. It didn't look busy yet, but she noticed The Fury members gathered around one of the leather sofas by the makeshift stage, deep in conversation.

"Hey, Steph." Andy jumped up to greet her as she walked through the door.

She smiled at him and said, "Hey, Andy. Great gig last night, I really enjoyed it." She nodded to James who looked up from tuning his guitar. His gaze lingered on her for a few seconds. She shuffled uncomfortably and looked across at Jack sprawled full length across one of the sofas, tossing and catching his drum sticks.

"Ah, it's the Kiwi. G'day, mate," he said putting on an accent.

Stephanie raised her eyebrows at him. "You sound like an Australian, Jack."

"There's a difference?" he teased. Everyone knew that New Zealanders insisted on being recognised separately from their geographical neighbours.

Stephanie glared at him, before breaking into a grin.

Dave waved at her from his seat beside James, and the fifth member of the band spun around on a bar stool and stood up.

"Liam," he said introducing himself. Stephanie recognised him as the lead singer. He was dressed in tight black jeans with a baggy grey shirt and several colourful scarves around his neck. His blond hair was tipped with red and stood straight out all over his head. He carried himself very confidently. Having seen him in action on the stage, she knew that he was an extremely charismatic character and a great singer.

"It's good to finally meet you. You've certainly made your mark in a few days," he said looking her over.

"Really?" Stephanie replied evenly. *God – what's been said?* Stephanie felt her heart sink.

"Yeah – Victoria tells me that you two are gonna be best buds," he answered slyly, gauging her reaction.

Stephanie tilted her head and frowned slightly as she studied him. "So you're a smart arse, as well as a singer?" she said lightly.

Liam looked slightly taken aback, but quickly recovered, "Wow – I think you just managed to squash every vowel in that sentence," he said.

Stephanie opened her mouth to retort, when Andy took her arm and rescued her. "This way – I should probably give you the formal induction," he said. With a sweep of his hand he indicated behind the counter. "This is where we make the coffee." She laughed, relieved to be out of the spotlight. When she glanced back at Liam, he was watching her with a 'don't take me on' expression on his face.

Bring it on, she thought, smiling sweetly at him.

It was a hectic night, but Stephanie thoroughly enjoyed herself. She was too busy to worry about Victoria and Liam and what people had been saying about her. The band played a couple of acoustic sets and the café was crowded. *Andy was right*, she thought. *This is the hottest venue in the village – although, there probably isn't anything else on in Carlswick on a Sunday night.*

Michael arrived around eight o'clock and started clearing

tables for Stephanie and then sat at the counter chatting to her as she made coffee and served thick slices of cake. Andy had enlisted one of the local ladies to bake for the café and the result was fantastic chocolate brownies, gourmet cupcakes and thick carrot and banana cakes, dripping with icing.

Matt and Fiona stopped by early on, with a group of friends.

"Steph," he boomed over the music. "I heard you were working here. Whatever for? I thought you were here for a holiday before uni starts."

"Just for fun, Matt," she said. "Can I get you guys a coffee?"

"Hot chocolate would be good," he said as he slid onto a bar stool in front of her. "Are you okay? I was worried about you last night – did something happen at the end?"

Stephanie shook her head. "Oh no, just tired – still a bit jet-lagged – I guess it caught up with me. Thanks again for taking me though," she smiled brightly at him.

"Any time, cousin," he said, sounding unconvinced as she started making their drinks, and added, "Steph – Knox is an arse – you don't want to waste your time on him."

Stephanie held her too bright smile. "Don't worry, I'm not," she said. "Tell me, is Liam always a dickhead?"

Matt straightened his shoulders and glared in Liam's direction. "What did he say?" he growled.

"Nothing Matt, I just wondered," she replied quickly. *The last thing I need is to have Matt fighting my battles for me.*

Andy wandered back and forth between playing his bass and helping behind the counter for the rest of the evening. He jokingly called 'last orders' at nine forty-five pm and shooed the remaining customers out at ten-fifteen.

The band continued jamming as Stephanie wiped down the tables and countertop for the last time and reset the tables and chairs. She loaded up the dishwasher with all the coffee-making equipment and switched it on.

Satisfied, she hung up her apron and retrieved her bag. She waved to Andy and mouthed, "See ya boss," above the music.

He stopped playing and called to her, "Stay for a drink, Steph?" Dave had produced bottles of Heineken from one of Andy's fridges and waved one at her. Liam stood swaying slightly, leaning his arm over the microphone stand, and watched her. He was clearly already several beers down.

"No thanks – gotta get home," she declined quickly, suddenly feeling uncomfortable with all the attention.

James looked up from where he was perched on an amp and caught her eye. After the humiliation she felt on Saturday night, letting herself think that he was actually interested in her, she was determined to not pay him any special attention.

But now he jumped up, putting his guitar on a stand.

"It's dark out – I'll walk you to your car," he offered.

"No it's okay," she replied hastily. Being alone with him was the last thing she wanted. What she really wanted was to get in her little car and go straight home to bed. In some ways it had been quite a stressful evening with all these egos bouncing around. She could feel her head beginning to pound.

"Since when have you been so chivalrous?" Jack asked, amused.

James pulled a face at him.

"Stephanie is immune to his charm, so she's safe," Andy added grinning at James.

"I'd be more worried about his hands than his charm, if I were her," offered Liam.

Stephanie smiled at the light-hearted banter and looking out into the dark night decided that maybe would be good to have someone with her until she was safely in her car. *Perhaps I've been watching too many episodes of Midsomer Murders, where the most gruesome slayings seem to always happen in a little English village at night.*

"Okay, thanks," she conceded. "But keep your hands where I can see them," she added in jest. The others laughed. James gave an insouciant shrug and held his hands up as if in defeat. He walked backwards in front of her to the door, once again giving her his trademark lazy smile.

The door banged behind them and they walked into the dark night and around the side of the building to the car park.

Stephanie glanced at him. "Hey, Andy's café is going to be a great live venue, eh?" she said. "You guys sound good acoustically as well as, you know, the other night." *Shut up, Steph. You are babbling,* she told herself. She didn't feel nearly as confident as she had the night before, teasing him at the pub. She unlocked the car and jumped in before he had the chance to say anything.

"Well, see ya," she called through the closed door, as she started the car and drove quickly out of the car park.

"Bye," he said to the back of her car, a bemused expression on his face.

Stephanie let out a shaky breath. *Stop it,* she told herself firmly. *He is with someone else.*

However, her heart betrayed her by thumping excitedly when she glanced in her rear view mirror and saw James standing with his hands shoved in his pockets, watching her drive away.

Chapter 6

Stephanie pulled her car into what seemed to be the only remaining empty parking space in the village, on Monday morning. She groaned inwardly as she glanced across and saw Victoria about to alight from her shiny new BMW.

They both got out of their cars at the same time. Victoria gave Stephanie's little Fiat a derogatory glance.

"I hope my car doesn't catch rust or something from your heap of junk," she said grimacing.

"Oh, I don't know, yours could do with catching a bit of style," Stephanie replied before she could stop herself. *How dare she insult my car?* she thought, annoyed.

Victoria scowled at her and with a toss of her head, stalked up the road.

Stephanie started in the opposite direction. She had offered to do her grandmother's shopping for her and Ellie had gratefully produced a list, which involved the post office, chemist, supermarket and newsagent.

She was just coming out of the post office, when she almost collided with James.

"Sorry. I wasn't watching where I was I going," she said, as he caught her arm, steadying her.

"That's okay. I was hoping to run into you," he said smiling. "Well, maybe not literally," he added.

"Yeah? Why was that?" she asked, blushing slightly as her skin tingled from where his hand had been.

"Well, I was thinking about you and I realised that I actually have no idea why our families don't speak. So I asked a few questions at home. I got a very chilly reception, but apparently something happened during the war," he said.

"Funny, you should say that," Stephanie replied, and relayed her conversation with her grandmother about the photograph which included his great-uncle. "She did say that we have nothing to do with your family, either."

"Huh – maybe, I'll have a look through our old photos at home and see what I can find," James mused.

"James," a voice called. They both turned to find Victoria crossing the road towards them, a scowl on her face.

"I think that's my cue to leave," Stephanie stage-whispered to him.

The corners of James's mouth turned up slightly.

"Hi, Victoria. Bye, Victoria," she said, turning and walking slowly up the road to continue her errands.

Half an hour later, shopping completed, she rewarded herself with coffee. She was surprised to find the café to be a hive of activity. The tables were filled with young mothers and slightly older women in sports gear. Classical music was playing quietly. She wandered up to the counter and perched on a bar stool. Andy was busy behind the espresso machine.

"What's this – Country Women's Institute?" she whispered across to him.

"I left some flyers at the Community Hall for coffee after yoga and hey presto," he said. He frowned and peered at her.

50

"Everything okay? You don't look your usual bubbly self."

"Nothing one of your macchiatos can't fix." She gave him a small smile. "Mind if I hang out here for a while?"

"Be my guest – you're always welcome," he said.

Stephanie selected an unoccupied armchair in one corner and picked up a magazine off the coffee table to read.

When Andy put her coffee down on the little table beside her chair, she was engrossed in an article on Michelle Obama.

He crouched down beside her and looked into her face. "Missing home?" he asked gently.

She gave a small smile. "It's nothing. Just finding my feet," she said.

"Don't let Victoria get to you. She can be such a bitch. She doesn't want James, but doesn't want anyone else to have him either," he whispered as he stood up and squeezed her shoulder.

"Thanks, Andy," she said and smiled gratefully at him, wondering how on earth he had guessed what was bothering her. She didn't think that she was that transparent. She was going to have to work on her 'game face' – first Matt and now Andy hitting the mark.

* * *

Feeling bored and a little restless later that afternoon, Stephanie threw on her workout gear and went for a run. She hated running. Actually, she hated any form of exercise, but it did seem to be the only thing that kept her weight under control.

She checked her phone when she got back to find a text message waiting, from an unknown number.

Found old photos. Pick up 7pm? James

Stephanie smiled and felt a stirring of excitement deep inside her, as she texted back.

Ok. S

Still grinning, she showered and wandered into her bedroom, wrapped in a towel – what to wear? It wasn't exactly a date – he was just showing her some photos. She selected black leggings and a red denim mini skirt. She rolled her hair into a knot and secured it with a large clip, letting the odd curl fall around her face. She touched up her mascara and added a slick of lip gloss. Studying the effect in the mirror, she decided, *no – it looks like I'm trying too hard.* She unclasped her clip and shook her hair out. Better down. She slipped off the skirt and leggings and pulled on jeans. Casual, but not scruffy. Satisfied, she slipped her feet into a pair of red Converse boots and skipped downstairs for an early dinner.

It was a little after seven pm, when she heard the crunch of tyres on the gravel. She picked up her bag, slung it across her body and slipped out of the main door, calling goodbye to her grandmother. It was too soon for introductions.

A red 911 Porsche was pulled up in front of the house. *Whoa!* James jumped out of the car and came around to the passenger side and opened the door for her.

"Thanks," she said. "Nice car."

"It's my brother's – I use it whenever he's out of town – which luckily for me is fairly often." He closed her door and climbed back into the driver's seat. "You look nice."

Stephanie blushed. "Thanks, how was rehearsal?" she asked, quickly changing the subject.

"Great," James was animated. "We have a couple of new songs which are coming together really well."

The car started with a loud roar and they drove down the driveway, past the pond, through the stone gateway and onto the lane. Stephanie glanced back at the house and saw the curtains twitching in the sitting room – her grandmother didn't miss a thing. *Although, a car like this is a pretty hard thing to miss*, she thought, feeling a little overwhelmed.

They chatted as James sped around the country lanes. Stephanie felt herself relaxing and was surprised to find that even though she now knew who he was, that they still had plenty to talk about and it didn't feel at all awkward. It was just like on the train. After about ten minutes, they drove through the sturdy wrought iron gates that marked the entrance to Knox Manor. To the immediate left was an old stone gate house. It was two-storeyed and lights shone in the downstairs windows. They continued up a winding driveway edged with massive oak trees. As they rounded the corner at the top of the drive, the house itself came into view. It was an impressive sight – a beautiful two-storeyed pale brick 17th century manor house with tall chimneys rising skyward, set in lush, manicured gardens. A long sweeping lawn ran from the front of the house down to a lake.

"Wow, we sure don't get houses like this in New Zealand. It's gorgeous," admired Stephanie.

James nodded. "Yeah, my family has lived here for almost one hundred years." He slowed the car to a stop at the front entrance. Unfolding himself from the car, he ran around to open her door for her. He held out his hand. "This way, mademoiselle," he said.

Stephanie bit her lip nervously, but let him help her from the car and continued to hold his hand as they walked under the stone porch and through a huge wooden door into a semicircular foyer with a spectacular white marble floor and a beautiful round centre table topped with an enormous floral arrangement. A sweeping staircase led up to the first floor.

"It's not exactly shabby inside either," Stephanie said, taking it all in.

"Is that you, James?" a woman's voice called. Stephanie turned as a middle-aged, grey haired woman walked through a doorway into the foyer, wiping her hands on an apron. "Oh, hello. I didn't realise that you had company." She smiled fondly at James.

"Stephanie, this is Grace, our housekeeper. Stephanie has just moved here from New Zealand," James said introducing them.

"Hi," Stephanie smiled. "Good to meet you."

"I've got the photos laid out in the library – this way," James said leading her up the stairs. He opened a door at the top with a flourish and ushered her in. It was a beautiful rectangular room lined on three sides with floor-to-ceiling bookshelves. A ladder rested against one of the shelves to enable the reader to reach the top shelf. Dotted around the room were several comfortable chairs, each with a side table and reading light. One end was dominated by a large oak desk in front of a fire place. Above the fireplace was a brightly coloured painting, of a man walking in the country, in a simple gilt frame.

"What a fantastic library, James. How many books?" she asked.

"Ten thousand apparently – mostly old volumes. My grandfather is the bibliophile. He spends the most time in here," James explained.

Stephanie walked around the room slowly, trailing her hand lightly along the shelves. She stopped by a shelf of the classics, selecting *A Tale of Two Cities*. "I love this book – I made my father take me to Paris as soon as I had read it."

James was watching her, smiling.

"Come and look at these photos – I've laid the best ones out on the desk," he said.

Stephanie replaced the book and followed him to the desk, where twenty old sepia photographs were laid out in neat even rows. Stephanie recognised her great-uncle David and great-aunt Sophie in a couple of them.

"God – you look like your great-aunt," James observed, stepping back to take a better look at her. "If you pulled your hair back from your face like hers," he said as he reached over and gently rolled her hair back around his hand, "you could be sisters." His hand accidently brushed her neck and she inhaled sharply.

"Which one is Edward?" she asked quickly, drawing the attention away from her and back to the photos. She hoped he wasn't looking too hard at her skin – it was a little patchy today, which she put down to the stress of coming here this evening. James let her hair slide through his fingers and pointed to a man in military attire in several of the photos.

"Wow – didn't he look dashing in his uniform?" Stephanie said.

"Really? Men in uniform? I didn't pick you as one of those girls," he teased.

She hit him lightly on the arm. "That's not what I meant. So tell me about him, what's his story? You said he was a war hero."

"Yeah – Battle of Britain, but he was also in a special forces type group who flew top secret missions into France, dropping people behind enemy lines and picking them up when possible.

Do you want to sit?" he asked, motioning towards a couple of chairs.

Stephanie sat down in one of a pair of armchairs facing the desk. She gazed up at the painting on the wall. It was stunning. From her limited art history knowledge, she guessed it was very early Impressionist in style, simpler than some of the later Impressionist works that she knew. She idly wondered who the artist was.

"Do your parents live here, James?" she asked instead.

"Not really. Dad died a few years back – heart attack. And Mum remarried last year – to a polo player half her age," he scoffed. "So they are on the global polo circuit, spending Dad's money." He sounded bitter.

"I'm sorry about your dad – that must have been hard," she sympathised. *Poor guy, maybe that explained his detached, devil may care attitude.*

"Yeah," James said matter-of-factly. "Such is life. What about your family, where are they?"

"Ah, it's a long story. Mum lives in New Zealand and Dad's in London. They have been apart since I was about three. Mum remarried a few years ago. My stepfather is okay, but I think I miss my four-year-old half-brother the most. He is so cool. I have been Skyping him and he kisses the screen goodbye – it's so cute." She finished quickly as tears welled up in her eyes. She looked down at her hands, blushing.

"So no boyfriend left behind in New Zealand?" James asked, arching an eyebrow.

She shook her head. "No, now you were telling me about Edward," she said, bringing the conversation back to something neutral.

"Ah, yes," he said, "he was quite a character."

She looked up and watched him as he spoke. He was animated, warming to his subject. Stephanie found herself very drawn to him. *I bet you've broken some hearts in your time*, she mused.

"From all accounts, Edward was something of a daredevil. He was always the one to run faster, climb higher, dive deeper than his older brother. If you wanted to see sibling rivalry in action, I believe that would have been a classic example. It kind of explains my grandfather in some ways. It must have been tough getting beaten at everything by your younger brother.

"If he lived today, I reckon Edward would be one of those extreme sports junkies. So when the Air Force started recruiting more pilots in the late 1930s, he was one of the first to enlist. He took to flying like a duck to water and moved quickly through the ranks.

"Edward was part of Group 11 Fighter Command when war broke out. You know Churchill's famous comment 'Never was so much owed by so many to so few'? Well, Edward was one of 'The Few'. He and his Spitfire fought against the Luftwaffe throughout August and September 1940 in the Battle of Britain," James said.

"Wow," Stephanie murmured, impressed.

"However, not long after your aunt's death, he volunteered for what many considered to be a suicide mission into France to rescue a number of key Resistance men who had been captured by the Nazis. Amazingly the rescue was a success, but they were shot down leaving the coast of France. Everyone bailed except Edward, who went down with the plane. A merchant navy vessel in the area picked up the survivors and saw the plane explode as it plunged into the sea."

Chapter 7

"So you don't really know anything about Sophie or her relationship with Edward or what happened between them to cause a feud that has lasted this long?" Stephanie asked.

"Just that she was a dreaded Wakefield," James grimaced, faking horror. "Our two families had some feud running before they met and would have nothing to do with one another. The fact that Edward and Sophie were having an affair scandalised both families. And then she died. A car accident, I believe."

Stephanie nodded, her expression thoughtful. "Hey, are you free tomorrow? We could ask my grandmother about her. She was her sister after all," she suggested.

"Yeah, okay. You've been courageous enough to come onto Knox land. I have to be brave enough to venture into Wakefield territory," he said, grinning.

"I love that painting behind the desk. Who is it by?" Stephanie asked, looking up at it again.

"I'm not sure, someone famous apparently. It was given to grandfather by a business acquaintance just before the war. I think it has hung here ever since," James replied glancing at it.

They chatted a little longer on university, the band and their plans for the summer.

"What are you studying at Oxford?" James asked.

"History and economics," she replied.

James looked surprised. "You are full of surprises. I didn't have you down as the business type," he said.

"There's a lot you don't know about me, James," she smiled at him.

"Well it's good that I have the summer to find out then, isn't it?" he smiled back at her, holding her eyes.

Stephanie looked away first and glanced at her watch; nine-thirty pm.

"Is it time for me to take you home?" She wasn't sure if she imagined the disappointment in his voice or whether she was simply hoping it was there. *Stop it,* she told herself sternly.

"Yeah, I think so. This has been really interesting. Thanks for showing me the photos," she said.

"My pleasure," he smiled at her, his gaze lingering on her eyes and dropping to her lips.

Okay, so maybe I didn't imagine that, she thought, her heart beginning to beat faster.

He leaned towards her, just as the library door swung open and a man burst into the room. His resemblance to James was striking, except that he was taller and broader across the chest. His dark hair was cropped and neatly parted and he was wearing an expensive looking dark blue suit. Even more surprising was the fact that he was the younger of the two men with whom her father had exchanged angry words in the village a few days earlier. *Of course, the Knox-Wakefield feud. How didn't I see the resemblance to James, then?* she thought, amazed at her lack of observation.

"Little brother – Grace said I'd find you here. You know we

don't like you entertaining your girlfriends in the library," he said condescendingly. James rolled his eyes as he pulled back from Stephanie and stood up.

"Alex – you're back," he said, his voice flat.

"Mmm, just drove down from London," Alex said rather pompously. "And you are?" He held his hand out to Stephanie who had also risen. He didn't seem to have recognised her.

"Stephanie," she said shaking his hand uncertainly. *Probably best if I don't mention my surname*, she thought, before adding, "Ah, pleased to meet you."

"We were just leaving, Alex. I'm going to drop Stephanie home," James said.

"Mmm. What are these?" Alex looked at the photos spread out on the desk.

"Just looking at some old photos. Stephanie is studying History at Oxford and I thought she might be interested in our famous ancestor," James said.

"Mmm, mmm," Alex replied sounding knowledgeable, "our war hero."

"See ya, Alex." James grabbed Stephanie's hand and pulled her towards the door.

"Bye," she said as she stepped through it, pulling the strap of her bag over her head and across her body.

"Stupid bastard," James muttered, pulling the door closed behind her. Stephanie raised her eyebrows, surprised. *Clearly there is no love lost between the Knox brothers.*

"What does he do, James?" she asked, following him down the sweeping flight of stairs to the main entrance.

"He's a 'fine art and antiques dealer'," he said mimicking his brother's voice. He curled his lip in disgust. "Enough about him – are you up for a slightly more open-air ride home?" he grinned at her.

"Sure?" she said, not at all sure.

"Wait here." He returned a minute later carrying two leather jackets and two motorbike helmets.

Stephanie grinned. "Ah, that sort of open-air ride."

James opened the front door for her and they were about to go through, when a deep voice called. "James?"

"Yes, Grandfather. Just dropping my friend home. I'll be back shortly," James answered politely.

Footsteps echoed across the marble floor of the foyer. Stephanie turned to see a tall, elegant, white haired man walking towards them. He was dressed in a formal shirt and trousers, with a deep blue smoking jacket buttoned up over them. He looked as though he had stepped straight out of a 1950s photo shoot. He was also the companion of the man who had confronted her father in the village.

His smile froze and turned to horror as he looked from Stephanie to James and back to Stephanie.

"W w who..?" he stuttered, his face going pale.

James rushed to his side. "Are you okay?"

The old man's composure returned and he waved his hand impatiently at James's fussing.

"Who is your friend? I don't believe I have had the pleasure?" He eyed her suspiciously.

"This is Stephanie," James said.

"Stephanie who?" the old man asked, not taking his eyes off her.

"Stephanie Cooper, sir. Pleased to meet you," she said as she held out her hand and smiled tentatively at him.

He recoiled as if she had hit him.

"Cooper." He practically spat the name. He shook his head,

turned on his heel and walked back into his study. "I will see you in my study upon your return, James," he ordered, shutting the door with a loud bang.

"Wow, I guess that'll be the feud, then?" Stephanie asked James, who was looking at his grandfather's retreating figure and shaking his head in disbelief.

"Yeah, sorry about that," he said looking embarrassed.

Stephanie followed him through the front door and along to a side gate, puzzled by the old man's reaction. *Feud, sure, but he looked like he'd seen a ghost.*

James led the way around the side of the house to an old stable which had been converted into garages and indicated towards his Vespa with a sweep of his arm. "My stead," he joked. "Here, let me help you." He held the leather jacket out for her and she slipped her arms into it. He pulled the helmet down over her head and attached the clip under her chin. He quickly did the same himself and stepped onto the Vespa.

"Hop on, Steph," he said. It was the first time he had shortened her name, as her old friends did. It sounded somehow very intimate coming from his lips and she hesitated for a moment before swinging on behind him slipping her arms around his waist. Beneath his helmet he grinned and accelerated through a gateway and down the long driveway past the lake.

"Thanks," she said shyly, several minutes later, handing him the jacket and helmet and running her hands through her hair to give it some lift after having the helmet pressed down on it. James lifted the seat of the bike and placed the jacket and helmet inside. He turned to her, removing his own helmet and put his arm around her waist pulling her towards him. They gazed at each other for several seconds before he dipped his head and kissed her very gently on the lips. Their kiss deepened as she twisted her fingers into his hair.

The sound of someone clearing their throat broke them apart.

"I think I should go," James said quietly, glancing over her shoulder before dipping his forehead forward to rest lightly against hers for a moment.

"Yeah, probably best," Stephanie agreed, feeling a little lightheaded.

"See you tomorrow?" he murmured.

"Okay, good night." With an effort she turned and ran up the front steps, slipping past her father who stood with the door open for her. She didn't meet his eyes, but turned briefly and watched James drive down the driveway and out onto the lane.

What about Victoria? she wondered.

Chapter 8

Stephanie slept late the next morning, and by the time she had come downstairs for breakfast her father had gone.

"What was Dad doing here last night?" Stephanie asked her grandmother, as she poured herself a bowl of cereal.

"He is hosting a conference in the guest house in a few days, so he was setting up, I suppose," she replied.

After breakfast, Stephanie popped into the village to get her morning coffee and agree her hours for the week with Andy.

She was leaning against the counter chatting to him when she felt someone close behind her.

"Hi, you," James bumped her shoulder gently with his. "Are we still on for seeing your grandmother later?"

"Yeah – come over around three?" she suggested. They stepped away from the counter as a group of people arrived and ordered coffee.

"Okay," he replied looking at her intently. "I really enjoyed last night."

Stephanie blushed, "Yeah, me too."

James raised an eyebrow "It would be good not to be interrupted next time."

Stephanie was still smiling as she left the café, and bumped straight into Matt, who stood blocking her way. His eyes slid over her slightly flushed face and shook his head over her shoulder at James, who glared back. Matt draped his arm around Stephanie's shoulders and pulled her outside.

"Wotcha doing, Steph? You don't want to become another of Knox's conquests, 'cause believe me, that bed post has quite a few notches on it," he said quietly as he walked her around to her car.

Stephanie blushed. "Don't be a killjoy, Matt," she said, slightly annoyed at having her happy bubble burst. "I'm just having fun."

"Well, I'm just looking out for you, cuz," he said gently. "I don't want to see you get hurt. Our family doesn't have a good track record when it comes to the Knoxes."

Stephanie struggled to shake her irritation as she drove home. *I don't think I'm quite as naïve as Matt suggested, but of course James is in a band and as we all know, musicians attract girls like mud attracts pigs. I am clearly going to have to be on my guard around James and not let things get out of my control.*

* * *

Three o'clock rolled around before she knew it, and the crunch of tyres on the gravel announced James's arrival. He was stepping out of yet another vehicle from the Knox garage, when she opened the door.

"Hey, come on in." She held the door open for him.

"Hi, Steph." He leaned over and kissed her lightly on the lips.

She felt a little shimmer of excitement run through her and tried to suppress Matt's voice in her head.

James looked around, taking in the wide curve of the

65

staircase, the oak panels on the walls and the mosaic tiles of the foyer. The scent of roses hung heavily in the air from two enormous arrangements on side tables on either side of the entrance hall, which were reflected back at each other by huge gilt-framed mirrors.

Stephanie motioned for James to follow her through a door into the sitting room. Ellie Cooper was sitting with a very straight back in an armchair by the window, a book open on her lap.

"There you are, darling." Ellie's smile disappeared as she looked past Stephanie at James. Taking in his mop of hair, tight t-shirt and skinny black jeans, she asked, "Who's this?"

"Grandma, let me introduce you to James Knox. He is in a band with Andy from the café," she said.

"Well, well," Ellie replied, a hint of amusement in her voice.

"Pleased to meet you, Mrs Cooper," James said extending his hand politely.

Ellie took his hand and looking him directly in the eye, said, "You are the first Knox to enter my house in more than sixty years."

"Really?" Stephanie and James said in unison.

"If it wasn't for your family, young man, my beloved sister would still be alive," she said sadly.

Stephanie and James exchanged looks. *Maybe we will get some answers about the origins of the feud,* Stephanie thought excitedly.

"Grandma," Stephanie said gently, "that's what we were hoping to talk to you about."

Ellie's eyes glistened with tears.

"But, if it's too hard…" Stephanie began, belatedly realising that her grandmother may not want to talk about her dead sister.

"No, dear, sit down. You too," she said, nodding to James. "I believe it's time you heard the truth about that family of yours."

James tensed, ready to defend his family's honour.

"James…" Stephanie started to say.

"Sit down, young man," Ellie said sharply. "Once I've told you the story of my sister and your uncle – then maybe you'll understand why we distrust your family."

James sat, but gave Stephanie a look which said, *I am only doing this for you.* She reached across and squeezed his hand.

Ellie began.

"The feud actually started with my father and your great-grandfather – no one remembers why, although we all thought as children it was over my mother who was something of a local beauty. Their wives, my dear mother and your great-grandmother, James, were friends before they married – and they continued to see one another socially – without their menfolk and not to their knowledge, I believe. However, my brother, sister and I grew up having very little to do with the Knox brothers.

"My sister Sophie turned eighteen at the beginning of 1939. She was very beautiful, kind and funny. With the country preparing for war – her debut into society was somewhat subdued. But she didn't care as she, like most other young women of the day, was desperate to help the war effort. However, Father forbade her to get a job, saying that war was men's business. He was very conservative, you understand. Sophie, however, had other ideas and she secretly planned to become a nurse. She was desperate to escape the confines of life in the country and craved excitement.

"Your great-uncle Edward, young man, was training with the RAF at Biggin Hill, near London. It was there that he met my brother David. They were two peas in a pod those two – both daring and brave and full of fun. Needless to say, they hit it off immediately. So when they came home in the spring of 1939 on leave, they weren't about to let their feuding fathers interrupt the social whirl that seemed to follow them wherever they went.

"Sophie and Edward didn't get off to a great start – in fact she hated him at first – years of hearing our father blustering about those awful Knoxes probably influenced her. They met at a dance over at the Lewises'. He thought she was beautiful and fiery, she thought he was arrogant and conceited.

"Throughout their two weeks of leave there were parties and dinners every night to which David would escort Sophie. Somewhere along the way she thawed and fell for Edward. By the time the boys were due back at base, Sophie and Edward were very much in love.

"In September of that year Hitler invaded Poland and war was declared. There was an awful row at home when Sophie announced at dinner one night that she was to begin training as a nurse at Great Ormond Street hospital in London. Father blustered and shouted, but with Mother's blessing, she left the following Monday. Father had to back down after Mother quite rightly pointed out that Princess Elizabeth was training to be a mechanic to help the war effort. I cried and cried, but Sophie wrote to me every week – you can read the letters if you would like, Stephanie – they were full of life on the hospital wards, the strict sisters and the dashing military men and of course, Edward whom she was seeing at every opportunity.

"They all came home again over Christmas. Sophie was

having dinner at the Knoxes' most evenings – much to the disgust of both fathers who each threatened to disinherit their offspring if they continued courting. But Sophie and Edward were so in love that there was no stopping them.

"You must realise that there was a war on and people were very aware that life was to be treasured.

"However, their happiness wasn't to last. Sophie came home one evening very upset. She had overheard a conversation between Edward's brother Charles and his father discussing where to safely store a number of valuable German paintings. Charles had caught her eavesdropping and shouted at her.

"There had been rumours in the village that the Knox family were spying for the Germans, but no one really believed it. Now David and Sophie started making a list of all the foreigners they had met at the Knox parties. They started asking lots of questions which didn't go unnoticed by Charles and his father who banned them from any further functions. David was furious and confronted Edward in the village pub about just what the Knoxes were up to. There was a huge row, with things said that shouldn't have been.

"Edward, being a Knox, defended his family's honour and he and David fell out."

"I'm not surprised," James muttered.

Ellie ignored him and continued with her story. "Soon the boys were flying again and Sophie was back working at the hospital, but the rumour mill continued. The Knoxes were shunned as whispers of 'collaborators' circulated. Officials from the Ministry of Defence arrived at Knox Manor to investigate. And although an inquiry exonerated them of any wrongdoing, it was a long time before the Knox family were welcome in polite society. Charles and his father placed the blame for their family's misfortune squarely with our family.

"Despite this Sophie and Edward were still very much in love and continued to see one another when their schedules allowed. The hatred between the families had deepened so much that they decided the next time they both had leave that they would elope.

"Sophie came home one weekend before the planned elopement and drove to Knox Manor to seek the blessing of Edward's mother. No one knows whether she got it or not, but the housekeeper recalled seeing her flee from the house with Charles in pursuit."

Ellie paused to dab a stray tear from her cheek with a lace handkerchief.

"She was found dead the following morning – thrown from her car. The official reports were that she failed to take a bend and slid on the wet road, but neighbours told David that they heard two cars speeding on the road, but the second driver never came forward," Ellie continued. "Charles, of course, insisted that he had not left the house the entire evening. No one had any reason to doubt him, except David, who always believed Charles to be responsible. He insisted that Sophie had seen something at the manor that night that she shouldn't have and that she had been killed because of it. My father, however, put a stop to any further investigation – nothing would bring Sophie back and as that family had already cost him one child, he wanted nothing further to do with the Knoxes.

"Edward was inconsolable, I'm told. He was killed during a mission to France several months later."

"Oh my God," Stephanie gasped when her grandmother had finished speaking. Tears threatened to spill from her eyes. She looked at James, whose hard expression softened slightly when he saw her emotion. "What a tragic story."

"What is even more tragic is that the accident was never investigated properly. The police answered to the landowners in those days – which didn't necessarily mean that the law was always upheld," Ellie said.

"I really don't like what you are insinuating," James said quietly, his anger tightly controlled. "Collaborators – I have never heard anything so ridiculous."

"Well, it is quite well documented. There was an investigation. You have to remember this was immediately after the war began and fear of the Germans was running high in England at the time," Ellie said.

"Yes – but it was just wild hysteria, and you said yourself, we were exonerated," James demanded, his expression dark.

"Yes the claims were never proven – although my sister had certainly come across something. Otherwise, why would they have killed her?" Ellie asked.

"Do you really believe that Sophie was murdered?" Stephanie was shocked. Her grandmother merely nodded.

James's voice was cold and a storm was brewing in his eyes. "Now you're accusing my family of murder – my *grandfather* of murder." He jumped up. "I've heard enough. I think I should go." He nodded at Ellie and strode to the door, fists clenched at his side.

"Your family loyalty is to be admired, young man, but you should ask your grandfather what really happened," Ellie called after him.

"I'll see you out," Stephanie whispered, through gritted teeth, following him into the entrance hall and closing the sitting room door behind them. "You shouldn't speak to my grandmother like that," she hissed, glaring at him.

"You expect me to sit there and listen to the bitter and twisted ramblings of an old woman, accusing my family of wartime collaboration and murder?" he asked incredulously, anger radiating from him.

"No smoke without fire, eh?" Stephanie retorted, then immediately regretted the words. She wished that she would stop and think before opening her mouth sometimes.

James went very still.

"Not you as well," he said, shaking his head at her, disgusted. Anger and something else that she couldn't quite place flashed in his eyes. She reached out to touch his arm, but pulled back, her pride getting the better of her. Instead she defiantly lifted her chin and matched his cold expression. Their passion of the previous night suddenly seemed a distant memory. They glared at each other for several moments, neither willing to back down.

"Don't let the door hit you on the way out," Stephanie said as she turned on her heels and strode back towards her grandmother. She jumped when the front door slammed shut behind her. She heard James's car door close with a loud thud and after a few seconds his car was speeding down the drive, stones flying in its wake.

Stephanie leaned back against the wall and closed her eyes, shaking.

"Stephanie?" Ellie was standing in the doorway.

"Arrogant bastard," Stephanie muttered. "Oops. I'm sorry, Grandma."

"Ah, don't be. It is not a story that I would have wanted to hear if I was him, either." She sniffed. "He certainly has the charm and good looks of the Knoxes, but they have a cruel streak to them, especially if things don't go their way."

"Oh, Grandma." Stephanie moved to Ellie's side, giving her a gentle hug.

"Actually, darling, you look a lot like Sophie did at your age," Ellie noted.

"Do I? James said something similar when we were looking at some old photos at his place. His grandfather nearly had a heart attack when he saw me," Stephanie said.

Ellie went pale and put a hand to her throat. "You've been to Knox Manor?"

"Yes, last night."

Ellie chuckled. "I'll bet old Charles thought he had seen a ghost."

"Yeah, he certainly wasn't very happy to meet me," Stephanie agreed.

"Don't worry about James," Ellie said, patting Stephanie's arm. "If he's anything like his great-uncle there will be a fine line between anger and passion."

Stephanie blushed and Ellie looked at her knowingly. "I have Sophie's diaries here somewhere. They may help you to better understand the difficulties of those times. But please be careful, dear – I'm afraid the Knoxes are not a family that I can trust."

Chapter 9

Stephanie saw James again sooner than she expected. He was leaving the café, just as she was arriving to start her shift, the next day. After an evening to reflect, she felt guilty that she had responded so badly to him the previous day. Her grandmother was right. Those revelations would have been hard to hear. She imagined that she would have reacted in a similar way if it had been the other way around.

"James?" she called, a feeling of nervous anticipation running through her.

"What?" he said stopping and glaring at her, his voice hard and his eyes distant. He didn't so much say the word as spit it at her. *Oh great*, she thought with a sinking feeling, *he's still angry.*

"I've come across some of Sophie's old journals – they are fascinating. Edward is mentioned quite a lot. Would you like to look at them?" she said. *Just say you are sorry*, an internal voice was telling her, but she just couldn't make the words come out.

He looked at her coldly and said, "No – I'm not interested in *anything* your family has."

Stephanie flinched and felt the sting of rejection hit her. *Ouch*, she thought.

"Good to see you've cooled off then," she said sarcastically.

"What? I think I'm entitled to be pissed off after what your grandmother, *and you*, insinuated yesterday," he said angrily.

Yeah that's right, take the moral high ground, Stephanie thought, annoyed. She slowly shook her head. "I see the Knoxes have taught their sons to hold grudges," she retorted.

"Us hold grudges?" James said incredulous. "Your grand-mother's been harbouring one for seventy years."

"Whatever, James – let me know when you decide to stop being such an arrogant git," Stephanie said, turning and walking quickly into the café, tears stinging her eyes. She wouldn't give him the satisfaction of making her cry.

* * *

Over the next few days, after dinner with her grandmother, Stephanie curled up on the sofa with Sophie's journals. She was enjoying being pulled back into another time. She had started reading at the beginning of 1939 and was now through to August. Sophie had been to a dinner party with Edward and her brother David, while they were home on leave.

> *David and I had dinner at Knox Manor last night. We were not the only guests. Edward's father and brother Charles were entertaining foreign visitors and looked none too pleased when we arrived. Edward was called aside and we heard the word Wakefield said in not a very nice manner!*
>
> *However, Edward's mother, always charming, intro-duced us to Baron von Katsburg and Herr Ritter, business acquaintances from Munich and Herr Hoffman, the*

curator of the National Gallery in Berlin.

Herr Hoffman was a curious fellow. He was very quiet at dinner and talked only with Charles. Only after dinner when Mr Knox and Charles retired to the study with their other guests, did Herr Hoffman join us in the drawing room.

He told a most unusual story about the Berlin Fire Brigade setting fire to countless items of irreplaceable art on the orders of Hitler himself! I do believe he had tears in his eyes as he described the beautiful paintings that he had witnessed being burned. He told us in a whisper, looking over his shoulder in the direction of the study, that he thought Hitler to be a madman. He didn't find anyone in our little group to contradict that opinion! He swore that he would spend the rest of his life trying to safeguard these irreplaceable paintings that were being needlessly destroyed!

Stephanie worked several afternoon shifts at the café during the week, while Andy rehearsed with the band. The conversation on Friday, as she made numerous coffees, teas and hot chocolates, was dominated by the fact that The Fury was playing at the pub again that night.

When her shift finished she collapsed on a sofa in the corner, with a flat white and her book. Michael arrived a short time later to discuss some updates to the band's website, with Andy.

"Are you coming tonight, Steph?" he asked. Stephanie looked up from her book, *The Origins of World War II.* Having spent the week reading her diaries, Stephanie felt like she was really getting to know Sophie. And that in turn, had rekindled her interest in mid-twentieth century European history. She had briefly studied it at school, but it somehow seemed more relevant, less abstract, living in England with family connections to anchor her to the past.

"No. I don't think I'd be very welcome," she said as she noticed James, who had arrived with Andy, holding court on the opposite side of the room. He caught her eye, scowled and looked away. *Ouch, you arrogant, conceited...*Stephanie quickly looked back at Michael. "And besides, I have an action packed evening with a bunch of dull old lawyers," she said with a wry laugh.

"Lucky you." Michael noticed the look that passed between Stephanie and James. "Hey, what's happened between you and Knox?" he asked. "I thought you two were getting cosy, but he's been shooting you daggers all week."

"Long story and one I won't bore you with. Suffice to say the feud between our families is alive and well," she said. She went back to her book, feeling miserable, while Michael sat up at the counter with his iPad open and chatted to Andy.

She heard laughter across the room and looked over and saw James, Jack and Dave with their heads together.

She sighed and gathering her things, waved to Andy as she walked to the door.

As she passed James's table, he glanced up. "What are you looking at?" he asked cruelly.

Stephanie stopped and very obviously looked him up and down. "I'm not sure, but there are a number of labels that could easily fit," she retorted grimacing.

Behind him Jack hooted with laughter and hi-fived Dave.

James's lip curled, "You little…"

With a toss of her hair she strode from the building before he could finish.

* * *

Stephanie arrived home to find her father's meeting was underway in the conference facility in the old guesthouse.

She flopped on the sofa in her bedroom and picked up Sophie's diary from 1940.

> *Dinner at the Knoxes' again. It's getting more and more uncomfortable. Only Edward's mother speaks to me – even the staff are rude! I know it's difficult for Edward – they are his family after all, but really! I am not my father. Their behaviour is the height of bad manners! Several foreign visitors tonight. One gentleman spent the evening speaking in whispered tones to Charles at one end of the table. It was very strange and they excused themselves to his study after the main course. When Edward went to get them for dessert, they were gone. It was as if they had vanished. Charles returned and said Herr von Gutenberg was tired and had gone up to bed. Strangely, Charles had dirt on his hands and cuffs and his usually tidy hair was dishevelled. It was all very mysterious.*

Stephanie paused thoughtfully. The next entry looked like it was written hastily.

> *Edward was in the drawing room when I arrived at Knox Manor last night, admiring a new painting that Charles had acquired. Quite where from with the war, I don't know.*
> *Edward showed me into Charles' study. It was jammed*

with all sorts of treasures. I had never seen anything like it – books, unframed paintings, various ornaments stacked on the bookshelves and mantel, and jewellery just lying on his desk. But it was the paintings that caught my attention. There was a Matisse, a Degas, a Chagall and a Monet among others. Unfortunately, he came in while we were admiring his art collection. He went mad! I don't believe I have ever seen anyone as angry.

He went so red in the face that I thought he might explode! We were ordered from the room. Edward told me today that I was not to mention our discovery to anyone. Apparently Charles is helping out some European friends by storing their valuables so that the Nazis can't get their hands on them.

Stephanie grabbed a notebook from her desk and turned to a fresh sheet. She began listing the names of the foreign visitors mentioned in Sophie's diary and the dates of their visits with the Knoxes. Very quickly, she had a list of twenty-five individuals. Opening her iPad, she started searching each name and artist mentioned by Sophie, on the internet. There were hundreds of combinations and potential website links. Interestingly a number of the searches came up with results relating to looted Nazi art, which distracted her momentarily.

There has got be a quicker, more accurate way of doing this, she thought, picking up her mobile and speed dialling Michael's number.

"Hi, Michael. I was wondering if you were doing anything this afternoon? I need some help doing an internet search," she said.

"Sure, Steph, I'll be there shortly." He sounded delighted.

True to his word Michael arrived about ten minutes later.

"Okay. So what are ya trying to search for?" he asked.

"Well, I'm trying to cross reference a list of artists with a list of people to see if there are any links between them. And I can't work out how to do it other than one by one. Even then I get hundreds of search results. I'm not sure how to narrow the search down," she explained, shrugging her shoulders and waving her hands in frustration at her laptop.

Michael nodded. "It's a common problem with search engines. You need a special programme to run a search like that."

Stephanie's face fell.

"However, I happen to have such a programme. I wrote it for computer science last year, but I haven't had a real world scenario to test it on," he said proudly.

Stephanie smiled. "Great! What do you need?"

"Just email me your lists and I'll get going on it," Michael said.

"Okay – but don't let me hold you up on your other work – this is just a side project," Stephanie said. Michael had a successful part time website building business, the proceeds of which would more than pay his way through university.

"Hey, it's no problem – I will have it running on a spare computer," he said.

Stephanie returned to Sophie's journals after Michael left. They were mainly filled with her love for Edward, but there were several entries concerning her dislike of his brother Charles, who frightened her. Stephanie checked the date – April 1940, before reading.

*Father gleefully slammed the newspaper down upon
seeing the main headline at breakfast this morning
announcing an investigation into the Knox family for
collaborating with the enemy! He said that this just
confirmed his suspicions that the Knoxes were rotten to
the core. 'They should all be shot as traitors!' he stated,
before forbidding David and me from ever setting foot
in their home again.*

Collaborators? That's treason!

I pray that Edward isn't somehow involved.

Hang on, Stephanie thought, her heart racing. *I'm sure an
official investigation would be part of the public record.* She picked
up her iPad and looked up a telephone number and dialled.

"Hello, Carlswick Museum and Historical Society," a pleas-
ant older woman answered.

"Hello, my name's Stephanie. I'm doing some research on
events in the village before and during World War II and I was
wondering if you could help me?" she said.

"I'm sure we can, dear," the woman sounded helpful. "Were
you after anything specific?"

"Actually, yes – I'm interested in the collaboration claims
made against the Knox family and the subsequent investigation," Stephanie said.

There was a brief hesitation on the line. "That's very specific,
dear. But I'm sure that we have some information here on
that. I would have to look it out for you. Can you come in
next week?" the woman said.

"Yes. Thank you very much. I'll pop in on Monday."
Stephanie clicked the phone off and kept reading.

Later that evening, the woman from the museum visited

her sister for their weekly gossip.

"I had an interesting phone call today from a young woman doing some research on World War II and the Knoxes. She wants a copy of the collaboration report," she said.

"Really?" her sister Grace answered. "Old Charles won't like that."

Chapter 10

Max Cooper's meeting adjourned at five-thirty pm and Stephanie and Ellie had been invited to join them on the terrace for drinks. Stephanie had rolled her eyes and sighed heavily at hearing her father's request the night before. Dinner with a bunch of corporate lawyers – just what she didn't need. *Maybe I can cite jetlag and escape straight after? Bit of stretch given that I've been here two weeks, but worth a try.*

She put on her favourite mini dress with blue knee-high boots and tied her hair up into a loose knot on top of her head. Ellie looked her over when she skipped down the stairs and smiled indulgently. "You are certainly not one to blend in, are you, dear?" she said.

Stephanie grinned and took her grandmother's arm, helping her out to the terrace. The ten lawyers were already sipping gin and tonics and admiring the view out over the countryside. The village was nestled into the hillside opposite appearing as if it were tumbling down into the valley, and the river wound its way lazily towards the coast. One edge of Knox Manor peeked out from the trees on the ridge opposite.

"Ah, here you are." Her father turned and smiled. Max was impeccably dressed in a charcoal suit, with a pale blue striped shirt and a red silk tie dotted with a pattern of tiny pale blue diamonds. "May I introduce you all to my mother and my beautiful daughter Stephanie – some of you will already have met?" There were nods and murmurs of hello from the group. Max took his mother's arm and kissed her cheek.

Stephanie looked over the group of lawyers – seven men and three women. All mid-thirties or older, except for one guy standing slightly off to the side with his back to her – there was something familiar about the way he carried himself.

Mm, she thought. *You're a little young to be one of the usual clones.* As if he sensed her looking at him, he turned, smiled and walked toward her. Stephanie gasped. Sam. She had dated Sam in London over the winter, before he had announced that he was off overseas on his gap year and broke up with her. All of the angry bitter comments that she had stored up to say to him the next time she saw him, suddenly eluded her. She opened and closed her mouth in surprise. *What is he doing here?*

"Well, this retreat just suddenly got a whole lot more interesting," Sam murmured conspiratorially, leaning down towards her. "How are you, Stephanie?"

Stephanie looked him over, catching the oddly familiar smell of the hair product he used – *funny what your nose remembers*. "Hi, Sam – I wouldn't let my father hear you say that," she said, recovering somewhat.

Six months in the sun hasn't done him any harm, she thought noticing how the tan he was sporting made his hair seem blonder and eyes bluer. He was dressed in a navy blue suit with a pale pink shirt and matching blue and pink tie. His straight hair had been cut shorter than she remembered, and was parted so that it swept across his forehead. His relaxed smile showed off straight white teeth and his eyes were full of mischief.

"Are you visiting too?" He held her gaze for a second or two longer than was necessary or comfortable.

She bit her lower lip to stop herself blushing at his obvious flirtation. *There is no way I am going to fall for his charm again. Despite what Anna says, there is no unfinished business here. But, a little harmless flirtation couldn't hurt, could it?*

"No. I'm spending the summer here, trying to keep out of trouble before uni starts," she said, glancing up at him through her eyelashes.

He chuckled, a low deep laugh that she remembered so well. "Somehow, I don't see that happening."

"I don't know what you mean," she exclaimed.

"Look at you," he replied, very deliberating looking her up and down. "And with that cute accent thrown in, those poor country boys don't stand a chance," he replied.

She inclined her head and smiled, acknowledging the compliment.

"What about you? How did you end up working for dear old Dad? I thought you were in the depths of South America," she asked. *Bedding as many voluptuous Brazilians as possible*, she thought.

"Internship before uni. My father insisted that I do some work after travelling," he explained. Sam's father, Peter Jones, was one of Max Cooper's oldest friends and business partner in his city law firm. "The boys and I spent the summer in Vietnam, Lombok, Laos and Thailand, before heading to South America – we surfed in Mexico, dived in Belize and partied at the carnival in Rio. I'd like to head back there for a holiday before uni starts."

"That is so cool." Stephanie couldn't help but be impressed. "I haven't been to South America," she said.

Sam reached out to brush away a stray hair that had blown across Stephanie's cheek. "Maybe you could come with me," he suggested.

Stephanie bit her lip again. The nerve endings in her cheek tingled where his fingers had brushed it. *Oh. I had forgotten how charming you could be,* she thought, a little wary, her senses on high alert. Still it felt really nice to have some male attention after the frosty reception she had been receiving from James all week.

"I do hope you are not flirting with my granddaughter, young man," a sharp voice called. Stephanie blushed and spun around. Ellie had ignored the wicker chair that Max had provided for her and was leaning back on her stick watching them with amusement.

Stephanie recovered her composure. "Grandma, you remember Sam. He's interning with Dad before uni," she said.

Sam extended his hand and said, "Hello again, Mrs Cooper." He flashed his charming smile at her. Ellie looked him up and down, unimpressed. "I remember your father at your age – Peter was good looking and charming too," she said. She turned to Stephanie. "I'd watch this one," she advised.

"Thanks, Grandma, I will," Stephanie said blushing again. *Damn, I wish that wouldn't happen,* she thought cursing her penchant for blushing at inopportune times.

They were interrupted by Max tapping the side of his glass and announcing dinner.

Ellie held out her arm for Sam to take. "Come on, young man – you can escort me to dinner and tell me all about your travels."

Sam graciously took her arm. Ellie winked at Stephanie behind Sam's back. Stephanie looked at her in surprise. Just what did her grandmother know of Stephanie's broken heart? Was she trying to protect her? Stephanie felt a rush of gratitude.

Stephanie found herself seated at the opposite end of the table between her father and one of his senior executives, an eternal bachelor named Steven.

"I hear you've been asking questions about the Knoxes," Max said to her as they finished the soup course. "Why's that?"

"It's nothing. You know me and history. And it seems that there is a juicy little feud between our families," she replied. "Actually, maybe you can shed some light on things for me?" she added.

"Probably not, Steph. From what I understand, there's nothing of interest there. If you want juicy family history, there's an eccentric uncle somewhere in the tree, who led a fascinating life – he was Governor in India or something…" Max said.

What? Stephanie thought. *That sounded like a fob off, if ever I heard one.*

"But didn't Aunt Sophie and Uncle David uncover some German connection with the Knoxes that possibly resulted in her death?" she asked, not willing to be put off that easily.

"Ah, you've been talking to your grandmother I see," he said smiling.

"Yeah and reading Sophie's journals. I was wondering if David left any memoirs?" she asked.

Max became serious. "Don't go there, Steph. What does the Knox boy make of all this?" he asked.

Stephanie frowned. "He's currently not speaking to me. He

wasn't very happy with Grandma's version of events," she said.

Max nodded, satisfied. "Good. Best keep it that way."

"Really? So the feud just continues into another generation then?" she asked, incredulous.

Max gave her one of those parental 'that's enough – we'll discuss this later' looks.

Rolling her eyes, Stephanie sat back as one of the women from a local catering firm placed the main course in front of her.

Looking down the table, she realised that Sam was watching her. *Trust Sam to walk back into my life like nothing had happened. But if he expects me to be running back to him, he has another think coming*, she thought petulantly. Sam inclined his head towards Ellie as she spoke and continued to hold Stephanie's gaze, giving her a slow smile.

Finally dinner was over and the party dispersed – some to the terrace for cognac, some to the lounge to check their messages and phone their families. Ellie excused herself to her room.

Sam slowly wandered to Stephanie's side, making a pretence of admiring the art works adorning the dining room walls.

"Do you think we can escape?" he murmured, leaning close to her, his lips brushing her hair. After a week of feeling hurt by James's rejection, Sam's familiarity felt somehow comforting. And even though she had absolutely no intention of rekindling anything with him, she knew that she would be guaranteed a fun night out if he was around.

Making a spur of the moment decision, she grabbed his hand. "I thought you'd never ask. Come on," she said. She led him out a side door and down some stone steps to where the Fiat was parked in front of the house.

"Don't worry. I've only had a few sips of wine," she said, slipping into the driver's seat. "How would you like to sample the local nightlife?"

"Sure. I didn't realise that they even had such a thing down here," Sam said as he let himself into the passenger seat.

Stephanie saw her father watching them from the terrace. She waved as she clicked her seatbelt across her body. She expected him to look annoyed at her kidnapping his young protégé – but instead he was smiling and looking satisfied. Stephanie frowned. *Of course*, she thought, *he's just happy that I'm going out with Sam and not James Knox.*

Still frowning, she glanced at Sam who was pulling his seatbelt across himself.

"What?" he asked, catching her expression.

"Nothing." She pulled her gaze away and started the engine, glancing in the rear view mirror at the retreating figure of her father.

"It's great to see you again, Steph. I've been meaning to give you a call," Sam said smoothly.

"Of course you have," she replied sarcastically.

"No really. I've only been back a week and straight into work," he said. "Hey, this is great, sneaking off with you. Feels just like old times." He reached over and brushed a piece of hair off Stephanie's face and tucked it behind her ear. "Remember when we used to sneak off and snog in doorways and mess around a bit?"

Stephanie shivered pleasantly at the memory and felt her blush rising, but somehow managed to keep a cool tone to her voice. "Well, that's so not happening again anytime soon." She put the car in gear and sped down the driveway.

Sam looked across at her and smiled as if accepting a

89

challenge. "Steph, you can't mean that."

Chapter 11

Ten minutes later, Stephanie pushed the door of the pub open. The smell of stale beer and roast meat hit her. She wrinkled her nose – these country pubs were so different to the modern city pubs that she enjoyed going to back home. However, it was crowded at ten o'clock on a Friday night and had a good vibe.

The band was playing. Stephanie scanned the room and saw Michael propped up on a stool at the bar with Mary and some other friends. They noticed her and waved her over. She took Sam's hand. "Come and meet some friends of mine," she called above the music.

She felt eyes on her as they crossed the room and she turned her head towards the stage. James was watching her as he played. He looked firstly at Sam and then down at his hand in Stephanie's and raised an eyebrow. She hastily freed her hand and Sam instead put his arm around her waist and put his lips to her ear. "Hey, isn't that The Fury? We saw them play in London in January, remember? – they're really good," he said loudly to be heard over the music.

"Yeah, they're from around here," she said, all of a sudden feeling very conscious of his hands on her and James's eyes on them both. She glanced back at the stage. James looked away as he continued to play. Stephanie shook her head at him. *Unbelievable – you were the one that pushed me away*, she thought. They made their way through the crowded tables to where Michael and his friends were sitting.

"Hey, Steph. You managed to escape legal aid," he said grinning.

Sam looked at her with an expression of mock surprise and said, "So that's what we are to you?"

She giggled and pointedly turned her back to the band and introduced Sam to the group.

"What are you having Steph? G&T?" Sam asked, about to order her usual tipple.

"No. Glass of red – that New Zealand pinot would be good," she said glancing at the blackboard behind the bar where the specials were written in chalk. She didn't like it that Sam considered her so predictable that he could just order for her after all this time. The barman heard her and nodded, reaching for a glass and twisting the screw cap off the bottle.

"And a beer for me," Sam added, indicating his choice. "Cheers. I'll get these," he said, as Stephanie went to hand him some cash. Sam paid the barman and handed her the drink, smiling.

"Sam's an old friend of mine who's interning at Dad's firm before uni starts," Stephanie explained to Michael, nodding her thanks to Sam at the same time.

Michael grinned and said, "So does that mean that you know where all the Cooper secrets are hidden?"

Sam laughed. "Yeah, whadda ya want to know?"

"Hey! I'm standing right here." Stephanie looked from Michael to Sam, shaking her head, laughing.

"Is James still not speaking to you?" Michael asked, looking towards the stage.

"Huh – he's being an arrogant little shit," Stephanie replied.

"Who's James?" Sam asked interested.

Stephanie nodded towards the stage. "The moody guitarist," she said. James was looking in their direction as he harmonised with Liam.

Sam raised his eyebrows. A mixture of possessiveness and jealously crossed his face.

"A muso, Steph – what a surprise," he muttered sarcastically. In a louder voice he asked, "What have you done to annoy him?"

"Long story, but put it this way, his family and mine have hated each other for more than seventy years and my generation doesn't look like altering that," she said sadly.

"Hey," Sam said, changing the subject. "Wanna dance?" The Fury had just launched into its summer hit and people were flocking to the dance floor. She looked over at the stage again and saw Andy looking their way. He grinned and she gave him a little wave.

"Okay," she smiled at Sam eagerly and followed him to the dance floor. They moved around each other in time to the music, bouncing up and down with the other dancers during the chorus. Stephanie didn't dare look up at the stage again, but she was sure that she could feel James's glare burning into her.

Stuff him, she thought as Sam caught her around the waist as the song ended. Around them the crowd clapped enthusiastically at the band.

"I had forgotten how much fun it was dancing with you," Sam said still holding her. "You'll have to have a weekend in London and we'll go clubbing like we used to," he called above the opening chords of the next song.

On stage, Liam glanced at James and followed the direction of his stare to where Sam and Stephanie were standing close together waiting for the next song to start. He grinned, seizing the chance to wind James up.

"Guys, let's do the new one," he called.

The song was a slower ballad. Sam's hands remained on her waist as they swayed to the opening chords. Stephanie closed her eyes, letting the music wash over her. This all seemed so familiar and comfortable. Before she realised what she was doing, she had twisted her hands around his neck and smiled up at him – then jumped back as a scream of feedback came from the stage. The music stopped abruptly.

"Sorry," James muttered into his microphone. "Broke a string. We'll take a break."

Liam started laughing, watching the emotions emanate from James, Sam and Stephanie. Stephanie was shocked at her momentary lapse of control, Sam was delighted that she had responded to him and James's fury was palpable. Liam caught James's eye and winked.

"You bastard," James mouthed at him, suddenly realising what Liam had done.

Sam turned back towards the bar where they had left their drinks with Michael. Stephanie looked up at the stage. The boys were jumping down and heading for the bar also. James threw his guitar off and glanced at her – a look of triumph. She glared back at him. He shrugged his shoulders innocently and indicated to his guitar. She looked down at it – not a broken string in sight.

"Huh," she sneered at him, unimpressed. She spun around and stalked back to Sam and Michael.

As soon as she turned her back, James's expression was replaced by a frown. "Who the hell is that guy with his hands all over Stephanie?" he quietly asked Andy. Andy shrugged.

Sam was chatting to Michael about his travels in South East Asia, with his arm loosely around Stephanie's waist, his hand resting on her hip, when James leaned across her and grabbed the beer that the barman had placed for him on the bar.

"Cheers, mate," James said, acknowledging the barman.

"Well that took ages to fix," Stephanie said sarcastically as she turned towards him, wriggling out from under Sam's arm. "Just as well you all took a break."

"Yeah, the dance floor was getting rather crowded anyway," he said, his eyes flashing. She tilted her head and raised her eyebrows, trying to determine whether that was a snipe at her. *Yeah, it probably was.* They glared at each other for a few seconds until she bit her lip and he was undone by the softening of her gaze.

"Steph."

"James." They spoke over one another.

Sam spun around and tightened his arm possessively around her. "Hi, we haven't met. I'm Sam," he said.

"James." James eyes flicked briefly to Sam, but he ignored his outstretched hand. "Steph, come and talk to me while I retune," he implored, indicating towards the stage with the nod of his head.

Stephanie hesitated, not wanting to be petty, but also not wanting to be at his beck and call.

"Ah, sure. Back in a minute," she said to Sam, who frowned and reluctantly watched her go. She followed James to the stage and sat on the edge while he reached for his guitar and fiddled with the frets. He looked down at her and held her gaze. She felt her heart give an extra thump.

Why does he do that to me – it's not that I'm some little groupie, she thought, annoyed at herself.

"Who is he, Steph?" James asked quietly.

"An old friend who now works for my father," she said.

James raised his eyebrow. "How convenient. I'll bet Daddy's pleased that his little angel isn't hanging out with a Knox anymore," he said bitterly.

"James – don't," she said quietly. She looked down at her hands, but couldn't help hearing a ring of truth in his comments. Her father had been furious to hear that James had been at the house, especially when he realised that was who she was kissing in the driveway a few nights earlier, and was pleased to learn that they weren't speaking. And then he had looked so smug, when he watched her sneaking off with Sam after dinner.

"I'm sorry we argued, Steph," James said in an odd voice.

"You have a funny way of showing it," Stephanie replied, still feeling hurt at his behaviour over the past week.

"Look, I know I'm stubborn and I hate to back down – but I have to tell you something. There's more to this family feud than either of us knows, and you *really* don't want to go there," he said. "Sometimes the past is better left where it is – in the past. OK?"

"Hey – how's that string going?" Sam interrupted them. Stephanie jumped up rather guiltily. James glared at him.

Sam put his hand on Stephanie's shoulder. "I hate to do this, but I've got a fairly early start in the morning, do you think we can go back now?" He smiled persuasively at her.

"Sure, absolutely," she replied quickly.

"Yeah, you could do with your beauty sleep. But I'm sure you can get a taxi or something – Stephanie and I haven't finished talking," James said, straightening up, his posture challenging.

"Beauty sleep? I'm not the one on stage wearing makeup," Sam countered condescendingly.

Stephanie shifted uncomfortably from one foot to the other as the two guys stared at one another, neither backing down.

"Sam, let's get my bag," she said tugging his arm. But he didn't move. He and James were glaring at each other, hostility rolling off them in waves. Reluctantly she walked back towards the bar on her own, where Michael was looking at her questioningly.

"What's going on, Steph?" he asked.

She rolled her eyes. "Chest beating and marking of territory," she said sighing.

"Oh hell." Michael looked past her. "Well, someone just overstepped the boundary." She swung around, following his gaze in time to see Sam shove James with both hands, knocking him backwards onto the stage. James steadied himself against the edge and then launched himself forward into Sam, knocking him to the ground. Stephanie's view was obscured by a sea of bodies rushing past to watch the fight. Andy and Dave pulled James off and the barman held Sam back, while Liam stood grinning from ear to ear.

"Okay, you two – that's enough." The barman turned to Liam and said, "Time to start your next set." He looked at Sam. "You – out."

Stephanie found herself being pulled to the door by Sam. She looked back over her shoulder at James. Victoria had appeared from somewhere and had her arms around him, gently brushing his hair out of his eyes. She caught Stephanie's eye and gave her a triumphant look. Stephanie felt a cold knot around her heart.

Outside, she looked at Sam, blood streaming from his nose. She turned on him –

"What the hell was that all about?" she shouted.

"Dunno – little bastard just leapt at me," Sam said innocently.

"What – after you shoved him, eh? You are pathetic, both of you." She stomped towards her car and unlocked it. Sam slid into the passenger seat, wiping his nose with the back of his hand.

"Get blood on my car and I'll beat you myself," she muttered. They drove back to the house in silence.

Chapter 12

The following night, Stephanie pulled into the little car park at the side of the café. She had been mulling over James's comments from the night before about the feud. He was so intent on her not looking into anything concerning their families, but her research into the mystery surrounding Sophie's death was just starting to get really interesting. It was like trying to find all the pieces of a puzzle, and some pieces seemed infuriatingly just out of reach. She was too intrigued to give up now.

Her intuition told her that something her great-aunt had stumbled upon remained unresolved. She kept thinking that James had been about to explain something else when Sam had interrupted them.

It was almost dark and the lights were on in the café. On the stage area in the front window she could see and hear the band playing an acoustic version of one of their songs. Taking a deep breath, she pushed the door open and wove her way between the tables to reach the counter where Michael was perched on a bar stool. She smiled at him, relieved to see his friendly face. He was chatting to the band's manager Cam, who was taking notes as they talked. Michael had designed the band's official website and he and Cam worked together regularly to keep it updated. Cam looked up as Stephanie approached.

"Stephanie, right? I hope to God you've come to make up – he's been like a bear with a sore head all day," he said nodding toward the band. Cam was in his mid-twenties and was beginning to make a name for himself as a talent manager. When he heard The Fury playing at a club in London, he had signed them on the spot. He was short and stocky, with a shrewd eye for business.

Stephanie followed his gaze. James was perched on the edge of an amp, tuning his guitar. She cringed as she registered the black eye that he was sporting, obviously the result of the previous night's altercation. His lip had been cut and was swollen. In his tight black jeans and a loose open-necked white shirt, he looked every bit the brooding rock star.

Stephanie felt her heart contract slightly – poor James, that looked sore and it was all her fault. She shouldn't have paraded Sam in front of him like that. But it wasn't like they were going out or anything.

As if he felt them looking at him, he suddenly looked up. Anger flashed in his eyes. When the song ended, he carefully set his guitar aside and sauntered over to where they were standing.

"What do you want?" he asked her coldly. "It's not your shift, so I assume you must be looking for me."

"James, sorry to break it to you – but the world doesn't revolve around you," she said scowling back at him. *Wow he can be so arrogant. The fact I am here to see him, notwithstanding,* she thought, not completely missing the irony in her response.

James rolled his eyes and said, "yeah, yeah whatever."

Stephanie was suddenly aware that the chatter in the café

had subsided to a low buzz. "But since you are here, my arrogant little friend – I do have a question for you. Outside?" she suggested quietly.

She gave Michael a little smile before walking to the door and opening it, suddenly keen to get away from the curious stares. James hesitated and then followed her, both of them conscious of everyone watching.

The door banged shut behind them as they stepped out into the dark night. He stood defensively, hands shoved in his jeans pockets, his face a mask.

She studied him for a moment. The black eye and swollen lip made him look somehow vulnerable, which gave her a strange feeling in the pit of stomach. *Damn it,* she thought annoyed.

"What did you mean last night?" she asked quietly. "It sounded like there is a lot more to this than simply my grandmother blaming your family for Sophie's death and your family being pissed off about the fraternisation claims."

Looking him directly in the eye, she tried to keep her breathing even, so as not to give away the turmoil that her emotions were in. *James has so many girls fawning over him already – it will make a nice change for him to have one who appears uninterested.*

He eyed her carefully, a taunting smile playing around his lips. "What? The Wakefield and Cooper women aren't enough to drive a family to war?" he said.

She sighed and shook her head. This wasn't going to give her any answers. Frustrated, she turned towards her car, pulling the keys from her jeans pocket.

James grabbed her arm, pulling her back around to face him. "Wait," he said.

101

She hesitated.

"Just leave it alone, Steph," he whispered. Their eyes locked.

"What? You said, and I quote 'you can investigate the bitter and twisted ramblings of an old woman if you wish'," she said lowering her voice, mimicking his accent, and shaking her arm out of his grasp.

"Yeah, very funny," he said. But he wasn't laughing. She could feel the tension building between them, like a dam that was ready to burst.

"Are you telling me that there actually *is* something and now you *don't* want me to look into it?" she continued.

A range of emotions crossed his face and he pulled his hand through his hair in a gesture of frustration.

"Let me spell this out for you. Leave *my* family alone. It's best if you just walk away from this," he said slowly, forcefully. He leaned down, his face close to hers and tilted her chin with his thumb, so that she was looking directly at him. "Do you understand?" he demanded, holding her gaze.

Stephanie gasped subconsciously at his touch and the force of his words. "Does that include us?" she said, her voice was barely a whisper. She lowered her eyes self-consciously, waiting for the sting of rejection.

"Oh – I think you made that perfectly clear last night," he said. The softness of a moment ago had gone from his voice, which had turned cold again. He straightened up and took a step back from her, his eyes hard.

Stephanie bit her lip. Last night he had said that he was sorry they had argued, but now? Now he was like a different person. One she didn't know. She could feel her own frustration and anger building like a tidal wave – there was no way she could bring herself to back down when he was being so cold and nasty. She would only make a fool of herself.

"As did you last week," she retorted, hands on hips.

"Then we both know where we stand," James said, his eyes flashing angrily. "Go now – I'm sure lover boy must be waiting for you to call."

He looked at her again – the hurt in his eyes raw for a fleeting moment before they became hard and distant again. She hesitated, "James," she began.

"See ya 'round, Steph," he said, backing away from her towards the café.

Stephanie turned away from him. She had to get to her car before the tears came.

James pushed the door of the café open and strode back past Michael towards the little stage.

"Don't be too hard on her, dude," Michael said softly as he passed.

"What? She left with that bastard last night," James said, stopping and turning on him.

"Yeah, but you didn't hear the row they had afterwards outside," Michael said, smiling broadly. "I followed her out of the pub to make sure she was okay and overheard her shouting at Sam. She told him where to go in no uncertain terms."

"Really?" James said, surprised.

"Oh yeah – he would most definitely have been on the sofa," Michael laughed. "Besides – it certainly looked like Victoria was going to kiss you all better," he said, looking knowingly at James. "And I know she made sure that Steph thought that."

James walked over to the band, returning Liam's hi-five, and looked out the window as he threw his guitar strap across his body.

"At least you came back in one piece," Andy said, trying to

lighten the atmosphere.

James glanced out of the window. In the light pooling from the street lamps he watched as Stephanie's Fiat accelerated out of the car park, gravel flying in her wake.

* * *

Stephanie woke the next morning with a headache. She hadn't slept at all well. Crying herself to sleep didn't help. In the cold light of day, she felt annoyed with herself. *Who is he anyway? A jumped up little wannabe rock star with an overinflated ego.* He had been annoyed about Sam though – far more than she thought he would have been. *What right did he have to act like that; it wasn't like we were together? And besides he was the one who had pushed me away.* Still, she felt miserable. *See,* she told herself sternly, rolling over and sitting up, *this is why you don't get involved. You only end up hurting.*

She shook her head. *Enough – time to move on.*

She hadn't dated that many boys, but she did know that really the only thing to ease the pain of rejection, was time and distraction. However, she didn't have the luxury of time to get over him, with her working for his best mate Andy, so it would have to be distraction. Still, she was surprised at the how much James's words had hurt her – after all she hadn't known him all that long and only kissed him that one time…..

*Stop it, s*he told herself firmly.

She crawled out of bed and pulled on her workout gear and forced herself out of the house for a thirty-minute run. After a hot shower, she sat at her desk, switched on her laptop and looked through the stack of information she had gathered. She had Sophie's journals, along with some old newspaper articles about the inquiry into the fraternisation claims that listed the names of several Germans who had supposedly visited Knox Manor in the immediate pre-war years. In addition, she had borrowed the autobiographies of some of the Knox and Wakefield family's contemporaries, such as the Mitford sisters, from the local library.

A good real life mystery – now that was just the sort of distraction she needed. James's insistence that she stop looking into the Knox family only strengthened her resolve to follow up on whatever Sophie and David thought they might have uncovered. James obviously knew more than he was letting on. She picked up the books and articles and curled up on her sofa to read.

If the Knoxes had been storing paintings and other valuables for European friends as Edward suggested to Sophie, what if they had kept some and not returned them after the war? she wondered.

She did a quick internet search on World War II and paintings. There were thousands of results. She clicked open the first search result which claimed to be the official site for research into looted art and scrolled through their first list. She was amazed. This was just something that she had never realised. There were literally thousands of works of art that had disappeared during those years that were still missing, presumed destroyed and lost forever. Specialist art theft units existed within police forces around the world tasked with recovering what they could, along with investigating more recent art thefts.

She clicked open an in-depth *New York Times* article from the previous year which explained how Hitler's men had systematically plundered the art galleries and museums of the countries they invaded and stolen valuables belonging to

105

many doomed Jewish families, such as the Rockefellers and Rosenbergs in Paris. The Nazis had meticulously catalogued their looting though, which had been an enormous help in the restoration process following the war.

The article went on to say that after the war, Allied soldiers had found famous art works by artists such as Picasso, Degas, Manet and Rembrandt, hidden in railway tunnels, underground mines and in the luxurious homes of the leaders of the Third Reich. The castle of Neuschwanstein had been a main repository of artworks stolen from France. It had taken a specialist team of Allied soldiers, the Monuments Men, six weeks to empty it. The Monuments Men were tasked with recovering and restoring whatever art, national monuments and treasures they could in Europe. Where they were able, many items were repatriated to their lawful owners, but countless others had simply disappeared.

Various efforts by governments and other groups in the years since the war ended, had recovered some of the art that had appeared in private collections and art galleries. But it wasn't always straightforward proving ownership; although museum collections had good records, there were many gaps in the documentation of art works that changed hands in Europe between 1933 and 1945. According to the article, it was likely that many major collections around the world could still hold pieces with dubious gaps in the history of their ownership.

As part of the war reparation process in the late 1940s a list of missing works had been compiled, using the albums that Hitler's men produced of the art work they had obtained.

Stephanie sat back at her desk and shook her head. This was unbelievable.

106

She spent the next hour reading other recent newspaper articles. Hitler had in effect tried to change Germany's view of what was appropriate art and what wasn't. He had labelled the art work of any modern, non-German artist as 'degenerate'. Stephanie was shocked at the famous names that had been considered degenerate in Germany – Dali, van Gogh, Picasso, Renoir, and Chagall.

This fits with the story that Hoffman told at dinner, according to Sophie's diary, she thought. *Imagine if Germany had won the war – much of Europe's cultural history would have been irrevocably altered and destroyed.*

Artwork thought demolished during the Nazi area was still turning up though. As recently as 2010 a set of sculptures labelled as degenerate in the 1930s had been unearthed during the excavations for an extension to the subway in Berlin.

Stephanie followed a number of links and came to a website which claimed to list one hundred paintings stolen by the Nazis. Some had been found, but many had never been recovered. She scrolled through the thumbnail pictures on the website. There were paintings by Gustav Klimt, Vincent van Gogh, Henri Matisse, Edgar Degas, Pablo Picasso, Marc Chagall and Johannes Vermeer.

Suddenly she stopped. She scrolled back up the page and peered at one of the pictures – it showed a brightly coloured painting of a man in a country scene. *It couldn't be. I have seen that exact painting before.*

Chapter 13

Stephanie enlarged the thumbnail of the painting on the screen. It looked exactly like the painting that was hanging in the library at Knox Manor. She had commented to James about it, the evening he had shown her the photos he had found of Edward and Sophie. She looked closely at the screen – there was no way that could be the same painting, was there? She would need to have another look at it to be sure.

She clicked into the detail of the painting. It was a self-portrait entitled *Painter on the Road to Tarascon* and the artist was none other than Vincent van Gogh. Stephanie did a double-take. She read through the history of the painting. The painting had originally hung in the Kulturhistorisches Museum in Magdeburg in Germany. From there the Nazis had confiscated it, considering it degenerate in 1938, and it hadn't been seen since. It was assumed to have been destroyed in the Allied bombing of Berlin in 1944.

Stephanie sat back, unsure what to do. Surely the painting hanging in the Knox library must be a copy, although James did say it was very old. Pity he was being so difficult or she could go back to the manor and take another look at it. One thing was certain; she would need to ensure it was the same painting before saying anything.

She had to think this through carefully, rather than run off and make a fool of herself.

Stomach rumbling, she skipped downstairs to have a late breakfast.

I wonder if Alex Knox's business has a website, she thought an hour or so later, her mind wandering. Back in her bedroom, she opened up Internet Explorer on her laptop and did a Google search and sure enough, there it was; www.knoxantiques.co.uk.

She clicked onto the website and spent the next ten minutes reading. It looked very legitimate – *well of course it would*, she thought. She noted that his area of expertise was late 19th and early to mid-20th century art and antiques. It appeared that he ran the business out of a shop in Green Park in London. She took a mental note of its location – could be worth a visit sometime.

Stephanie was interrupted a little while later by a visit from Michael. He arrived at the same time as a courier, who handed him a large bouquet of flowers.

"Hi, Steph," he called knocking quietly and poking his head around her open bedroom door. "Here, these were just delivered for you." He handed her the flowers.

Wow. Maybe James has gotten over his mood after all, Stephanie thought. She felt her own mood lift and her breath hitch. She laid the flowers on the end of her bed and pulled out the card.

Sorry about Friday. Look forward to seeing you again soon. Love Sam

Stephanie let out the breath she had been holding. She felt disappointed and then immediately annoyed with herself.

Michael watched the myriad of emotions cross her face.

"Not from the person you hoped?" he asked with surprising insight.

She shrugged, but didn't answer. She tossed the card aside onto the bed. It landed face up and Michael saw Sam's name on the bottom.

"I thought I'd check you were okay after last night. I know you and James argued and you looked upset when you left," he said, shuffling uncomfortably.

"I'm fine," she said, dismissing his concern. "It seems that James and I have agreed to disagree on just about everything – especially when it's to do with to our families."

"James is really sensitive about his family. He was absolutely devastated when his father died. Not only were they really close, but I think he protected James from his brother," Michael said. "Alex has beaten the crap out of James on several occasions since then. He's got a foul temper."

"What about his mother? Surely she wouldn't let that happen?" Stephanie said.

"She hasn't been around much of late. She remarried fairly quickly and he hates his stepfather," Michael said. "I think James feels pretty betrayed and abandoned by her, although he puts on this tough front."

Stephanie looked away. *Great.* Her natural instinct was to feel sad for James. *Don't make me feel sorry for the arrogant little git.*

Michael perched on the arm of the sofa beside Stephanie's desk. Her laptop was open with the Knox Antiques home page displayed.

He looked at her quizzically. "So what does Alex Knox's antiques business have to do with the search you have me running for you?" He picked up Sophie's journal and turned it over in his hands. "What are you up to, Steph?"

Stephanie blushed. "I'm not quite sure yet. Can you trust me for a few days, if I promise to tell you once I have uncovered a little more? It might be nothing." She carefully took the diary from him.

"Okay – I will hold you to that promise though," Michael said.

After Michael went home, Stephanie felt restless. Despite what he had said, she refused to allow herself to feel sorry for James. *He's made his feelings for me pretty clear. I need to just move on*, she thought.

While she arranged Sam's flowers in a large vase, the painting in the library continued to play on her mind. If only she could get another look at it. The seed of a plan began to grow in her mind. However, it depended on James's whereabouts. She wandered into her wardrobe and selected a casual hat. She piled her hair up on top of her head and pulled the hat on. The brim partially covered her face. She grabbed her bag and car keys and ran down the stairs to the front door.

"Just popping to the village," she called and let herself out the front door.

The Fiat was parked in the front of the house, where she had left it the night before. She drove into the village and along the main street, slowing as she approached the pub. Through her open window she could hear music coming from the café across the road. As it came into view, she scanned the car park. There it was. The red Porsche 911. That meant James was with Andy and his brother was out of town again. *Two out of the way*. She took the next right turn and headed out of the village and up the valley towards Knox Manor.

A few minutes later she pulled her car over to one side of

the driveway under a large oak tree and took a deep breath as she got out and looked up at the imposing house.

She walked cautiously up to the front door and rang the bell.

Please don't let it be the old man, please don't let it be the old man, she recited under her breath.

Her assumption that someone like him wouldn't stoop so low as to answer his own front door bell, was a good one. The housekeeper, Grace, opened the door.

"Hello?" she smiled when she saw Stephanie. "James isn't here, love."

"Actually I didn't come to see him. It's just that I think I must have dropped an earring in the library the other night. You haven't found it by chance? They were a gift from my grandmother and rather special to me." Stephanie held up an earring to show Grace. Its mate rested securely in her pocket.

Grace opened the door wider. "Why don't you come in for a look, dear," she said kindly.

Stephanie cautiously stepped through the door, her heart racing. Today, the dark foyer seemed menacing and she suppressed a shudder as Grace led the way up the staircase to the library. She held the library door open for Stephanie.

"Now where were you sitting?" she asked.

Stephanie walked over to the desk, glancing up at the painting. Her hand itched to pull the printout of the missing work from her pocket and compare the two, but Grace was watching her from the door.

"Well, we were here and then sat over there," she said, reluctantly turning her back on the painting and looking around the armchairs that they sat in. She straightened up.

"No, it's not here either," she said. Stephanie took a long look at the painting. She would love to have touched it to see if it was original. It certainly looked it. But one thing she was now certain about was that it *was* the same painting mentioned in the missing art list. Maybe it was a copy? Although James said that it had hung here since his grandfather had been given it just before the outbreak of World War II. And her research had shown that the original hadn't been seen since 1938.

There was the sound of a door opening in the distance. A deep authoritative male voice called, "Grace."

Stephanie jumped, alarmed. It was Charles, James's grandfather.

"Coming," Grace called. She hesitated.

"It's okay – I'll let myself out. I'm just going to crawl under the desk in case it fell under there," Stephanie smiled at her. "Um, Grace, James and I have had a bit of a falling out – do you mind not telling him that I was here – I feel a bit stupid now that it looks like I've lost the earring somewhere else," Stephanie said, trying to look embarrassed.

"Of course, dear. It'll be our secret," she said, patting Stephanie's arm. "Just close the library door behind you. The front door is straight down the stairs."

"Thanks," Stephanie said and smiled gratefully at her. Grace hurried out of the room and along the corridor away from the library.

As soon as she was out of sight, Stephanie pulled the chair from the desk over to the wall and stood on it, carefully lifting the painting down. It was heavy. She stepped off the chair and laid the painting gently on the desk.

Needs an expert, she thought shaking her head. She reached out and tentatively touched a corner of the canvas – it was definitely not a print, but the signature was not neat, it was half scrawled, difficult to make out. *I need to rehang this before I get caught*, she thought anxiously.

Heart racing, she cast a surreptitious look at the library door, as she carefully lifted the painting up, turning it so that she had it in the right position to rehang. Writing on the back of the canvas drew her attention. She balanced the edge of the painting on her knee and leaned in for a closer look, gasping as she noticed a distinctive mark on the back – a black swastika.

Chapter 14

Stephanie paused, and hearing no footsteps in the hallway, she quickly stepped back up on the chair and carefully rehung the painting. She replaced the chair and rushed toward the door.

She looked back at the painting and as an afterthought pulled her mobile phone from her pocket and photographed it. Then she slipped out of the library and ran lightly down the staircase to the front door, her mind racing. According to the Monuments Men article she had just read, every piece of art requisitioned by the Nazis was stamped on the back with a black swastika. Holding her breath, she let herself quietly out of the house.

I did it; she congratulated herself, hardly believing her own audacity.

Stephanie ran to her car and quickly drove away, casting furtive glances in her rear vision mirror. She turned left at the end of the long drive, back onto the main road towards the village and breathed a sigh of relief. She came towards a sharp bend in the road and her mind drifted to Sophie. She pulled over to the side, leaving the car idling and took a couple of deep steadying breaths.

This must have been where she crashed – it's the only big corner between here and the village. She looked down the straight road ahead of her with the village nestled at the end and felt a wave of inexplicable sadness. A large oak tree hung part way across the road. *I wonder if that's the one she hit?* Stephanie pulled out again. *There wouldn't be any evidence here after seventy years.*

She suddenly glimpsed a flash of red speeding towards her. *James. That was close,* she thought, her heart thudding loudly. He slowed as he recognised her car. She kept her eyes straight ahead and accelerated away, but could feel his angry glare as their cars passed each other on the bend.

Stephanie checked her watch as she pulled in at the café; three-thirty pm, it was safe now that she knew James had gone home. The café was quiet, just a few customers.

She ordered a takeout coffee from Andy.

"Sure – whatcha been up to?" Andy said.

"This and that," she said, feeling the adrenaline rush start to ease. Although her hands were shaking, she tried to ensure her features looked relaxed. She didn't want Andy picking up on anything. He was surprisingly perceptive for a guy, so she changed the subject. "Hey tell me, your family have lived around here for years, haven't they?" When Andy nodded, she continued. "Well, I was wondering what you know about the feud between the Wakefields and the Knoxes?"

"What? The ancient grudge or the new mutiny?" Andy smirked.

Stephanie rested her chin in her hands, elbows on the counter. "Both?" she asked hopefully, her eyebrows raised.

"Ha," Andy gave a short laugh. "I'm not getting involved in the current one, but from the little I know of the old one it goes back to before the war. The story in the village has always been about accusations of collaboration and then someone

116

was killed. But I don't know on which side," he said.

"Mmm, it was my great-aunt who died, but the Knoxes did have a large number of German visitors before and during the war, from what I've read. You can understand people at the time feeling uncomfortable and jumping to conclusions," said Stephanie.

"Oh, Steph," Andy shook his head. "If you made comments to James along those lines, then I can understand why he's so mad. Despite what he says about his brother and mother, he's fiercely loyal to his family."

Stephanie let out a sigh. "Great," she said despondently. "Actually, between me and my grandmother, we made worse allegations than that." Stephanie grimaced at the memory of James's reaction at her house that day.

"Yeah?" Andy said.

"Oh yeah, we threw in murder and theft for good measure," she said. "Now saying it out loud again, it does sound ludicrous." She put her head in her hands. "Andy, what have I done?"

Andy reached across the counter and patted her on the shoulder and said, "James never stays mad for long. He'll come around. Hey, who was that guy on Friday night – your boyfriend?"

"Ex-boyfriend," she mumbled from behind her hands.

"What, ex as in after Friday's little altercation?" he asked.

Stephanie looked up. "Oh no – ex as in months ago," she said.

"Looked like he was keen to become the current boyfriend again," Andy observed, placing a coffee in front of her.

"Nah. He was just playing – I think he could tell that he was annoying James. Speaking of which, tell me about the history between James and Victoria," she asked.

Andy shook his head and held his hands up in front of him. "Oh no, you are going to have to ask him about that," he said.

"Maybe I will if he ever speaks to me again," Stephanie said sadly. She picked up her cup and stood up from the bar stool. "Thanks for the coffee. I'll see you tonight."

Stephanie's thoughts on the drive home were of Sophie. She had mentioned visits from a number of wealthy Europeans, any one of whom could have left the painting.

Once back in her room, she quickly downloaded the photo from her phone onto her laptop and brought up the picture from the missing artwork website. She put the two pictures side by side to compare them.

She studied them carefully – they were identical! Right down to the scrawled signature in the bottom left hand corner.

What if, rather than storing valuables for European friends as Sophie's diary entries had indicated, the Knoxes were storing items looted by the Nazis from the museums and art galleries of the occupied countries or stolen from their own people? What if everything hadn't been returned after the war?

Any one of those items would be worth millions now. And who better than an antique dealer to quietly move it on? No wonder Alex had been so annoyed that they were in the library. The question was, though, what did James know? Had his innocent act surrounding the painting simply been a performance? Did he kiss her to just distract her?

Stephanie squeezed her eyes shut and rubbed her temples. There were too many questions for which she had no answers.

Stephanie was dreading that evening at the café, but James was nowhere to be seen and Andy had the sense not to mention him. Andy had organised a poetry recital, with amateur poets reading their compositions and Victoria and her friends sat in the corner laughing and commenting on each would-be poet. *Nasty cow,* Stephanie thought. *Maybe now that she has James back, she will leave me be.*

About halfway through the evening James and Liam arrived and sat with the girls. Stephanie kept her eyes down and worked quietly.

She went out to the back room to get some more milk to refill the small refrigerator behind the counter at one point. As she came back in she heard her name mentioned and paused to listen.

"….not her usual bubbly self," Andy said to someone.

"James is an idiot," an unknown voice, possibly Dave, said. "He's crazy to let some old feud get in the way. I mean, look at her, she's gorgeous."

Stephanie blushed, embarrassed. She wasn't used to hearing herself talked about that way. *I wonder what he would say if he saw the gawky and overweight kid I was a couple of years ago?* She made a loud noise with the milk crate as she walked back into the café, which stopped the conversation. Sure enough, Dave was perched on a bar stool across the counter from Andy. He raised his eyebrows in greeting and gave her a friendly smile.

Towards the end of the night, James came up to the counter and was talking music with Andy as Stephanie cleared dirty coffee cups and plates from the tables. She came back into the kitchen, deposited a full tray on the bench and bent to open the dishwasher.

"Nice drive this afternoon?" James enquired.

"Yeah," she answered lightly, straightening up and leaning against the bench and confidently looking him in the eyes. "I was doing a bit of sightseeing – dangerous bit of road, from what I hear," she said, deliberately baiting him.

"Stephanie," he growled, a warning note in his voice.

"What?" She looked up at him, her blue eyes wide and innocent. She put her hands on her hips and crossed one leg over the other.

He sighed looking away. "Remember what I told you," he said, clearing his throat.

"Yeah, yeah, whatever," Stephanie replied, turning his own flippant remark from the night before back on him. Turning away, she began noisily loading the dishwasher.

"That smart mouth will get you into trouble one day," James sneered.

"James," Victoria called from across the room.

Stephanie glanced at Andy, who was busy frothing milk and studiously ignoring them. She leaned across the counter towards James and whispered, "I think you are being summoned, jingle boy. Now run along." She patted the back of his hand, as one would a child.

James flushed an angry red and narrowed his eyes at her. He opened his mouth to say something further, but Andy shook his head at him.

"Huh!" A muscle in James's jaw clenched and his mouth contorted into a thin angry line as he thumped his fist on the counter and stomped back to Victoria's table.

Chapter 15

Michael arranged to meet Stephanie at the café after her shift on Monday afternoon. The café's menu now had a New Zealand flavour to it. Andy had sampled and enjoyed the flat white that Stephanie had made for him, after initially teasing her by pretending to choke on it. When Michael arrived, she was standing on a chair and adding it to the blackboard on the back wall, drawing a kiwi and the New Zealand flag beside it, just so there was no doubt as to its origin. They sat at a table by the window and he handed her a manila folder containing the results of the search he had run for her.

"Basically I cross-referenced the twenty-five names you gave me with each other and the list of artists, and here are the top five results for each name. Several had no matches. But a couple of them gave a lot more than five positive results. I've saved it all onto a USB drive for you." He fished around in his pocket and produced a slim USB stick which he handed to her.

"What's a positive result mean?" she asked.

"That's where both the person's name and the artist are fully mentioned, not just combinations of the words," he explained. "What you have here are at least one hundred websites to visit and review, although some are just different pages within the same website – I've highlighted those in the same colour so that you can knock them off quicker. It's all on the drive, but sometimes it's easier to digest this much information and the cross links on paper. This guy Hoffman for example, he had lots of matches. Was he a collector?"

"No, a museum curator, I think," Stephanie said. "Reading all of this is gonna keep me out of trouble for a while." She smiled at Michael. "Thank you so much for doing this. Remember it's just between me and you. okay?" she said.

"Sure thing, Steph. Are you ready to tell me what this is all about?" he asked.

"Hey, you two look like you are plotting," a voice interrupted them.

Stephanie instinctively slammed the folder shut and jumped to her feet. Jack stood in front of them grinning. He reached out a hand and steadied her as she overbalanced into him.

"Whoa, there, Steph. Sorry, didn't mean to startle you," he said.

Stephanie blushed. She slipped the USB stick into her jeans pocket. "That's okay," she murmured.

Behind Jack she noticed James leaning against the door frame, watching the interchange with interest. How long he had been standing there and what he had overheard, she didn't know. His eyes were hooded. She quickly looked away.

"Thanks, Michael," she said as she picked up her bag, shoving the manila folder into it and walking quickly towards the door. "Excuse me," she said quietly to James who was blocking the doorway.

"What are you up to, Stephanie? You look guilty – like you are doing something you shouldn't be." He tilted his head to one side and studied her.

"Nothing," she mumbled. "Gotta go." She went to push past him.

He put his hand across the doorway, blocking it further, "What? No more smart-arse comments?"

"Yeah, sorry – all out of those right now. Now, excuse me!" she said.

He didn't move, so she had to slide under his arm to get through the doorway. He held her gaze defiantly as she squeezed through. *I could never be a spy,* she thought, her heart thumping. *He's right, I feel guilty.* She walked a few steps and glanced back over her shoulder. James stood there watching her, his face unreadable. She scowled at him and hurried away. She hoped that he and Jack weren't going to be too tough on Michael and that he wouldn't cave and tell them. It wouldn't take James much to conclude that she was still looking into something related to his family. And she knew what his reaction to that would be.

She walked down the hill towards the village green where the local museum was situated. It was housed in a sympathetically restored building with whitewashed stone walls and a thatched roof. She had to duck her head as she went in through the low doorway. While she waited for the lady behind the reception desk to retrieve the information that she had requested, she took a wander around. According to the exhibits, Carlswick had been a haven for smugglers back in the days when the sea came right up to a harbour in the little town, before it steadily silted up over the last two to three hundred years. The stories of daring smugglers were numerous and included rumours that some of the larger homes nearby had tunnels from the old harbour linking up with their basements and cellars to aid the smugglers. Stephanie gave a shiver. *How exciting, I'm going to have to read up on that.*

"Here we are, dear," the lady called from the front desk, a large manila envelope in her hand.

"Thanks," Stephanie said as she opened it. It contained a photocopy of the official report into the collaboration claims and note suggesting that she could try the library for any local memoirs or diaries from the war.

Saying her goodbyes, she went and sat on a bench in the sun scanning the report – the claims were explosive, but James was right, the Knoxes had been completed exonerated. Read with 21st-century sensibilities, it did just seem like hysteria. Interestingly though, a lot of the names mentioned in Sophie's diary were in the report. So someone other than Sophie and David had been taking note of who was visiting Knox Manor too. There were no mentions in Sophie's diary that she had been talking to the officials. In fact she had seemed shocked by the investigation.

Stephanie continued to ponder the painting in the library and what to do about it. She was really no further ahead in discovering anything more about it or how it came to be there. It would only make the feud between her family and the Knox family worse if she started throwing around unsubstantiated allegations, and probably just make her look like an idiot in the process. *What to do?*

The week passed slowly. Between working at the café, Skyping Toby, who had excitedly told her that they were flying over to have Christmas with her, and devouring the history pre-reading that she had been set, Stephanie managed to keep a low profile. She had downloaded Robert Edsel's *Monuments Men* to her iPad and was learning more about the extent of the Nazis' looting during the war.

James continued to outwardly ignore her, although she could have sworn that he watched her carefully whenever he was at the café. She assumed that he hadn't discovered her extracurricular activities. She was sure that he would have confronted her if he had. *Whatever – I won't give him the satisfaction of even acknowledging him*, she decided.

I am completely off guys, she told herself, *especially those of the musical variety.*

Andy called Stephanie early on Thursday morning to see if she could work during the day, as the band was rehearsing at the pub, for an upcoming musical festival.

It was a long day. Stephanie was beginning to rue the fact that she had agreed to work quite so much, as the sun beat down outside. There was quite a crowd across the road at the pub, obviously gathering for the free live music.

Stephanie breathed a sigh of relief when Andy arrived at four pm to help her close up. She said goodbye as he locked the door behind her and wandered across the road to the pub car park, where she had parked the Fiat that morning. As she approached, the hairs on the back of her neck stood up – something was amiss. She slowed and walked cautiously towards her car. She gasped as she saw that her windscreen was smashed and a brick was lying on the driver's seat amidst shards of glass. Written in black letters on the brick were the words:

You may look like her, but don't end up like your aunt

Chapter 16

Stephanie jumped back as if stung. She quickly looked around her. There were a few people milling around, but no one appeared to be taking any notice of her. She stood rooted to the spot, unsure what to do.

"Hey, Steph," a voice called. Matt pulled his car over to the curb, and then jumped out, after seeing the distraught look on her face. "Are you …." He broke off and stared at her smashed windscreen. "Steph, what happened?"

She shrugged, a sick feeling gripping her.

He beckoned to the bar manager, who was clearing tables in front of the pub. He came over and looked at the damage, horrified. He hurried away wordlessly to call the police. Michael appeared from somewhere and together they helped her pick up a few larger pieces of broken glass from around the car and sit them in a pile at the curb.

He leaned in the window and read the words on the brick, and turned, looking at Stephanie with one eyebrow raised. She glanced at Matt, who was checking under the car for any glass, and shook her head at Michael, silently asking him not to say anything.

Flashing lights signalled the arrival of a police car.

"What's happened here?" the constable asked, stepping out

and putting his hat on.

He looked into Stephanie's car and carefully opened the door. More glass tinkled to the ground. He lifted the brick out, reading the words as he did.

"What happened to your aunt, Miss?" he asked.

"Stephanie," she corrected. "I think it means my great-aunt – she was killed in a car accident many years ago, although there's some debate about whether it was an accident or not," she said.

A crowd had now gathered, attracted by the flashing lights of the police car. She saw James push through and glare at her as he overheard the conversation. She looked away. What was he still doing here? Rehearsal had finished an hour ago. This was undoubtedly the work of his family. They all seemed to think she looked like her aunt. A sudden thought hit her; maybe he had done it – he would have had time, wouldn't he? She shivered uncomfortably, fingers of fear crawling up her back.

She glanced nervously in his direction, and watched as he turned and walked away.

"Do you have any idea who might have done this?" the police officer asked.

Stephanie shook her head, not trusting herself to speak. *I am trying so hard to fit in here, I don't need this,* she thought miserably.

The police officer made a phone call and arranged to have Stephanie's car taken to the local garage to have the windscreen repaired. He gave Michael a broom and dustpan from the boot of the police car and instructed him to sweep up the remaining broken glass while he bagged the brick as evidence.

"This is probably just a prank, albeit a nasty one," he said quietly. "But I will of course make note of it and if you think of anything else, call me." He handed her a business card with the local police station's contact details. "Now, Stephanie, would you like a lift home or is there someone who can drive you?"

"I will," said Matthew taking her bag. "I couldn't help but overhear you talking to the cop – is this something to do with Knox?" he asked. Michael glanced sharply at Stephanie.

"I don't know, Matt," she answered simply.

"Leave it with me," he muttered starting his car.

Stephanie sat looking out the window as Matt drove her home. *Why would someone send me a warning like that?* she wondered. *Maybe it was James. Maybe he does know that I am still looking into what happened back then and decided that since his verbal warnings weren't enough to stop me, he would try to frighten me. He would have had time too; he was at the pub all day.* She shuddered at the thought. She was beginning to think that James Knox wasn't all he appeared to be on the surface.

Later that evening, Stephanie opened the bulging file on her desk and sorted through to find the newspaper report of her aunt's accident. There were a couple of grainy, yellowing photos of the accident site that she'd printed from an old newspaper on the internet. There was no suggestion in the article that it had been anything other than an unfortunate accident. Stephanie looked hard at the photos. The passenger side of the car was all bashed in, although the newspaper said it was the driver's side that hit the tree. Still, maybe the car had rolled. The news report didn't say. It was too long ago to make any sense of the limited information there was. *What a shame Sophie's brother David hadn't left any notes on his investigation.*

Stephanie started reviewing the websites that Michael had

identified, focussing on the ones that had any reference to van Gogh. Some were fascinating reading, others just drew blanks. None shed any further light on the Knoxes' painting.

Frustrated, she settled down on the sofa with her laptop and her iPod – might be a good time to download some new tunes. Despite her determination that she had moved on, it still hurt every time she listened to The Fury, so best delete them.

She had just hooked up to iTunes when her mobile phone rang. She picked it up and saw from the caller ID that it was her friend Anna.

"Hi, Steph. Are you okay? I hear that you had a little car trouble today," Anna said.

"Who have you been talking to?" Stephanie replied, surprised.

"Facebook," Anna said.

Stephanie groaned.

"Who did it?" Anna asked.

"I'm not really sure, but I think it's part of a much larger story," Stephanie replied.

"Really? Why don't you come up here for a few days and you can tell me all about it then? Please? You haven't been back to London since you arrived. What's keeping you in the country? Is it that hot guitarist?" Anna teased.

"Huh, that arrogant bastard," Stephanie said.

"Stephanie Cooper! That's so not like you. What's going on?" Anna asked, surprised.

"Like I said, long story. Tell you what, I'd love to come and stay for the weekend," Stephanie said, making an immediate decision. They arranged that she would catch the train up to London the next morning.

She had just clicked her mobile phone off when it chimed

with a text from Sam. He'd obviously been on Facebook, too.

You ok?

I'm fine

Wanna get away for the weekend?

No thx. Got plans.

See you soon?

Sure, Stephanie keyed the text and closed her phone, throwing it on the sofa beside her. She rubbed her temples. *A weekend with Anna, away from car trouble, boy trouble and mysterious paintings is just what I need.*

Chapter 17

The train pulled in to London's Charing Cross Station at nine-fifty the next morning. Stephanie stepped off lifting her small wheelie suitcase onto the platform. Somehow, despite her love of clothes, and shoes in particular, she had learned the art of packing lightly – probably from the years of sitting on her mother's bed watching her pack as little as possible for their trips to England. She set the case down on the platform, extended the handle and walked away from the train towards the station, pulling it along behind her.

Charing Cross Station was still crowded at this time on a Friday morning. Stephanie made her way towards Embankment and onto the eastbound Circle Line platform.

She wrinkled her nose at the smell – a damp metallic scent mixed with sweat and perfume. *Mmm – funny how I have gotten used to the fresh country air after only a few weeks*, she thought. *I never used to find this smell so offensive.*

Her father's office was located near Tower Hill. The Tube ride took around fifteen minutes – she was lucky enough to get a seat and popped her iPod on and zoned out for the journey.

The offices of Cooper, Reynold and Jones were in a modern low rise glass and concrete building on a busy corner. The area was a mixture of old and new London. A quaint old pub was on the opposite corner, next to a thirty-storey steel and glass structure that was home to an investment bank.

Stephanie wheeled her suitcase up the ramp entrance of the building and walked through the revolving glass door and into the sleek air-conditioned foyer. The atmosphere was one of quiet prosperity. The walls of the reception area were hung with expensive looking modern art, and pots containing tall indoor trees with shiny leaves were dotted around here and there. To one side was a small café with a coffee machine whizzing away quietly and the occasional clink of china as cups and plates were laid out. Comfortable chairs were clustered on both sides of the reception area and stacks of unread glossy magazines adorned the low coffee tables.

In the centre a large reception desk dominated, attended by three attractive young women all wearing telephone headsets. As Stephanie approached the desk, one of them looked up and smiled.

"Can I help you?" she said.

She must be new, Stephanie thought, *she doesn't know me.*

"Yes I'm here to see Max Cooper, please," Stephanie replied pleasantly.

The receptionist looked her up and down. Stephanie was suddenly conscious that her black skinny jeans tucked into burgundy boots with stiletto heels were well outside the corporate mould, despite the tailored red jacket and layers of necklaces. She grinned to herself.

"Is he expecting you?" the young woman asked.

"No, but I'm happy to wait if he's not free," Stephanie replied.

"Mr Cooper sees people by appointment only," the receptionist said politely, as she clicked at the keyboard in front of her searching. "He has an opening next week."

"He will see me," Stephanie paused, enjoying herself. "I'm his daughter."

The receptionist smiled. "Yes, of course, Miss Cooper. I will see if he is free." She quickly tapped on her keyboard and spoke into her headset.

Stephanie leaned back and looked around the reception area. She groaned inwardly. There was Sam, leaning against the counter of the coffee shop, takeout in hand, laughing with two smartly dressed women. There was no avoiding him. Their eyes met at the same time. Sam excused himself and strode straight over.

"Stephanie," he said, leaning over and kissing her cheek.

"Hi," she replied, her inbred manners taking over, despite the fact that she was still really annoyed at him over the events of the previous weekend.

"His current meeting is about to finish, so you can go straight on up," the receptionist interrupted them.

Stephanie smiled at her. "Thanks."

She took the handle of her bag and started walking towards the bank of lifts hidden behind the reception desk by a partition. Sam fell into step beside her.

"I didn't think I would see you *this* soon," he said enthusiastically.

"Me neither," she agreed. "I'm spending the weekend with Anna, so thought I'd take the opportunity to have lunch with Dad." *Why am I feeling the need to explain myself to him?*

A bell announced the arrival of the lift. They waited for three people to get out, before Sam held his arm across the door allowing her to get in.

"Thanks," she murmured. The silence was awkward as they rode the elevator to the 12th floor.

"Here we are," Sam said brightly as the lift stopped. "Ah, Steph, you wouldn't have time to have dinner with me while you are here? I feel bad for what happened last weekend and I'd like to make that up to you."

"No sorry. I'm completely booked," she smiled apologetically at him.

"I could join you and Anna – it would be great to see her again," Sam suggested, his tone light.

"Girls weekend – you know," Stephanie said making an excuse.

"Okay," Sam said reluctantly. "But I'd like to catch up with you again soon."

"Okay," she stepped out of the lift and let the doors close on Sam.

She breathed a sigh of relief. *That was a lucky escape*, she thought. She hadn't forgotten his part in her bust up with James. Still it was unlike Sam to be so persistent; he used to leave it to her to do the chasing. But maybe that was because he was used to her just saying yes, whenever he asked her out. And surprisingly, she really didn't want to. After all the months of wanting him back, it dawned on her that she now suddenly didn't. She felt a weight lift off her as she walked away from the lifts.

The partners' floor was even more luxuriously decorated than the rest of the building. It was a hive of activity with people hurrying about with folders in their arms, telephones ringing and various meetings going on in the glass-fronted meeting rooms.

She had to walk the length of the floor to get to her father's corner office. She stopped just short of the corner as she overheard loud voices coming from the partially open door.

"We have left this too long already," a heavily accented male voice said somewhat impatiently.

"Yet we must exercise caution – if he gets wind of this, you can guarantee it will disappear or the deal will be called off," Max Cooper's steady clipped voice replied.

Stephanie hesitated; she didn't want to interrupt one of her father's meetings. She was about to go and wait by the lifts, when she heard the accented voice ask;

"What about your daughter – have you stopped her involvement?"

Stephanie took a sharp intake of breath and stepped backwards so that she was hidden behind a bookshelf. *Daughter? What?*

"Oh, yes. She was merely friendly with the youngest son, but that's been taken care of," her father said.

"Good. You don't want her anywhere near the location when we drop in," the foreign voice said.

What location? Stephanie was puzzled. *I am missing something.*

"Now, the rest of the team fly in tomorrow morning. We will come directly here at noon for a strategy meeting," the man said.

Stephanie could hear the creak of furniture as the two men stood up. She looked around wildly and saw the door to the ladies toilets to her left. She quickly slipped inside holding the door slightly ajar, so that she could see whoever it was who left her father's office.

The two men paused at the door to the office and shook hands.

"Thanks, Max. It will be good to finally get resolution on this one," the other man said as he stepped into view.

He was well over six feet tall, with olive skin and short cropped dark hair. He was very muscular and wore a dark suit that pulled slightly on his broad shoulders, with a black t-shirt underneath. The way he carried himself screamed military. Stephanie shuddered.

"Yes, Eli. I will be happy to see that man behind bars," Max agreed. They walked down the floor, past Stephanie's hiding place, to the lifts.

Stephanie slipped out of the bathroom and quickly walked around the corner to her father's personal assistant's desk.

"Hi, Emily," she said perching on the edge of the desk.

Emily looked up and smiled. The two chatted for several minutes until her father came back.

"Stephanie. What a lovely surprise. I didn't know you were in London," he said as he leaned over and kissed her cheek. He looked a little unsettled. "I didn't see you waiting here."

"Oh, you were busy with a client, so I chatted with Emily," she replied lightly. If Emily saw any reason to contradict her, she didn't show it.

"How long are you in London – are you staying at the house?" Max asked.

"No. I'm staying with Anna for the weekend," she said. He'd obviously not heard about the incident with her car so she decided not to mention it. He had enough to worry about here. Besides, she was trying to convince herself it was just a prank. It was probably Victoria or one of her friends.

"That's great," he sounded relieved and quickly added. "I'm sure you must miss her, being down in the country. I mean you two have been inseparable every time you came to stay."

Stephanie looked at him confused – how unlike her father to babble, he was normally such a succinct orator. "Do you have time for lunch, Dad?" she asked.

Max looked at his watch. "Just a quick coffee. I am due in court at noon." To Emily he said, "I'll be about twenty minutes."

Max took Stephanie's bag from her and they caught the lift back down to the coffee shop in the foyer. They ordered their drinks and sat opposite one another on a pair of leather armchairs, to drink them.

"Are you busy, Dad?" she asked.

"Always busy, sweetheart – you know that," Max replied.

"Yes, but are you working on anything interesting?" she asked clumsily. She couldn't quite work out how to ask who his client had been, without raising suspicion that she had overheard their conversation.

He eyed her carefully for a moment. "Oh, just various cases."

Stephanie sipped her coffee as Max changed the subject. She screwed her nose slightly. The coffee wasn't up to Andy's standard.

"Have you seen Sam? He's been asking about you," Max asked smiling.

"Yeah, just before and no, Dad, I'm not going there again," she replied.

Max raised his eyebrows, but said nothing. She was about to try a different line of questioning about his mysterious foreign client, when a man approached them and cleared his throat.

"Excuse me, Max," he said.

Stephanie looked up and groaned inwardly. Vince Burgess worked for her father as a kind of private investigator. He was apparently very good at what he did, but he gave Stephanie the creeps. He was always popping up out of nowhere.

"Ah, Vince," Max stood and shook his hand. Vince stood at attention, his close cropped hair emphasising his stocky build. "You remember my daughter, Stephanie."

Vince glanced at Stephanie and nodded once. "I have that information you are after," he said, returning his attention to Max.

"Great. Let's head upstairs," Max replied, his demeanour suddenly serious. "Sorry, darling. I have to go," he said to Stephanie, leaning down and kissing her cheek. "See you in a few days?"

"Okay, Dad. Vince," she smiled goodbye to the two men.

Stephanie sat in the foyer for a little while longer, finishing her drink and musing over what had just happened.

Why was she being discussed by one of her father's clients? And what did he mean that her friendship with the younger son had been taken care of? Were they talking about a deal with the Knoxes – that would be a little strange, especially after the scene she had witnessed between her father and James's grandfather and brother in the village a couple of weeks ago? *What's going on here?*

Chapter 18

Still puzzling over the conversation she had overheard, Stephanie caught the District Line to Embankment and joined the crowds of people spilling out of the station. She walked up the road past Charing Cross, dodged black cabs to cross The Strand and walked the block to Trafalgar Square passing St. Martin-in-the-Fields church. It was a lovely summer's day and a large number of tourists were milling around in the square, enjoying the sunshine. The National Gallery, located in a magnificent Georgian building, was on the northern side of the square. Stephanie made her way up the front steps and through the imposing double doors.

She left her suitcase in the coat check room in the basement and climbed the wide marble staircase to the second floor, which housed the gallery's early 20th century collection. Her attention was taken by Monet's *Bathers at La Grenouillère*, when she noticed a woman enter the room and speak briefly to the gallery assistant seated adjacent to the doorway, watching the visitors.

"Excuse me?" she called as she hurried towards them. *Why do librarians and people who worked in art galleries all adhere to the same dowdy uniform of navy skirts, flat rubber-soled shoes accessorised with glasses hanging around their necks?* she

THE CARLSWICK AFFAIR

wondered idly.

Stephanie noticed that they both wore photo ID which introduced one as Dr Margot Pierce and the gallery assistant as Caroline Jones.

"Hi. I'm working on a project about lost artworks during World War II and I was hoping to find someone to talk to about the missing so-called Degenerate Art works," Stephanie asked politely, as she approached.

Caroline nodded. "Sure."

Stephanie pulled a notebook out of her bag and continued. "Now I know from my research that any sort of art work that didn't meet the Nazis' criteria of what a good painting, for example, should be, was considered degenerate. And that all such art work was confiscated and some pieces were incorporated into a travelling exhibition designed to ridicule the work and influence the cultural views of the German people," she said.

"That's correct," Caroline said pleasantly.

"What would have happened to the art after the exhibition?" Stephanie asked.

"Well, I believe anything of value was sold at auction outside of Germany before the war, and everything else was destroyed," she answered.

Stephanie thought back to Sophie's diary. Her meeting with Hoffman had mentioned that art was being destroyed. It also mentioned art being stolen from Jewish families.

"What about the more famous pieces that were forcibly taken from German and Jewish families?" she asked.

"Same thing," Caroline said

"So who would have bought them?"

"Other museums and galleries and wealthy collectors,"

Caroline answered.

Stephanie's mind was racing. This made sense. The Nazis had sold the pieces they had stolen to help fund their war. It seemed unlikely that Hoffman was selling degenerate or stolen art for the Nazis, but perhaps he was doing his own deals on the side? she thought.

"So, some galleries and individuals potentially still have stolen Nazi art in their collections?" Stephanie asked.

"Most definitely. If the provenance couldn't be established after the war, they remained where they were," Caroline agreed.

Dr Pierce interrupted. "I don't like what you are insinuating, young lady."

"Oh no. I didn't mean, the National Gallery," Stephanie said, her eyes wide.

"Mmm," said Dr Pierce, sounding unconvinced. She looked at her watch. "Was there anything else?" she asked frostily.

"No. Thank you for your time," Stephanie said as her mobile chimed with a text. "Actually there was one thing – how do you establish, what did you call it, provenance?"

"Dealers and the larger galleries have research departments that have set procedures for reviewing documentary evidence such as bills of sale and photographs. There are a number of journals and publications that assist in proving the legal ownership of an art object," Caroline replied.

"So with stolen art, there would be a break in that documentary chain," Stephanie said.

Caroline nodded and Stephanie thanked them again for their time. She flicked her mobile open and saw the text was from Michael.

Michael: *Hey, hacked the secure section of Knoxes website!*

Stephanie: *Michael!* :-o

Michael: *Interesting client list. From a supposed mafia boss to the Nat Gallery!*

Stephanie: *That's where I am right now.*

Michael: *Some woman from there is mentioned a lot.*

Stephanie: *Who?*

Michael: *Dr Margot Pierce.*

Stephanie: *That's who I am talking to!*

Michael: *Get the hell out of there – u don't want anyone letting Knox know u r snooping, especially after yesterday! Call me. U owe me an explanation!!*

Stephanie hurried towards the stairs, glancing over her shoulder. Dr Pierce was standing in the centre of the room staring at her. Stephanie took the stairs two at a time back to the lobby. Jeez, Michael obviously didn't buy the prank theory.

Dr Pierce watched her go and then hurried to a nearby office and closed the door. She picked up the phone and dialled a number.

"I have had a young Australian woman here this afternoon enquiring about missing Nazi art in galleries and private collections," she said quietly into the telephone.

"No, not any one specifically, but I thought it odd, given the current situation."

She walked over to the window and looked down into Trafalgar Square.

"Yes, she has just left," she said pausing to listen. "Yes, that's right, dark hair, late teens. She is heading towards Charing Cross now."

"Okay. Goodbye." She pressed 'end' on the handset, replaced the phone on the desk and continued watching until Stephanie had walked out of sight.

Stephanie hurried back towards the underground station, wheeling her bag behind her. There was no way the woman would link her queries with Alex. Was there? She felt the back of her neck prickle as though someone was watching her. Nervously, she glanced over her shoulder. People were going about their business, taking no notice of her. *Stop being paranoid,* she thought, annoyed for letting her imagination get the better of her. She joined a stream of people walking down the road from Charing Cross to Embankment, where she caught the District Line, changing at Earls Court for Parsons Green.

Anna's flat was on the south side of the Green. Stephanie walked past the White Horse Hotel where a few groups of people had gathered under the umbrellas to enjoy a lunch time drink. She crossed the road, walking up the front steps to a red door on the end of the row of terraced houses. She rang the buzzer for the top floor flat.

"Yes?" A voice crackled through the intercom.

"Hi, it's me," Stephanie said.

"Come on up." The door clicked as Anna unlocked it remotely from upstairs. Stephanie pushed it open and pulled her bag into the entrance hall. She carried it up the stairs which were carpeted in a plush red with swirling patterns. The walls were wood panelled. The effect would have been dark and forbidding, had it not been for the large picture window on the landing at the top of the stairs, which looked back out over the Green. She continued up another flight to the top of the building where a smaller window overlooked the tree tops.

Anna was waiting at the door of her flat and threw her arms

around Stephanie. Anna was gorgeous. Tall and slim with long auburn hair which curled as it hit her shoulders and spilled down her back. She had sparkling blue eyes, luminous skin and a very pretty smile. Stephanie returned her hug. Anna's family lived in the same apartment complex in Chelsea as Stephanie's father. Being the same age, Anna and Stephanie had quickly become firm friends from the age of four.

The flat was light and spacious. The walls were painted white and the floorboards had been polished and shone. The living room, kitchen and dining area were all one and the doors on the far side of the room led to two bedrooms and a bathroom.

It wasn't the sort of flat that a jobbing actress should have been able to afford, however, Anna's father had bought it for her, as he couldn't bear the thought of his only daughter living in squalor.

"So are you going to tell me who or what's been keeping you so busy?" Anna asked filling the kettle.

"It's a long story, but…." Over a pot of tea, Stephanie filled Anna in on meeting James, Sophie's journal, the feud and the mysterious painting in the Knox library, the reappearance of Sam and finally the brick through her car window.

"Wow – you have been busy. I don't know what to say. But I don't like the thought that you are being threatened. Do you really think it could be James?" Anna asked, frowning.

Stephanie hesitated. She had no real evidence to link James, but she was feeling increasingly suspicious, and slightly afraid of him.

"Don't know. I keep telling myself it's probably just a prank. James has an ex-girlfriend who has taken a dislike to me. Although I am also wondering if the Knoxes – " She broke off shaking her head. "I want a night off all that tonight."

"Well that's good, because I have a great night planned. We'll grab a bite at that little Italian by the Tube and then we are heading into the West End to see a band. Hey – I have to say I told you that you and Sam had unfinished business," Anna teased.

Stephanie shook her head. "No way."

"Actually, Anna, there's something else I haven't told you," she said hesitantly, unsure how to start.

"Yeah?"

"When I went to visit Dad today, he had a foreign military type guy with him and they were discussing the Knoxes and talking about me," she said. Saying it out loud, she felt a strange twinge in her chest.

Anna looked surprised. "What did they say?"

"Just that Dad had made sure that I wasn't hanging out with James anymore and they don't want me at a 'location' when something happens. What do think is going on, Anna?" she asked.

Anna shook her head, curls bouncing. "No idea – that is really strange. What have you stumbled into?"

Chapter 19

"James," Alex shouted, annoyed.

James tried to slip out of the house through the kitchen. But the smell of freshly baked biscuits made him pause and he grabbed a handful that were cooling on a wire cake rack on one of the granite kitchen benches. That was his mistake.

"Hey," Grace called across the kitchen. "Thief!" But there was a smile in her voice.

Unfortunately, her calling out had alerted Alex to James's whereabouts and he came bursting into the room.

"There you are, little brother. My office. Now." He turned on his heel and strode back across the hallway towards his open study door.

James hesitated, sorely tempted to continue his escape out the side door.

"It'll be easier to just get whatever he wants over and done with," Grace advised, sensing his indecision.

James sighed. "I suppose." He grabbed another couple of biscuits, receiving a smack on the hand from Grace, and sauntered after Alex.

Alex's office was dominated by a huge polished antique mahogany desk. On one wall was a row of bookshelves and opposite was a glass fronted cabinet containing collectible rare volumes. A large chesterfield sofa had a variety of antique chairs clustered around it.

James loitered in the doorway. "What?" he asked sullenly. "I was just on my way out."

"Sit." Alex raised his voice and pointed to a chair, his eyes steely.

James sighed, but did as instructed, dropping heavily into the nearest chair and rocking back so that he was sitting on two legs rather than four.

Alex rolled his eyes. "You do realise how much that chair will cost you if you break it?"

It was James's turn to roll his eyes, but he eased the chair back onto its four legs.

"Now, I thought Grandfather and I had made it very clear that you were to stop that Cooper girl from snooping around." He looked accusingly at James. "Why is she up in London now, making enquiries at the National Gallery regarding works of art that we may or may not have in our possession?"

"What. Stephanie is?" James said, confused.

"Well a girl fitting her description was. Seems a little coincidental, don't you think? You do know she was back here the other day with some flimsy reason to snoop around in the library?" Alex said.

"Was she now?" James said slowly, thinking back to the previous weekend when he'd passed her on the road outside the manor. "Did you see her?"

"No – Grace let her in," Alex said.

James was thoughtful for a moment. "What's so important about this anyway?"

Alex went very red in the face, battling to control his temper.

"What's so important? I'll tell you what's important. I have been working on this deal for the last five years and secrecy is of the upmost importance. I. Will. Not. Have. It. Fall. Through," he finished, shouting. "Do you realise how much the upkeep on this house is? With our darling mother traipsing all over the world spending our inheritance, someone has to raise enough money to keep this place going. Playing a few gigs down at the pub certainly isn't going to do it."

James stood and backed towards the door.

"Okay. Don't get your hair in a knot. I'll tell her again, but I can't see what she would have to do with one of your deals," he said.

"No you wouldn't, but she must be stopped before she does some damage. Her drawing attention to us now could ruin everything! I need her kept out of this for another three or four days and then you can do what you like with her. If this gets screwed up, I will hold you personally responsible and you know what that means," Alex said menacingly.

James held his hands up as if in defeat. He had suffered enough of Alex's beatings over the years to fear getting on the wrong side of him. "Alright, leave her with me. I'll find out what she's up to and put a stop to it."

Alex nodded and said, "Just make sure you do. Because if you don't, I will find someone who will and it won't be pretty."

Chapter 20

L ater that night when Stephanie and Anna arrived at the club in Covent Garden, there was a long line of people spilling out of the door and snaking their way along the footpath. Anna took her hand and pulled her to the front of the queue. The bouncer was about to send them to the back of the line, when he suddenly smiled.

"Hey, Anna, in you go," he said.

"Thanks, Tommy," she said as she leaned up on tiptoes and gave him a quick peck on the cheek.

He unhooked the velvet cord, letting them through the door. Stephanie looked at her amazed.

"We have auditioned together a number of times. He's a great guy," Anna said by way of explanation.

"Useful person to know," Stephanie said.

The club was an in an old warehouse. It had high ceilings with exposed rafters and concrete pillars running in lines, like solders, down the centre. It was dimly lit. Along one wall was a long shiny metallic-topped bar attended by several very handsome barman in crisp black shirts with the club's logo on a breast pocket. *So this is where one finds all the out of work actors and models*, Stephanie thought.

At the far end of the cavernous space was a raised stage. A

red velvet curtain covered the back and the stage was set with drums, guitars, and several microphones. Off to one side of the stage was a large mixing desk. Tonight's band was sitting on the edge of the amps tuning their guitars and chatting with the various people who milled around them.

The girls checked their coats and headed towards the bar.

Anna had just ordered when the guy beside Stephanie put his hand on her arm. She looked up into the face of Andy.

"Andy! What are you doing here?" she exclaimed.

"We've come to see the band. Liam knows the lead singer," he said.

Anna turned around to see who Stephanie was talking to and recognised Andy. She smiled flirtatiously at him.

Andy's grin widened.

"Andy, this is my best friend, Anna. Anna, this is Andy," Stephanie said.

Anna gave Andy a dazzling smile and said, "Hi."

Andy invited the girls to join them, but Stephanie shook her head.

"I dunno," she said hesitantly. "Is James here?" She most definitely didn't want to spend the evening sitting anywhere near James. She craned her neck, looking around trying to see if she could see him.

"Yeah – but so are plenty of other people – it'll be fine," he said, smiling encouragingly at Anna.

"Come on then – lead the way," Anna said, making the decision for both of them. She took his arm. She winked over her shoulder at Stephanie, who couldn't help but laugh. Anna usually had men falling at her feet – although Stephanie wouldn't have thought that Andy, who had his pick of pretty girls, would have tripped quite so quickly. She reluctantly followed them to a table down the front.

And sure enough, there sat James, along with the other members of The Fury and a few of their friends. Stephanie groaned. Her great 'forget about everything' night out with Anna was taking a wrong turn and there was seemingly nothing she could do to control it. James looked furious to see her and her heart twisted painfully. *You bastard,* she thought.

"Stephanieee," Jack called and patted the bench beside him, saving her from having to sit at one of the empty seats next to James. She smiled at him and sat down, taking care not to look at James. Anna sat across the table from her, curiously watching the interaction between the two of them.

"Thanks, Jack," Stephanie murmured, gratefully. Andy introduced Anna around the table and then turned so that he had her to himself.

"God, don't tell me I have a stalker," James muttered.

Stephanie felt her face go hot. She had the sudden urge to lean over and scratch that arrogant look off his face. Instead she sat on her hands and resisted the impulse. Which was just as well because Liam and Peter, who was the singer in the band they had all come to see, chose that moment to stop by the table.

"Anna. Steph. Jess said you might be coming. How are you? It's been ages," Peter said before leaning over and kissing each of them in turn on the cheek. Anna had gone to school with Peter's younger sister Jessica, and the three girls had spent quite a lot of time at her house. "You know, the last time I saw these two, they were with my sister, climbing in through her bedroom window at two am!" They all laughed.

Stephanie allowed herself a triumphant look at James. Stalker? She knew the band better than he did.

To his credit, James had the grace to look embarrassed.

However, it was Stephanie who felt uncomfortable for the rest of the evening. She was annoyed that James being there had spoilt her night out with Anna. Once the band started, they all hit the dance floor, so at least she didn't have to sit at the same table as him for very long. She stayed well away from him, instead dancing with Jack, Andy, Anna and the many people who seemed to orbit their circle. James seemed to have a different girl twirling in front of him every time she looked his direction – although she tried her best not to glance his way too often. Oddly enough, he looked miserable and disappeared from the dance floor before the first set was finished. The band was really good and they were all thirsty after dancing, so in the break Stephanie went to get a round of drinks. She took orders and wandered up to the bar, squeezing into an empty spot. She soon realised to her dismay that the guy waiting to be served beside her was James. She let out a heavy sigh and turned her back to him.

After a few minutes of pointedly ignoring each other, James broke the silence.

"So, what have you had Mikey working on for you?" he asked.

She didn't answer immediately. *I have to be careful here – James isn't just making polite conversation, he is fishing.*

"He was just helping me get my technology all set up for Oxford," she replied.

"Yeah, right, Steph. Wanna try again?" he said.

She shook her head, trying to look indifferent.

"I will make him tell me, if I have to," he said. He lowered his voice. "Stephanie – I do hope you are still not looking into my family. Stay out or there will be trouble," he said roughly.

152

She looked up at him and frowned. He had carefully arranged his features and she couldn't read what he was thinking.

"Are you threatening me?" Stephanie could feel her temper rising.

"I just don't want to see you get hurt, that's all," James said.

"And who's going to hurt me, James, eh?" she challenged, her eyes flashing in annoyance.

He gave her an exasperated look, before suddenly changing the subject.

"I had a visit from Matt yesterday," he said.

Stephanie groaned inwardly, but said nothing.

"I think I convinced him that I had nothing to do with your smashed car window, but you didn't have to send your cousin to do your dirty work, you could've just asked," he said.

"I didn't know he had done that," she said quietly.

"Did you really think that I'd thrown a brick through your car window?" he asked.

Stephanie looked at her feet, unsure what to say. "Ah well, the writing on it said how much I looked like my aunt and that I could end up like her. And I do recall you saying how alike we were," she said, raising her chin defiantly and looking him directly in the eye.

His eyes went wide. "What?" he almost shouted.

The barman caught her attention as James grabbed his bottle, pivoted and walked away. He flicked his phone open, speed dialling as he walked.

Oh no, she thought, with a sinking feeling in her stomach, this was getting confusing. James really seemed only interested in stopping her looking into his family. Yet he seemed to provoke a strong reaction from her. She needed to avoid him as much as possible for her own sanity.

Frowning, she returned to the table balancing the drinks and squeezed in beside Anna, who was tossing her hair and giggling at something Andy had said.

Stephanie sat back and surveyed the crowd. On the opposite side of the room she could see James talking animatedly on his phone, waving his arms around as though he was arguing with someone.

Shame I can't overhear that conversation, she thought. *Ah, but maybe I can.*

She told Anna that she was off to the bathroom and skirted around the back of the crowd, so that she came up behind James. She stood on the other side of the pillar that he was leaning against and listened to his side of the conversation.

"I don't care. It's not the way to do it," he said angrily into the phone.

"Look, give me a bit longer. I'm trying to find out what she knows, so I can stop whatever it is that she's up to." He paused listening. "Okay – I'll call you back."

He clicked the phone shut with a frustrated sigh and shoved it in his pocket. He looked back over at the table where they were all sitting and then scanned the room, as if looking for someone.

Stephanie flattened herself further back against the pillar that was hiding her. *Don't turn around*, she prayed.

With a puzzled expression on his face, he slowly started walking back to their table. Stephanie slipped quietly behind him and through the doors leading to the bathroom.

What was that all about? She was suddenly feeling scared again. He had to have been talking about her. Find out what she knew about what? The painting? She looked at her watch. Eleven-thirty pm, she had to get out of there, but first she would have to drag Anna away from Andy.

She reapplied her lipstick and opened the bathroom door, stepping into the corridor leading back into the club. Her senses were suddenly on high alert and the skin on the back of her neck prickled. She spun around and gasped. James was leaning against the wall outside the door waiting for her.

She felt a shiver of fear crawl down her spine. She started backing away from him towards the door which led back into the club.

"Steph, we need to talk," he said, his voice was gentle, but the look in his eyes was not.

"Okay – but let's do it back in there," she said, edging towards the door.

He crossed the corridor in two large steps and grabbed her arm, spinning her around against the wall.

"No," he said firmly. "Let's talk here."

At that moment the door to the club opened and one of the bouncers came through.

James put his hands either side of her head on the wall and leaned towards her as though he were about to kiss her.

"Get a room," the bouncer chuckled as he ambled past.

Stephanie went to call out for help, but James put two fingers against her lips and whispered "Sshhh" as he looked sternly at her. She froze. The bouncer disappeared through a doorway further down the corridor.

Now she felt really frightened. She quickly assessed her options. There really wasn't anything he could do to her here – the corridor was too much of a thoroughfare –but she would be happier to be back in the bar with Anna and Andy close by. She tilted her head up as if to kiss him back and heard his breath catch in his throat. She acted quickly and shoved him really hard in the stomach so that he stumbled back. She ducked under his outstretched arm and ran for the door. But he was too fast. This time he got both arms around her from behind and held her tight.

"Stop. I am trying to help you," he said fiercely in her ear.

"Yeah, right. Let me go." She struggled and tried to stamp her heel down on his foot.

"Steph – stop. If I let you go, will you promise not to run? I just need to talk to you," he said, his breath hot against the side of her face. His chest was pressed up against her back, and she could feel his heart hammering.

"Okay," she reluctantly agreed.

He slowly released her, testing whether she was about to bolt again. Suddenly the door burst open and two guys walked through laughing. One of them held the door open for her and she gratefully rushed through it. Behind her, she heard James swear. He caught up with her and walked back to the table, his hand on her elbow. She looked around wildly for Anna and Andy, but they were nowhere to be seen.

"What were you looking for at my place last Sunday?" he asked as he slid in beside her at their now empty table. She spotted Anna and Andy on the dance floor throwing themselves around, and let out a shaky breath.

No. Grace told him.

"I thought I had lost an earring in the library when we were looking at the photos," she lied.

"Try again," he said coldly. "I don't believe you."

"Believe what you want," she answered, trying to sound annoyed rather than frightened. Her heart was racing in her chest and she could feel a cool trickle of sweat running down her back.

"What has Michael been doing for you – hacking something maybe?" James asked.

Stephanie feigned shock, her eyes wide. "Last I heard helping someone set up their laptop, wasn't called hacking."

He shook his head. He clearly knew more than he was letting on. "Stephanie, you have gotten involved in something that has nothing to do with you. I don't want to see you get hurt."

"And there you go, threatening me again." Stephanie replied equally as vehemently. She couldn't believe what she was hearing. She could feel her anger rising and overtaking her fear.

James looked at her long and hard, and with a deep sigh, stood up and walked away from the table.

Stephanie sat there stunned for several moments. *Holy crap – what was going on with James? Maybe I've had a lucky escape. The guy is like Jekyll and Hyde. I sure know how to pick them.* She looked around – no one had been close enough to overhear their conversation or appeared to have taken any notice of them arguing.

Dave came back to the table and slumped down beside her, clearly the worse for wear. He turned to her and said, "Tell me, Stephanie, why would a nation name itself after a small oval brown fruit?"

Distracted, she looked at him, uncomprehendingly. "What?"

"You lot. Kiwi. Fruit?" He repeated.

She couldn't help but laugh. "We are called Kiwis after a small native flightless bird, not a kiwifruit, you idiot!"

Dave just grinned drunkenly at her and got up and wandered away as Anna and Andy came back to the table giggling and flopped down beside her.

"Anna, I'm not feeling well. I'm really sorry, but can we go?"

Stephanie asked quietly, a pleading look in her eye.

"Sure." She turned back to Andy and whispered something to him. He leaned past her and looked at Stephanie concerned, "Are you okay?"

"I think I have a migraine coming on." She winced at lying to him.

He jumped up. "Let me see you two into a cab, then." He leaned down to kiss Anna, whispering something that made her giggle.

Stephanie made her way through the crowd to the coat check and retrieved their jackets. She stood and waited for Andy and Anna to join her once they had exchanged phone numbers. She felt a hand on her arm and turned expecting Anna. It was James.

"Not you again? What now?" she asked. She roughly shook his arm off. Over his shoulder, she could see Andy and Anna pushing their way through the crowd towards them.

"Look, I'm sorry if I sounded harsh before, but I am trying to help you," he hissed as they approached. Andy looked from James to Stephanie and back, trying to assess the situation.

"You two okay?" he asked.

"Yep, just peachy," Stephanie replied flippantly. "Don't worry about seeing us out – I'm sure we can find our way to the Tube, just fine."

Andy put his arms around Anna and gave her a lingering kiss goodbye. Stephanie and James looked in different directions, the atmosphere between them tense and uncomfortable.

"Okay – what's going on?" Anna asked as soon as they got outside.

"Anna – I'm really sorry – I know you were having a great time with Andy, but James was really scaring me – he knows something and keeps telling me to stop looking into his family or I'll get hurt."

"It's okay," Anna said, "It was time to leave anyway – didn't want Andy thinking I was too keen." She hooked her arm through Stephanie's. "Now let's walk down to Embankment and you can tell me exactly what he said on the way. And then you can tell me everything you know about Andy."

Their footsteps echoed among the brick buildings as they walked along the narrow lane. It had rained lightly while they were in the club. There was a slight mist rising off the Thames, diminishing the impact of the street lights. Stephanie shivered and began explaining the evening's events. Just as they neared the bottom of the lane, she felt the hairs on the back of her neck rise again.

Suddenly out of nowhere an engine revved and a black SUV with its lights on full came hurtling towards them. Stephanie grabbed Anna and pulled her into a doorway as the car veered past them. Anna screamed as its tyres hit a puddle of water, splashing them both with dirty oily water.

"God – that was close," Stephanie said. "What an idiot."

The car screeched to a stop at the top of the street and began reversing.

The two girls looked at one another, terrified.

At that moment, the door to the club opened and half a dozen people spilled out and began walking down the lane towards them. The car stopped reversing and instead accelerated forward around the corner out of sight.

Chapter 21

The girls slept late the next morning. They had sat up talking, going over the events of the day and Stephanie had lain awake for a long time after Anna had gone to bed. She couldn't be sure, but she hoped it wasn't James driving the SUV. *That would have been pretty extreme. He wouldn't have had time to get to it after they had left the club. Would he? But he had been really insistent that I stop looking into his family or I would get hurt. The thing is though, I haven't really looked into his family, just my aunt and...* She sat up in bed. That was it. James must know about the painting. Sophie's last entry had been just before she died when she was on her way to Knox Manor to visit Edward's mother. Maybe she had seen something there that she shouldn't have. This had to be all about the painting. What was a piece of art that had been requisitioned by the Nazis doing hanging in the Knoxes' library all these years? But the bigger question was; who else knew?

Anna popped out to pick up coffee and bagels the next morning, while Stephanie made a few phone calls. She had opened Anna's refrigerator earlier in search of food instead finding it to be sparsely populated – some long life milk, cheese and several bottles of wine.

Her first call was to her father's office. Although it was Saturday morning and most staff wouldn't be working, she suspected that her father would have Emily there, even if it was just to make coffee for his meeting. It was a good guess. Emily answered in a professional clipped voice. When she realised it was Stephanie on the other end, she relaxed into her usual midlands accent.

"Your dad's asked not to be disturbed before his meeting at noon – shall I leave him a message for you?" she said.

"No, that's okay – don't tell him I called. I was just going to see if he wanted lunch. Does he still have his foreign visitor with him?" Stephanie said.

"Yes and more coming. We will have half of Israel here soon," Emily said. "Steph – you might have to call your dad on his mobile if you need to talk to him today as they are all driving down to Carlswick straight after the meeting. I've had to organise five estate cars and book a whole lot of rooms at the hotel."

"Are they?" Stephanie said. She couldn't keep the surprise out of her voice. "Well, I hope he doesn't make you work too long today." She said goodbye to Emily and hung up.

Anna returned with coffee, which Stephanie gratefully grabbed as she was dialling her grandmother's number. It rang four times before it was answered. Ellie was delighted to hear from Stephanie.

"Grandma, there is something that you may be able to help me with. You mentioned the other day that your brother David conducted his own investigation into Sophie's death. Did he make any notes – leave anything written that you might have?" she asked.

"I don't have anything, dear. But the library in the village has his memoirs," Ellie said.

Stephanie gave a sharp intake of breath. *Have I caught Dad in a lie?* She clearly remembered her father telling her at dinner that David didn't write a memoir. Stephanie felt a sharp pang of guilt. She shouldn't be suspecting her father of anything untoward. It was possible that he didn't know that David had written anything. Although the thought felt false, especially as she knew what a history buff her father was. *Where else did I learn to love the subject?*

"Now, when are you coming home, dear? It's very quiet without you coming and going," Ellie asked.

"Later today, I think," Stephanie said.

Stephanie ended the call and stared at the phone for a few moments. *Funny that Dad failed to mention yesterday that he was heading to Carlswick this weekend. And David did leave a memoir. This is getting stranger all the time. One thing's certain; I need to get hold of that memoir,* she concluded.

She scrolled through the phone book on her mobile phone and pressed the telephone symbol beside Michael's name.

After a brief conversation, he agreed to drive into the village and see if the library would allow the memoir to be loaned out, and hold it for her until she got home later in the day. She couldn't guarantee that she would get back to Carlswick before the library closed, what with British train services being as unreliable as they were.

"Can I read it?" he asked.

"Of course, if you have time – I'm keen to know what it says about his investigations into the Knoxes and my aunt's death," she said.

"Okay. So this is what you've been looking into. But I don't see what your Sophie's death has to do with old paintings?"

Michael mused, mentally linking the internet search he ran with Stephanie's current request.

"I am hoping the memoir will shed some light on that," Stephanie replied.

"Okay," he replied. "Hey, I'll pick you up from the station. Text me when you're on the train."

Stephanie thanked him and said goodbye, clicking her phone shut and gulping the last of her coffee.

"Anna – that foreign guy at Dad's office yesterday was Israeli. And there is a meeting scheduled at midday with more of his colleagues and then they are all driving down to Carlswick. I'm going to do a little research here this morning and then do you fancy coming back down to the country with me for a few days?"

Anna grinned. "Yeah. Apparently, there's a great coffee shop in your village that I must try."

Stephanie laughed and curled up in a comfy armchair with her iPad and continued reviewing the websites that Michael had identified which mentioned Hoffman. What had become of him? Her mind wandered to her father. What was he up to? She was beginning to wonder if he wasn't somehow involved with the painting too. Trips to Carlswick with Israeli military types – maybe they were looking for stolen Jewish art? No. That would be too coincidental. But then again her father was relieved that she was in London which was strange given how delighted he was that she was spending the summer with her grandmother. It was all very confusing.

Anna's mobile phone ringing interrupted her thoughts.

"Sorry, Steph," Anna said after she ended the call. "I can't come back with you. That was my agent. I have an audition for that movie, tomorrow morning."

"That's great," Stephanie said. Anna had been actively campaigning for an audition for a role in what was touted as the next blockbuster, ever since the production company had announced their intention to make the movie. "Why don't you come down after the audition? I'm sure Andy would love to see you," she added suggestively, waggling her eyebrows.

Stephanie spent a little longer surfing the web. It appeared that in 1941 Hoffman had been replaced as curator of the Nationalgalerie in Berlin. But she could find no reference to him after that time. *I am missing something here*, she thought frustrated. *I need Michael's computer wizardry.* She closed her iPad and quickly packed her things.

"There's a train back to the village at one-thirty pm so I'd better go now, if I'm going to make it. See you tomorrow?" Stephanie said, hugging her friend goodbye. "And good luck for the audition or break a leg or whatever it is that you say."

"Thanks. I'll text when I'm on my way," Anna replied, returning her hug.

"Great. I'll pick you up. Thanks for last night. Sorry I had to spoil it with all this," Stephanie said, waving her hand vaguely at her iPad.

"It's fine. We just need to get to the bottom of it. I have a feeling that whatever your dad is up to will resolve this," Anna reassured her.

Unfortunately Stephanie was not sure which side he was on. She shivered, feeling icy fingers running down her back. Surely he was not involved with the stolen painting?

Chapter 22

A little while later, seated on the train, she sent Michael a text to let him know that she would be arriving at two forty-five pm.

He didn't reply, but she guessed that maybe he was still at the library. If they hadn't allowed him to borrow the memoir, he may have had to stay there to read it. She sighed and closed her eyes, only opening them again when the driver called her stop over the intercom. Quickly gathering up her things, she jumped off the train as the doors opened. She looked up and down for Michael, as the train pulled away, but she was the only person remaining on the platform.

She walked through the little station waiting room out to the car park. Being a Saturday, there was no commuter traffic, so only a few cars were parked there. Michael's wasn't one of them.

Strange, she thought, *he must have forgotten the time.* She pulled her phone out of her pocket and sent him another quick text. A few minutes later, she still hadn't heard from him and was about to walk up the hill to the library, when Matt drove past and screeched to a stop.

"Hello. You look like you are waiting for someone?" he called, opening his passenger window. "Do you need a lift?"

"Actually I'm waiting for Michael to pick me up, but he seems to have gone AWOL," she said.

Matt's face fell. "You haven't heard," he said.

"Haven't heard what?" she responded slowly, a knot forming in her stomach.

"Michael had a car accident earlier this afternoon. He was run off the road. The other driver didn't stop," he said.

Stephanie gasped and put her hand over her mouth, feeling nausea rising. "Oh my God! Is he…?

"He's still unconscious from what I understand. He's up at the hospital. Do you want me to take you to see him?" Matt said.

Stephanie's hand was already opening the passenger door. "Yes please." She lifted her bag onto the back seat before climbing in the front. They drove quickly to Carlswick Memorial Hospital.

Michael's mother was sitting on a chair outside his hospital room looking pale, when they walked down the corridor towards her several minutes later. She stood and gave Stephanie a hug.

"How is he?" Stephanie asked in a whisper.

"They are just running some tests. He's still not conscious, but otherwise appears to be uninjured," Mrs Morgan explained.

"It's my fault. He was on his way to pick me up." Stephanie could feel her eyes filling with tears.

"It's not your fault, dear," Mrs Morgan said, patting her arm kindly as Michael's door opened and the doctor came out and explained that there was no change, but he was stable and they could sit with him.

Matt offered to drop Stephanie's suitcase at their grandmother's house, and said he would come back later to visit. She hugged him goodbye and followed Mrs Morgan into Michael's room. He looked peacefully asleep and without his glasses, a lot younger. She felt a huge stab of guilt. This was too much of a coincidence – first the SUV last night in London and now this. She reached out and took Michael's hand. The back of it was covered in superficial cuts, probably from broken glass, Stephanie guessed.

"Sorry, mate. I would never have asked you to help if I knew I was putting you in danger," she whispered, before sitting on a chair beside the bed.

"What did the police say, Mrs Morgan?" she asked.

"They don't really know. He was sideswiped and spun off the road just outside town and the other driver didn't stop," she said. "There were no witnesses apparently, but his car has black paint down the side and is a real mess."

"Poor Michael. He will be upset about the MG," Stephanie said.

"I know," his mother agreed. "But it can be repaired."

They sat in silence for a few minutes. Stephanie looked around the sterile hospital room. On the cabinet beside the bed were Michael's belongings – his glasses, wallet and a single piece of paper. Stephanie's eyes picked up on the writing. It was a receipt from the Carlswick Library for a copy of Lt. David Cooper's *Memoir*.

So he had got it. Stephanie picked up the receipt and showed Michael's mother.

"Do you know if Michael left this at your place?" she asked.

Mrs Morgan looked at the receipt. "Is that for your great-uncle's book? Michael showed me. He was very excited about it and he was bringing it to give to you." She looked around the room. "It's not here, is it? The police emptied out the car and brought his jacket and iPad, but there was no book," she frowned. "I wonder if it was thrown from the car?"

Or stolen from the car, Stephanie thought grimly.

But to Michael's mother she said, "It's not important now. We can look for it once Michael is back on his feet."

A thought suddenly crossed her mind. *The receipt was for a copy of the memoir, which meant that the original must still be at the library.*

Stephanie glanced at her watch. It was four o'clock. Hopefully, the library would still be open.

"Mrs Morgan, I'm going to have to go – Grandma is expecting me at home. I came straight here from the station as soon as I heard. But I will pop back in after dinner, if that's okay," she said.

"Of course, Stephanie. Give me your number, so I can let you know if there is any change," Mrs Morgan said, pulling her mobile phone from her pocket.

They exchanged phone numbers and Stephanie hugged her goodbye and gave Michael's hand a squeeze.

She hurried from the hospital, down the hill to the library. It was still open. She had guessed correctly. Michael had checked out a copy, but the original was still available to be read. She sat in the library's tiny reading room, wearing cotton gloves, so as not to damage the fragile book.

David's writing was hard to read. She quickly scanned through the early sections on his childhood, education and air force training – she could come back and read those later. Her heart began to race as she reached the section entitled World War II. She had to force herself to slow down and read carefully. He mentioned that his sister Sophie was seeing his friend Edward Knox and several dinners they shared whilst on leave. She and David had begun to suspect that all wasn't right with the Knox family and their many foreign house guests. Other people had obviously noticed too, as the Ministry of Defence launched an enquiry into the family. Edward had been livid and he and David had argued.

Stephanie looked at her watch. It was ten to five – she would get thrown out of there shortly. She flicked over a few pages; an entry dated June 1946 caught her attention:

> *I do believe that old man Knox is storing artworks stolen by the Nazis, but as yet I have been unable to prove it! All of the visitors before and at the start of the war had one thing in common – they were wealthy Germans, and we now know for a fact that Hitler was forcibly confiscating art works, particularly those belonging to Jews or by artists he deemed to be Degenerate. And of course, we were to find out after the war, that he would also plunder all the major galleries and cultural institutions of Europe.*

Stephanie gasped. *Oh my God – I have come to a similar conclusion about the Knoxes, so there is something going on here.* She kept reading. There were more pages on the subject, covering his investigations and conclusions. However, at that moment the librarian came into the room and told her time was up and they were closing. She was welcome to come back when they were open again.

Stephanie looked longingly at the memoir. She felt it still had more to tell her. In fact she hadn't read anything on Sophie's death and from what her grandmother had told her, it was David who believed that it wasn't an accident, so he was sure to have written a lot about that.

Stephanie sighed and reluctantly handed the book and gloves to the librarian. It would have to be Monday now, as the library was closed on Sundays, but she checked with the librarian, just in case that had changed.

"No, we are closed now until Monday," the librarian confirmed. "It must be a good book. You are the third person to enquire about it in as many days."

"It's my great-uncle's memoir," Stephanie replied. "My friend Michael borrowed a copy of it for me, as I was out of town, but who else wanted it?"

The librarian went back to the front desk and tapped on the computer. "It doesn't say who requested it, I'm afraid. I wasn't here, but I know that when I went to retrieve it for Michael, it had already been brought out of the archive and was waiting to be put back. It was only when I scanned it for him to take into the reading room, that I noticed that there was a copy, which is the one that I loaned out to him," she explained. "We have started copying the old memoirs as some of the pages are deteriorating."

"Okay. Thanks," Stephanie said, the cold feeling engulfing her again. She seemed to be several steps behind whoever else was looking into events in the village during the war.

Chapter 23

Dusk was beginning to fall when the librarian locked the door behind her. Stephanie walked back up the hill to the taxi stand outside the hospital and took a taxi back to Wakefield House.

The Fiat, parked in front of the house, was dwarfed by half a dozen black estate cars. Stephanie was relieved to see that the windscreen had been repaired. *The garage must have returned it, while I was in London,* she thought, giving it a welcome home pat.

There were lights on in the guest house, but the blinds were drawn, so she couldn't see who was inside.

Ellie had left a note stuck to Stephanie's bedroom door, letting her know that she was visiting friends and would be back later. Stephanie's stomach suddenly rumbled. It had been a long time since her coffee and bagels at Anna's. She cooked herself a quick plate of scrambled eggs on toast and washed it down with a glass of orange juice.

After dinner, Stephanie wandered restlessly around the house studying the various photos that her grandmother had hanging on the walls and in frames on the piano in the sitting room, hoping they would give a clue to the family mystery. But the faces simply smiled back at her, retaining their secrets behind the glass.

Bored, she decided to drive back into the village and visit Michael again. She packed a small container of muffins and grapes to take for Michael's mother, in case she hadn't managed to get any dinner. The hospital café was sure to be operating on similar hours to the library in a village this size.

Her mind was still going over all the events of the last few days as she drove down the lane. *If Dad and his guests are planning on 'dropping in' to the Knoxes, then I wonder if the Knoxes are expecting them?* She puzzled over this for a few minutes. It just didn't sit right that her dad would be working with Alex, especially if it was to do with art of questionable provenance. *I wonder what's happening at Knox Manor?* An idea began to take shape in her mind as she parked at the hospital. *Once it's dark I will pay Knox Manor a visit and see what is going on there. Maybe I'll see Dad arrive for whatever meeting he was planning.*

There was no change with Michael. His mother was grateful for the food and they sat and chatted quietly for a while, with Michael sleeping peacefully beside them. A nurse bustled in and checked on Michael at regular intervals, each time pronouncing that he was doing just fine and giving a reassuring smile.

After about an hour, Stephanie said her goodbyes and promised to visit again the next day.

She drove out towards Knox Manor and turned into a farm gateway about a kilometre from the house. Pulling a small flashlight from the glove compartment as she jumped out, she carefully locked the car. She shrugged her long jacket on over her jeans, buttoning it up to the neck. The evening was still, crisp and clear and the stars were scattered across the sky like a sprinkling of glitter. She shivered slightly and could feel her heart starting to beat a little faster as adrenaline kicked in. The old wooden gate shuddered and creaked as she climbed over it.

Switching on the flashlight and pointing it at the ground, she walked across two gently rising fields until the chimneys of Knox Manor came into view. Quickly crossing the next two fields, keeping close to the hedgerows that served as fences, she stumbled once or twice on the uneven ground. She came to the tall stone wall which bordered the gardens of the manor and skirted along it a little way looking for an opening. Her breath was coming faster and forming condensation in front of her. A little way along there was a break in the wall. The gap was filled by a rusty looking metal gate and she gave it a gentle push with her foot. To her surprise it swung open, but made a loud creaking noise. She froze and flattened herself against the outside of the wall, desperately listening in case the creaky gate had attracted attention.

There was nothing but silence. Cautiously she crept through the gate, leaving it open so as not to make any further noise, and carefully wove her way between the trees, shrubs and garden borders towards the house.

She crept around to the front corner and took up a position beside a row of low trees where she had a good view in one of the rooms. The lights were on and she could hear the murmur of voices. Suddenly Alex sauntered across the room, glass in hand, talking to someone out of her line of sight. She was so focussed on what he was doing that she didn't hear the crack of a twig to her left until it was too late. It was all she could do not to scream with fright.

"You just don't listen, do you? Why are you hanging around outside my house after dark?" James sneered. "I don't think I could have been any clearer, when I said, keep away from us."

Stephanie said nothing, she was suddenly too frightened. In the darkness, she realised just how much bigger than her he was. She opened her mouth to speak but the words wouldn't form.

"Do you really have nothing better to do on a Saturday night?" he taunted.

"It's not like that," she blurted out, suddenly indignant. *You conceited prat.*

Movement in the window momentarily distracted them both. Victoria came into view laughing – glass of wine in her hand. Stephanie groaned inwardly.

"What's *she* doing here?" James murmured, as Stephanie took a couple of tentative steps away from him, readying herself to run. A hand clamped on her arm.

"Where do you think you are going?" James said.

Laughter came from the study and they both looked up as Victoria stopped by the tall wing-backed chair in which someone was reclining, and bent to kiss them. Stephanie felt James stiffen beside her.

"What the?" he began.

The person in the chair rose and pulled Victoria into a passionate embrace. When they pulled apart, he turned his head slightly. James gasped. It was his brother, Alex.

Suddenly the front of the house was bathed in light. Two dark cars, followed by two police cars, with their lights flashing blue and red, sped up the driveway and around the lake.

This time Stephanie didn't miss the opportunity of James being distracted. She violently pulled free from his grasp, shoving him roughly away and leapt over the box hedging at the edge of the garden and began running as hard as she could away from the house and driveway, back towards the gate in the wall. Her heart was racing. She could hear James's footsteps behind her.

"Steph. Stop," he called out in an urgent whisper.

Yeah, right, she thought, frantically trying to remember the way she had come.

She zigzagged through the trees at the edge of the garden trying to lose him, but got herself lost in the process.

"Stephanie. What's going on here?" his voice sounded close behind her.

She made the mistake of hesitating trying to decide which way to go and found herself slammed into the ground.

"Ouch," she cried indignantly, struggling under his weight to get free.

"Sorry – stay down," he said as a powerful flashlight swept over where they had been standing. "What are the police doing here?" he whispered in her ear. He eased his weight off her onto his elbows and knees, but she could still feel his breath against her cheek.

There were the sounds of loud voices and running footsteps back at the house.

"How would I know – I'm just a stalker, remember. Now get off me," she said.

"Steph….." James began, as he loosened his hold on her.

She pushed him away and scrambled to her feet. Her emotions – anger, fear and frustration – all rose to the surface in one hot bubble and overflowed. "No. You listen to me. First the brick through my car window, then a car trying to run me down outside the club in London last night, and now Michael is unconscious in hospital and my great-uncle's memoirs that

175

he had with him are missing." She paused and took a deep breath. "I don't know what you and your family are up to, but I've had it. I will *not* be your next victim," she said in a low sharp voice.

He leapt to his feet and stood in front of her looking confused. "Wait – Mikey's in hospital?" he said.

She saw red. *How can he stand there and act so innocent when he is clearly right in the middle of whatever Alex and his grandfather were up to?* "Oh sod off, James," she hissed and punched him in the face. A hard right hook. She was suddenly grateful for having a mother who insisted she take self-defence classes with her. James went down. Stephanie turned and ran for her life. This time he didn't follow. Somehow she managed to find the gate in the wall again and bolted through it to freedom.

Stephanie was shaking and out of breath when she reached her car, still parked where she had left it tucked in the farm gateway. She got in and drove quickly home, letting herself in through the kitchen entrance.

The lights were still on in the guest house and she could hear muffled voices. She crept up the stairs and into her bedroom, and throwing off her coat and kicking off her shoes, changed out of her dirty jeans and top and into a simple wrap dress. Exhausted by the events of the last few days, she collapsed on her sofa, nursing her bruised knuckles and picked up Sophie's diary to re-read her last entries.

A little while later she stuck her head into her grandmother's bedroom. The old lady was back home and tucked up in bed with a book open on her lap, reading.

"I thought I heard a car, a little while ago. Did you have a nice time in London?" Ellie asked.

"Yes, Grandma, but I'm tired, so I'm off to bed. Who does

Dad have here with him?" Stephanie said.

"Don't know, dear. Some legal matter. Oh, I almost forgot. How's Michael?" she enquired.

Stephanie leaned over and kissed her grandmother's soft wrinkled cheek. "Still unconscious, I'm afraid. Mrs Morgan said that she will text if anything changes."

"Oh dear." Ellie laid a hand on one side of Stephanie's face and smiled indulgently. "I'm glad you are home safely."

Instead of going straight to her room, Stephanie skipped downstairs and out across the driveway to the guest house. She was surprised to see a man standing to attention outside the closed door. He looked as startled as she was.

"Who are you?" he demanded.

"I could ask you the same thing," she replied, matching his tone. "Is my father here?"

He stared at her for a few seconds and said, "One moment." He turned, knocked and opened the door. Stephanie peered past him into the room. Around the large oval oak table were seated at least twelve men. She recognised none of them except Vince, who was standing writing on a white board. Stephanie shuddered. What was that creepy guy doing there?

"….and without a search warrant, we couldn't find anything," a bodiless voice spoke from a speaker on the centre of the table.

"Excuse me, Mr Cooper. Your daughter?" the man on the door said, interrupting.

The room instantly went silent and Max appeared in the doorway. He nodded to the doorman and the door was immediately closed behind him. He took Stephanie's arm and led her away from the meeting and back across the driveway towards the house.

"What are you doing home? I thought you were spending a

few days with Anna." He sounded slightly annoyed.

"I was, but Michael's had a car accident, so I came home to visit him in hospital," she replied, thinking on her feet. "What's with the meeting – must be pretty serious for a Saturday night?"

"Oh yes, you know how negotiations go sometimes. Now I have to get back in there – so they don't make any decisions without me," he laughed humourlessly. "Was there anything in particular that you needed?"

"No, Dad, just thought you'd like to know that I was home. Goodnight," she said as she reached up her tiptoes and kissed his cheek and walked back inside, leaving him looking warily after her.

She suddenly wasn't sure that she wanted to share the result of her investigations with her father. It was a strange sensation, but she felt as though she didn't completely trust him anymore. *All those years of visiting as a child and actually, I don't really know anything about him,* she mused sadly.

Chapter 24

There was a quiet knock on Stephanie's bedroom door a little while later.

"Come in," she called, expecting it be her father or grandmother. James slipped in quickly; breathing heavily as he quietly shut the door behind him and leaned against it.

"This place is worse than Fort Knox," he complained.

"Well I guess you would know, Mr Knox," she said, shocked to see him standing there.

James chuckled.

"What are you doing here? Are you stalking me now?" Stephanie asked.

He saw fear flicker across her face, along with the defiant tilt of her chin, as he strode over to where she sat. Stephanie jumped up, knocking over a small table with a glass on water on it. She moved away from the sofa, feeling the sudden need to put some distance between them.

"I am not involved with whatever it is that you think my family is doing," he said bluntly.

Her eyes flashed with anger. "Really? Then why have you been threatening me?"

James sighed. "Alex said he had a deal on that you were putting in jeopardy with your snooping around. He said I had to warn you off or he would. And believe me – you would rather it was me," he said.

Stephanie didn't answer immediately. She couldn't decide whether to trust him or not. All her instincts where screaming *No*, but there was measure of sincerity in what he was saying. "Why didn't you just explain that?" she said eventually.

"Like that would have stopped you," he said quietly.

"Oh so now *I* am unreasonable too," she said.

"Come on, Steph. I haven't come here to fight. This is doing neither of us any good," he implored.

They stared silently at one another for a few moments. James's cheekbone was shiny and red from where she had hit him earlier. It looked like he would have a bruise on it the next day. She knew she should be feeling frightened, but for some reason, she no longer did. The image she had built of him in her head over the last few days had been of some monster out to hurt her, but instead it was just James standing in front of her; the same James that she had kissed passionately a week earlier, but then had argued so bitterly with. He seemed to bring out such strong emotions in her.

"Steph, there's a lot more going on here than either of us realise. It's more than just bitterness over what happened all those years ago," James said.

"Yeah, I know. Have they sent you to extract everything I know, before they kill me too?" She eyed him suspiciously, only half-joking.

"Yeah, just call me Bond," he said, laughing quietly.

"No, James, I'm serious," she said. "I'm a bit out of my depth here, so I'm really not sure who to trust. You aren't very high on the trustworthy scale right now and the one person I did trust has ended up unconscious in hospital."

James moved towards her, holding out his hand in a gesture of peace. She looked at his hand, torn with indecision. Her instincts were telling her not to trust anything he said, but her heart was betraying her by thumping loudly and excitedly in her chest.

A loud knock on her door made them both jump. James looked at her in alarm.

"Stephanie – are you okay? Can I come in? It's Vince," a voice called.

They both froze.

"Quick – in here," she whispered, making a hasty decision and pushing him towards her walk-in wardrobe. "Get behind the curtain."

"Hang on," she called. "I'm not decent." She quickly pulled off her dress and pulled a light summer dressing gown around herself.

James raised his eyebrows appreciatively, before ducking behind the curtain. Stephanie glared at him, her cheeks burning, and rushed to the door.

"What's up, Vince? I was just getting ready for bed," she asked as she opened her door and stuck her head around it, trying to keep her voice calm.

"A security alarm went off and your father asked that I check on you and your grandmother," he said, looking past her into her bedroom. "May I come in for a look?"

Stephanie hesitated, but stepped aside to allow him into the room, "I didn't realise that we had such high tech security," she said.

"Who were you talking to?" Vince asked, ignoring her comment.

"Was probably the internet – I was just downloading some

new music." Stephanie waved her hand toward her laptop and iPod lying on the sofa.

Vince's trained eyes scanned the room. His eyes stopped on the spilled glass of water and upturned side table.

"Are you okay?" he mouthed silently to her.

Stephanie felt a shiver of fear. "No, I mean yes. You banging on the door startled me and I knocked it over when I jumped up," she explained. She walked as calmly as she could over to the small table and righted it, picking up the now empty glass. "I'll just get a towel to mop this up," she said walking into her ensuite bathroom. Vince followed, looking behind the door and in the shower. He paused to look into her walk-in wardrobe. He walked directly to the curtains covering the window of the small room and pulled them back. Stephanie gasped, but it was empty behind them. Vince visibly relaxed and smiled at her.

Where was James? Stephanie could barely look.

"Okay – all clear in here. I'm sure it's just a false alarm," he said walking back to the door of her bedroom. "Lock yourself in though – just in case." He nodded to her and went out into the hall.

Stephanie closed the door behind him and quickly turned the key in the lock. She momentarily leant on the door and let out the breath she had been holding, before rushing over to the walk-in wardrobe and pulling the curtains back herself. "James?"

"Here," a low voice sounded from behind her. She spun around and stumbled into him.

"Thanks," he said quietly, not taking his eyes off hers.

Stephanie stood still, her heart beating furiously. She wasn't sure if it was from the fright of nearly being caught in a lie or from the fact that he was standing so close to her – probably a bit of both. He left his hands gently on her shoulders where they had steadied her a moment earlier. They stood like that for several moments, looking into one another's eyes, each trying to assess what the other was thinking. Stephanie lowered her gaze to his lips and before she realised what she was doing, she reached up on her tiptoes to kiss him.

The kiss was gentle at first, until James ran his hands down her back and pulled her firmly up against him. She responded by winding her hands around his neck and into his hair. He flicked his tongue over her bottom lip and with a low moan in the back of her throat she opened and kissed him back. Their bodies pressed together, the pent up feelings of the past weeks spilling over.

When they finally pulled away, they stood silently gazing at each other, their breathing uneven.

Wow, Stephanie thought, quickly trying to gather her scattered thoughts.

"Um," she said eventually, breaking the silence. "How are we going to get you back out of here undetected tonight?"

Stephanie took a step away from James, trying to physically put some distance between them to allow her to think clearly. *What has just happened here? Why am I kissing someone that I don't completely trust? Is it because it feels a little dangerous?* Yet strangely, it somehow felt right, at the same time.

"I don't actually think I'll be going too far tonight – even if I wanted to," he smirked.

She took his hand and led him to the sofa.

"You wait here, while I get changed," she instructed, pushing him onto it.

"You really don't need to," he called quietly to her retreating

183

back, with a smile in his voice.

"Oh no, I really do," she replied, pulling on dark blue jeans and a rose pink hoodie. She needed a couple of minutes alone to regain her composure. *Careful, Steph*, she warned herself, *you don't know what he is up to.*

She came back into her bedroom and sat cross-legged at the opposite end of the sofa, studying him.

"You know it's not just my family guarding secrets," James said, leaning towards her and gently pushing her hair back where it had fallen over her face.

Stephanie flinched slightly at his touch. A hurt expression at her reaction flashed across James's face, and then was gone. "Well, why does your eighty-five-year-old grandmother have an ex-SAS officer here?"

"What? Vince? He works for Dad," Stephanie frowned. "Actually, that does make sense. He is very military, isn't he?"

"Check him out, Steph, and you'll see I'm right. He served two tours in Iraq and two in Afghanistan," James said.

"So now you've been looking into *my* family," she stated, frowning at him.

"He's not your family," James replied evenly.

"What about Victoria, James?" she asked, unsuccessfully trying to mask the bitterness in her voice. "Do you and Alex take turns?"

James flushed and blew out a breath. "Long story – but I was as surprised as you to see her with Alex tonight. She and I were finished months ago. Not terribly mature I know, but I was just trying to make you jealous after seeing you with Sam. She doesn't care for me – too busy being in love with herself or maybe Alex," he said. "Although how anyone could love Alex is beyond me."

"Yeah, but why this sudden change of heart? You've ignored me for days, you were really quite nasty at the café last Saturday, you threatened me at the club in London and frightened the hell out of me earlier tonight," Stephanie said.

"You are actually very hard to ignore," he said, laughing.

Stephanie let out a frustrated sigh. "Stop avoiding my questions, eh?" she said.

James moved closer to her on the sofa and put his hand under her chin and lifted her face to meet his. "I'm sorry – I really am. My grandfather hates your family for what happened during the war and will never forgive them for their part. The thought of me hooking up with a Cooper was too much for him. He made all sorts of threats. I've been disinherited several times in the last few days, whatever that means. After that night I showed you the photos in the library, he and my brother insisted that I cease all contact with you immediately 'for the good of the family'. And then your name kept coming up and Alex made it very clear that he would deal with you if I couldn't stop you looking into our family history. He has some top secret deal on and you were asking questions about us and drawing unwanted attention. You don't know him. He is ruthless when anyone gets in his way and I couldn't stand you getting hurt." He dropped his hand and sat back, watching her reaction carefully.

Stephanie bit her lip. *It all sounds very plausible, but can I trust him?* She shook her head, trying to process what he had said. The usually confident James was gone and a vulnerable looking James sat in his place. *But it could be just an act to find out what I know?*

"Steph, can I ask you something?" he said suddenly.

She nodded.

"Sam…" he began. "Are you and he…?"

She sighed. "No. We were together, but it ended six months ago," she said.

"Andy was right," he said as much to himself as to her.

She half smiled. *So he has been talking to Andy about me.*

"So, James, what now? Because I have uncovered some information that you are really not going to like. And I think that it's going to be a problem, because something is really off here and since someone keeps trying to stop me, I have to see this thing through," Stephanie said moving away from him. "I owe it to Michael to at least find out who ran him off the road."

"You think that's related, don't you?" he asked.

"I know it is," she replied with certainty.

James took a deep breath. "Okay – why don't you tell me what you think you have found," he said.

Stephanie hesitated. She couldn't just tell him bits, she would have to tell him everything and she still wasn't sure. She was beginning to believe that maybe he was sincere, but there was still that nagging doubt that he might use whatever she told him, against her.

James sensed her uncertainty and sat back from her, giving her space. "Let's start with what were the police looking for at my place tonight?" he suggested.

"Okay," she agreed, "I don't know, but I suspect that some of Alex's business deals are not all above board." *I will test the waters with that one.*

"Okay, somehow that doesn't surprise me," James said looking thoughtful. "The cops tried to blag their way in without a search warrant. It seemed that they were looking for one thing in particular. Do you know what that might be?"

It was Stephanie's turn to take a deep breath. "The painting in your library."

"What – the little one?" he asked.

"It's a van Gogh which is on a list of stolen artworks, missing from Germany since World War II," she said.

Silence.

"No." James shook his head. "Grandfather was given that by a business acquaintance, many years ago."

"How many years ago?" Stephanie asked.

"Before the war, from what I understand…." His voice trailed off. "How do you know that it's not just a copy?" he said.

"Well, the Nazis marked all the artworks they acquired with a black swastika and yours has one on the back," she said.

"And you know that, how?" James frowned.

Stephanie blushed. *Oops.*

"Ah – the day you were looking for your 'lost' earring. Right?" he said remembering his conversation with Alex. When Stephanie nodded, he continued. "Jeez, Steph – that took some nerve – you could have been caught at any moment."

"I know," she agreed quietly. "Here, I will show you the information on it." She stood and walked over to her desk, grabbed the large file of papers and her laptop and brought them back with her to the sofa.

"You think Alex is trying to sell it," he said drawing his own conclusion.

"I don't know. But it is worth millions," she said.

"Mmmm. It disappeared from the library a few days ago," James said quietly. "I asked Grandfather about it and he said it was being cleaned."

Stephanie looked at him long and hard and made a decision.

She shuffled along so that she was sitting beside him. She sat forward on the front edge of the sofa so that her feet were flat on the floor. Her leg pressed against his as he settled comfortably beside her resting one arm on the sofa behind her and leaning in against her shoulder. She opened the folder across their knees and proceeded to take him through everything that she had found. He interrupted with questions every now and again. She showed him the file she had saved on her laptop comparing her mobile phone photo with the screen shot of the missing painting.

After about half an hour, James sat back and ran his hands through his hair. "Bloody hell, Steph. I don't know what to say."

"I don't either. Part of me thinks I should take this to my dad. Those guys that came to your place tonight with the police are from Israel, I think; military or law enforcement of some kind. They are downstairs having a meeting right now."

"What? Here? Now?" he asked, surprised. "Hey, tell me honestly, what is Michael's involvement? He has been helping with more than setting up your laptop."

Stephanie blushed. "Yes," she admitted. "He was helping me with an internet search to cross reference German visitors to your place before the war with the list of missing Nazi art. You see many of them had valuable paintings in their art collections that haven't been seen since the war and Sophie's journals mention that your grandfather and his father were acquiring new art and other valuables long after war was declared. Here I'll show you," she said, flicking to the relevant pages in Sophie's journal.

After reading over her shoulder for a few minutes, he sat back deep in thought. "So why exactly do you think Michael was targeted today?" he asked.

"He had a copy of David's memoir from the library with him, but it's missing," she sighed and leaned into him slightly, feeling a strange relief at having shared all the information that she had gathered, and having him believe her at last. "I just don't know what my dad's involvement in this is. Maybe he is on the other side of Alex's deal? Although, I can't believe that he would be involved in anything illegal, but then I'm sure that you think that about your family."

"That's where we're different. I could so believe that about Alex. It's all about money and power with him. I don't know your dad, so I can't comment on him," he said.

"Maybe Alex doesn't realise that the painting is stolen," Stephanie mused.

James laughed. "This is Alex we're talking about. He's an art dealer. If the provenance is dodgy – he will know. It certainly explains why he has been so concerned with you looking into our family around World War II."

Stephanie walked over to her desk to return the folder and laptop.

A movement outside caught her attention. Vince and another man were out on the front lawn with torches and headsets. She gasped. James vaulted the sofa and was at her side in an instant. She pushed him away. "You need to stay away from the windows – they're still searching." A sudden thought crossed her mind. "Did you drive here? Will they find your car?" She felt a sharp stab of panic.

"No – the Vespa is stashed in a hedge about a kilometre back on Ridge Road. They won't find it," he said.

Stephanie breathed again, relieved.

James yawned and looked at his watch. It was midnight. He

pulled out his phone and tapped a text.

"Just letting Grace know that I won't be home tonight – not that anyone will notice, but still," he said, his voice trailing off.

Stephanie didn't know what to say. She stood studying him for a few moments. She really wanted to trust him. He yawned again.

"You're tired." Stephanie could see the dark circles under his eyes and the bruise that was beginning to show on his cheek. He looked worn out.

"Yeah – it's been a long day. Can I sleep on your sofa tonight?" he asked shyly.

"Of course," she said.

James kicked off his shoes and stretched out on the sofa. Stephanie went to get a spare duvet from her wardrobe and laid it over him. She wandered into her bathroom to get ready for bed. When she came out five minutes later, he was fast asleep.

She curled up on the chair opposite the sofa for a long time, watching him sleep and thinking. Finally, she decided that he was truly asleep and that she was safe to do the same. She stood and stretched. James looked so relaxed and somehow younger when he was asleep, with one arm thrown back behind his head and his hair flopping down over one eye. She leaned over him and gently brushed it back. He murmured and stirred. She very gently kissed the top of his head and climbed into her bed and fell into a restless sleep.

Chapter 25

Sunshine streamed into Stephanie's room the next morning. She rolled over and bumped into James who was stretched out on top of the covers beside her.

"Good morning, sleepyhead," he said huskily. She smiled and ran her hands self-consciously through her sleep tousled hair.

"I thought it was a dream – I didn't think that you were actually here," she said, the memory of their kiss the night before springing unbidden to her mind and causing her breath to catch in her throat.

"At least it was a dream and not a nightmare," he said, arching an eyebrow.

In the morning light, the bruise on James's cheek had darkened and was swollen. Stephanie reached over and gently ran her fingers over it.

"I'm really sorry for hitting you – I lost my temper."

He reached up and held her hand in place with his.

"It's okay, Steph. I was being a prat. I deserved it."

A loud knock on her door and the handle turning, startled them both.

"Steph – it's me, Sam," the person on the other side called.

Stephanie froze. Thank goodness she'd locked the door the

night before.

James looked at her through narrowed eyes. "What's he doing here?" he demanded angrily in a low whisper.

"Honestly, I don't know, James. I thought he was in London – you have to believe me," she whispered.

"Steph – wake up. Open the door. I need to talk to you," Sam called urgently from behind the door.

"Hang on – let me get dressed," she called.

"That's not really necessary," Sam said, a smile sounding in his voice.

Beside her James swore.

"What do you need to talk about this early?" she called, stalling for time and sitting up in bed holding the sheet to her chest. "Is Dad still here?"

"No, he left earlier. You *must* have been sound asleep – he took the helicopter. But he's just found out about the brick through your car window and wants you away from here for a few days. He thinks that maybe James Knox was behind it and wants you where he can't get to you," he called through the closed door.

"Oh?" It was Stephanie's turn to glare at James. She shoved him hard, which caught him by surprise and he fell off the bed with a crash.

"Steph, are you okay?" Sam sounded concerned and tried the door handle again.

"Yeah – just tripped," she called through gritted teeth as she rounded the bed to confront James. "Go and make me some coffee and I'll be down in a minute, eh. I just have a bit of a mess here to clean up."

"Okay, see you in a couple of minutes." She heard Sam retreat along the passage towards the staircase.

"Oh come on, Steph. You don't believe that, do you?" James protested, getting up from the floor and holding his hands up in front of him, as if to defend himself.

"It's an interesting conclusion for my father to come to though, isn't it?" she accused in an angry whisper, hands on her hips, her eyes blazing.

"For God's sake. Sam turns up and you believe him over me?" James was getting annoyed now.

Stephanie groaned and put her hands over her face. "Who do I believe? Everyone is putting a different slant on things."

James gently pulled her hands away from her face and tilted her chin to look at him. On one hand she looked so cute with her messy bed hair and smudged mascara and on the other she looked incredibly sexy in her camisole and pyjama pants that he had to force himself to let her go. "Go and see what the bastard wants. I'll wait here," he said roughly and then added, "Please trust me, Steph."

"How do you know that I won't tell them that you are up here?" she challenged, but with less defiance in her voice.

"I don't. Now I'm the one trusting you," James replied evenly.

Stephanie sighed and disappeared into the walk-in wardrobe and reappeared a moment later wearing her skinny black jeans and a blue hoodie, which somehow reflected in her eyes making them seem a deeper blue than usual.

James was standing to one side of the large bay window near her bed, looking outside. He turned as she walked back into the room. She gave him a small smile and unlocked the door, letting herself out of the room and closing it behind her.

Stephanie walked down the wide hallway to the staircase that curved down to the entrance hall, skipping down the stairs past the portraits and photographs of her family. She headed towards the kitchen where she could hear the low murmur of a conversation.

The voices abruptly broke off as she strode into the room. Sam was leaning against the counter talking to Vince.

What the hell is he doing standing in the kitchen like he owns the place? Stephanie thought, irritated and a little wary.

"Hi." Sam smiled, walking towards her. He ran his eyes up and down her body and leaned to kiss her cheek. She stiffened. "Vince was just telling me they thought there was an intruder last night," he said.

"Just a false alarm wasn't it, Vince?" Stephanie asked, stepping away from Sam and helping herself to coffee from the percolator bubbling away on its stand.

"Look, Steph. After that brick was thrown through your car window and Michael's hit and run, your father and I think it would be safer for you to come back to London with me today," Sam said with the air of someone taking charge. "That way we can make sure that you are safe until we can find out what's going on."

"I think I'm pretty safe if Vince is still here – you should have seen him last night, Sam," she responded light-heartedly. "It was like a full scale military operation." She looked slyly at Vince, who returned her gaze steadily and said nothing.

"Nonetheless, Steph, I'm just following your father's instructions," Sam said.

Stephanie thought quickly.

"Well, okay," she said, acquiescing. "Give me a little while to cancel my plans for the next few days, have a shower and pack a bag. What time did you want to leave, Sam?"

"No hurry," said Sam, sounding surprised. He'd clearly been expecting her to put up more of a fight.

Stephanie refilled her coffee mug and headed back upstairs to her room where James was waiting beside the window, his back to the door. She locked the door again behind her and walked over to him, handing him the coffee. He smiled gratefully. His fingers lingered on hers momentarily as he took it from her.

"Sam is here to take me back to London with him – 'to be safe,'" she mimicked Sam's London accent.

"No," said James shaking his head, his eyes stormy. "That bastard – trust him to use the situation to his advantage." He sipped the coffee, frowning.

"Hang on, though," Stephanie said. "I've had an idea and I've bought us a little time. Why don't you slip out the back way now and go and get your moped. Text me when you get there and I'll meet you at the front gates. You can kidnap me. That will give me some space to decide what to do."

James thought for a moment. Then a wide smile spread across his face. "Perfect," he said, leaning down to kiss her on the lips. "I can't wait to see Sam's face when I spirit you away before he gets the chance." He took another gulp and put the coffee cup down on her desk and grabbed his hoodie and leather jacket off the back of the sofa. Glancing out of the window he said, "I don't think I'm going to need all these clothes – it looks much warmer today."

Stephanie sat on the edge of her bed watching him as he pulled his t-shirt off and picked up the hoodie to pull it on. She ran her eyes over his firm chest and abs – James was very toned with muscular arms. His jeans hung low around his hips.

He grinned as he caught her staring him and sauntered over to where she sat, dropping the hoodie on the floor as he walked.

He stood with his legs either side of hers and leaned down, cupping her face between his hands and gently kissed her. She placed her hands on his chest as he pushed her back on the bed, deepening their kiss as he did so. Stephanie wrapped her leg around his thighs and deftly twisted so that James was thrown off balance on to his back.

She sat up, straddling his legs with hers, her breathing slightly faster than normal. They both laughed. "You can do that to me anytime," James said in a low voice, as he reached up and put his hand behind her head and pulled her into another lingering kiss. He slipped his hands up under her top and began stroking her back, a small moan escaping from his throat.

"James." She broke from his kiss and sat up again. His eyes sparkled with desire and she could feel his body responding to hers. "Get your clothes on and let's go – enough gratuitous flesh for one day." She placed her hand on his chest and laughed, sliding off the bed, pulling him up as she did.

"You weren't complaining a moment ago," James said. "But you're right, you'd better show me the best way out now or we'll never leave your bedroom. I think you greatly overestimate my self-control," he said, his voice huskier than normal. He picked up his discarded hoodie and pulled it on, followed by the leather jacket.

Reluctantly, she quietly unlocked her door and poked her head out. All clear.

"Come on," she whispered. He held her hand as she led the way along the corridor to the right of her room, until they came to a back staircase. They ran lightly down the stairs. Stephanie opened a door at the bottom and peered left and right. Directly in front was a short stretch of lawn bordered by trees.

"Okay – run to the trees and follow them along that way," she said pointing, "You should get to Ridge Road in about ten minutes."

"I'll text you when I get back to the bike." His lips brushed hers lightly and he was gone – sprinting across the grass and disappearing into the trees. Stephanie was about to close the door and go back up the stairs when she heard footsteps coming down.

She quietly let herself out and staying close to the wall hurried around to the side of the house. Heart thumping, she slipped in through the kitchen door. She could hear Sam talking in a low voice on this mobile in the hall. She paused to eavesdrop.

"I don't know what she has done or said – but something has really got Knox upset. We need her out of here before she does some damage."

He paused, listening.

"Yeah, I know. I thought the brick would have had frightened her enough to go back to London, but it doesn't seem to have had that effect….."

Stephanie froze. *No*, she thought, *no. That doesn't make any sense. He can't mean that my father organised that? Why would he do something so public to stop me looking into the past? Surely he would have spoken to me instead? Actually he kinda did at the lawyer's dinner...*

Sam's voice was getting harder to hear. He was clearly walking towards the sitting room. *I've got to keep moving, work this out later.* Stephanie felt for her mobile phone in her pocket and switched it to vibrate. No need to alert Sam to the text she was expecting in a few minutes. She reached the staircase and ran up, taking two steps at a time. Her grandmother's door was slightly ajar in front of her.

"Grandma," she called, pushing the door open.

"Yes, dear, I'm just coming downstairs. Bridge game at eleven o'clock, you know," Ellie replied as she walked across the room towards her.

Stephanie gave her a kiss on the cheek. "Grandma, I'm popping out for a while, but not with Sam – can you trust me and cause a diversion for me in about ten minutes?"

Ellie had a faraway look in her eye.

"My sister said a similar thing to me once, dear. What are you up to? Is it that Knox boy?" she asked.

Stephanie blushed.

"What is it with that family?" Ellie said shaking her head. "Go now, but be careful."

Stephanie hugged her grandmother, stunned at her perception.

She ran along the passage to her room. Grabbing a large over-the-shoulder bag from her wardrobe, she selected a couple of tops, sandals, underwear and a dress that rolled up small and didn't crush. She pushed them into the bag along with the necessary cosmetics and accessories. Rushing over to her desk, she picked up Sophie's journal and a handful of printouts and stuffed them into a pocket in the side of the bag. *What else*, she thought? *Warm Jacket, iPad, wallet*, she mentally checked off a list.

Pulling on a pair of flat deep red knee-high boots over her jeans, she spun around feeling eyes on her. Sam was standing silently in the doorway.

"Wow – I don't think I've seen anyone pack so quickly," he said with a forced laugh. "Are you in a hurry to leave with me?

It's just that we didn't part on the best terms last time I was here."

Ugh. Stephanie shuddered involuntarily. "Sam, I'm a bit scared after what's happened to Michael – it will be good to get away," she said, smiling weakly at him.

He strode over to her and put his arm around her shoulders and kissed the top of her head.

"Poor baby – you should have called me. I would have come straight away," he said.

Stephanie's mobile vibrated in her pocket. She pulled away from Sam. "I'll just get my toothbrush and then let's go downstairs and get something to eat before we go," she said lightly.

In the bathroom she flicked her phone open. The text from James was there:

Got bike – yours 2 mins.

Time to move. Adding the toothbrush to her bag, she pulled on her jacket and they headed downstairs. Her grandmother was loitering in the entrance hall.

"Hi, Grandma," Stephanie said cheerily, walking past her to the front door and giving her a big wink.

"Steph – didn't you want breakfast?" Sam called after her.

"I thought I'd put this in your car first – throw me the keys." She held out her hand and caught the key as he flung it to her.

She skipped down the front steps and into the bright sunshine, pulling her sunglasses out of her hair and over her eyes.

"Now, Sam – can you help me into the sitting room please?" she heard Ellie ask.

"Certainly," Sam answered smoothly, offering his arm.

In the distance, Stephanie could hear the drone of the Vespa getting closer. She pocketed Sam's keys and pulled the long strap of the bag across her body, and started walking across the courtyard to the top of the long driveway. She allowed herself a backwards glance and saw her grandmother talking to Sam, who had been positioned with his back to the window. *Clever old lady*, Stephanie thought affectionately as James drove into view. He pulled up beside her and handed her a helmet. She quickly pulled it on and jumped onto the bike behind him.

"Hey," shouted Sam. He was running down the front steps after her. James floored the bike, sending stones flying out behind them. They both looked back at Sam's angry face and James cheerfully flipped him the finger and they were gone – speeding down the driveway.

"How long until he catches up?" James shouted back to her.

"Quite a while, cause I have his car keys," Stephanie said as she pulled them out of her back pocket and showed James before throwing them into the pond beside the house as they zoomed past it.

Chapter 26

James drove straight into the village and pulled into a small service alley behind the main street.

Removing his helmet, he turned to her and said, "Food. I need to eat or I can't think straight."

She hopped off the bike and adjusted her bag. It was heavy. James helped her with her helmet and then lifted the bag over her head.

"Here, let me carry that," he said. He closed the gap between them, his knee brushing her thigh as he settled her bag across his back.

"That was a blast – thank you. Did you see the look on his face?" Stephanie cracked up laughing, with relief more than anything. "You don't think he'll come looking for me in town, do you?" she asked, becoming serious.

James put his hands on her waist. "Don't worry – even if he does, what can he do in the middle of a busy street?" He brushed her hair out of her eyes and pulled her close, kissing her gently on the lips. Stephanie sighed and relaxed into his embrace, enjoying a brief moment of respite.

Hand in hand they walked through a narrow gap between the old buildings to the front of the tea rooms. Once inside they ordered breakfast – James a full English breakfast,

Stephanie, one poached egg on grainy toast, and a big pot of tea between them. They chose a table in the window behind a pretty lace curtain that hid them from the street, but allowed them to look out. Stephanie poured the tea and they sat hand in hand smiling at each other waiting for their food.

"I know I said it last night, but I am really sorry that I was so horrible to you over the last couple of weeks," James said softly. "I was mad at first with you and your grandmother, but seeing you with Sam that night at the pub made me just crazy. And then Alex got involved."

Stephanie squeezed his hand and smiled at him.

"Just so long as you know that I was trying to protect you from Alex," he continued. "And his threats." He shuddered.

The waitress interrupted them with their breakfasts. James tucked into his pile of food with gusto. Stephanie nibbled her egg and toast and looked wistfully at James devouring bacon, eggs, sausages, sautéed potatoes, tomato, baked beans and mushrooms. After everything that had happened over the last few days, she had lost her appetite.

"Okay – so Andy and I have a song writing session today out at his place. The others are still up in London and not due back until later tonight. Do you want to come?" James asked, wiping his mouth.

"Won't I just be in the way?" Stephanie said.

"No – I'd like you to be there. It will give us a little more time to work out just what is going on. And you will be safe, from everyone," he said.

Except you, she thought, but hastily pushed that thought away. *I've made my decision. Now is not the time to start second guessing myself.*

After breakfast, they drove out to Andy's parents' farm.

Several years earlier, when the boys first put the band together, Andy's father had let them turn an old unused shed into a practice space. They had spent days, during one school holiday clearing it out, painting and redecorating it. About a year ago, when it became clear that they were actually going somewhere with their music, Andy's father had installed heating and plumbing in the shed, and it now sported a bathroom and kitchenette.

Andy was already in the shed strumming away on an acoustic guitar. He looked up as they walked in.

"Hey, dude." He did a double take. "Steph."

"Hi, Andy. I promise not to get in the way. I just need to hang out here for a while," she said.

"It's fine with me, darlin'. I'm just a little confused to see you two together. Last time I saw you, you were mouthing off at one another. What's happened?" he asked.

"I realised that I was being an idiot," James replied simply.

"Really, dude? You've only just realised that?" Andy said. They laughed.

Andy suddenly registered the shiny bruise on James's cheek. "Aw, Jamie, who have you been fighting with now?"

James grinned and said, "I have Steph here to thank for this one."

"What?" Andy was incredulous. Stephanie rather sheepishly held up her bruised knuckles. "What did he do to deserve that?"

"He tackled me," she said.

"Only to stop the police finding you outside my house in the middle of the night," James replied.

"Maybe," she conceded, "but then he kept acting ignorant of what his brother is up to and after everything that has happened over the last few days, I saw red and lost my temper."

"Hang on," Andy interrupted. "I'm missing quite a lot here."

"Actually, it's a bit complicated. Steph, okay if I fill Andy in?" James turned to her and asked.

She nodded.

"Let's sit." James led her across the wide rehearsal space to an area with mismatched sofas and armchairs at the back of the room. Stephanie looked around the shed. Three of the walls and the ceiling rafters were all painted white, making the room seem even bigger than it was. The third wall, opposite the door, was painted with a mixture of splashes of colour and words. James saw her looking at it.

"That's the result of one of Liam's artistic expression phases," he explained, rolling his eyes.

At the opposite end of the room from the seating area, the band had all their equipment set up on a series of rugs. Drum kit in the centre, keyboard off to one side, a couple of racks of guitars, microphones and amps littered the area immediately in front.

Andy had walked to the kitchenette at the side of the sofas. It, of course, contained an industrial sized espresso machine. "I sense we will need coffee?" he said.

James threw himself down on one of the sofas and grabbed Stephanie's hand, pulling her down onto his lap. She landed awkwardly sprawled across him, laughing. He leaned his head down and kissed her. She struggled to a sitting position and sat sideways across his knee, resting her back against the arm of the sofa. He reached up and stroked her hair, gazing into her eyes as he did. His other hand ran down her leg from her thigh to the top of her boots and back again. He rested it there absentmindedly tapping out a beat as he leaned over and kissed her just below her ear.

"Okay – here we go," said Andy, clearing his throat as he deposited three lattes on the coffee table in front of them. "Am I going to have to separate you two to get anything sensible out of you?" he teased.

They spent the next half an hour filling Andy in on what had been going on.

"What do you think?" Stephanie asked when they had finished. "Is it just a coincidence that my dad is down here?"

"As Einstein once said, 'Coincidence is just God's way of remaining anonymous'," Andy said. "I think your dad is involved somehow." He turned to James. "Do you really think your grandfather's been hiding a piece of stolen art all these years and has just now decided to sell it?"

"It has to be Alex, my grandfather is too far gone to be involved in anything like that," James said.

"Maybe my father is working with people to buy the painting from Alex. And I got in the way by getting friendly with you," she said, looking at James. "Sam mentioned something about scaring me off, so maybe he was behind the brick through the window, so that Dad could get me out of the village and up to London while some deal went down."

"Well, Alex did say that I had to keep you away for three or four days and then I could do what I liked with you," James said.

"Charming," she replied sarcastically. "You obviously couldn't wait that long!"

"I thought it unnecessarily cruel to make you wait any longer," he said grinning.

"Huh. The only thing is, I just can't believe Dad would have Anna and me followed to that club and have someone try to run us down outside. He wouldn't do that," Stephanie said, shaking her head. "He might want me out of the village for a few days, but he wouldn't hurt me to do it."

"Yeah – you never finished telling me about that," James said thoughtfully. "Alex also knew you were at the club. That's who I was talking to on the phone."

"I have to admit, I thought it might have been you driving the car," she said, looking sideways at him.

James looked hurt for a moment.

Andy shook his head. "There's no way that it could have been. He was with me after you and Anna left, being a miserable git," he said. James threw a cushion at him.

"Nothing adds up here. I feel like there is something that I am missing," Stephanie said, frustrated.

"Jack and I were talking to our grandfathers at the pub the other night. They were both teenagers when war broke out," Andy said. "I was asking them what they remembered about your feud. They didn't really know anything, but they do remember a very active black market operating in Carlswick during the war."

They talked in circles for a while longer until Stephanie looked at her watch. "Okay – I've held you guys up long enough. Go and write a song or whatever it is that you do and I will try and do some more research," she said. She stood up from James's lap and pulled him to his feet. Andy wandered over to the guitars and selected one. James put his arms around Stephanie and slipped his hands into the back pockets of her jeans, squeezing her butt gently. She jumped against him and giggled. He bent down and buried his face in her hair and whispered, "I can't wait for all this to be over, so we can properly spend some time together." She shivered pleasantly at the thought and knew that he had felt her reaction, because he wore a suggestive smirk as broke away from her.

"Don't go getting too sure of yourself, Knox. I am by no means a certain bet," she called to his retreating back.

He stopped and turned back to her. "I'll remember that when you are begging for it," he said, quietly laughing.

"Cheeky, much?" she muttered and pulled her iPad from her bag. She settled herself on the sofa and quickly became engrossed in her research.

In the background, the boys ran through chord sequences, putting lyrics together with new melodies. After a while she realised that they had stopped playing and had their heads together talking quietly. James, as if he felt her looking, glanced over and winked at her. She felt a tingling sensation flood through her. *I really hope he is for real and that I haven't made a mistake trusting him?* She mused and then pushed the thought from her mind. She had made the decision to trust him, now she had to follow it through.

She sat back and closed her eyes. A little while later she felt her iPad being pulled from her hands and she opened her eyes. James was leaning over her.

"Sorry. I didn't mean to wake you. I just didn't want you to drop this on the floor," he said gently. He placed the iPad on the table.

"I can't believe that I fell asleep," she murmured.

"I can. You have had a couple of strange days. Lie down and sleep some more. You are safe here," he said kindly, laying a blanket over her.

Stephanie lay on her side, with a cushion beneath her head, watching him walk back over to Andy. She closed her eyes and slept.

A couple of hours later she woke feeling refreshed. She lay on the sofa watching Andy and James for a few minutes. It was almost as if they had forgotten she was there and were strumming and singing together. The song was one she hadn't heard before. She looked at her watch; four-thirty pm – where had the day gone? She stood up, stretched and walked over to the small bathroom.

When she came out, they had stood up and were plugging their guitars into the amps.

"Hey, sleepyhead," James called.

"I like that song you were singing before. Is it new?" she replied.

"Yup. Now you are awake we'll plug in and you can tell us what you think," he said.

They launched into the song – it started softly with just James's voice and then hit the chorus with a wall of sound bouncing off the walls. Andy harmonised with James's husky tones. They had written a really sweet love song, about a girl who had gotten in behind a boy's well-constructed defences, but he wasn't able to tell her how he felt, as she was with someone else. But they played it with the speed and attitude of a punk number. It was fantastic.

They both looked to her with enquiring eyes when they finished. "Obviously it has to have better drums and keyboard and Liam's dulcet tones, but what do you think?" Andy asked.

"Amazing. How do you make such a sweet song sound so raw and energetic and full of promise?" she said stunned.

James and Andy hi-fived each other.

"That's exactly the reaction we want," Andy said, pleased.

"How long has it taken you to write it? You didn't just do that this afternoon?" she asked.

The boys exchanged glances. "About a month," James replied cautiously.

"Yeah, his inspiration kept pissing him off, so it would go from love to hate and back again," Andy said, cracking up laughing at James's glare. "What – better that she knows you wrote it for her than anyone else, dude."

James flushed and busied himself unplugging his guitar.

Andy rubbed his arms. "It's cooling down. I'm just gonna pop into the house and get a sweater." He loped to the door and winked at Stephanie.

She wandered over to James, who was studiously ignoring her.

"No one has ever written a song for me before," she said shyly. James reached over and pulled her into him and kissed her hard on the lips. "I seem to be able to write about the stuff that I find too difficult to say." He looked at her hesitantly.

She smiled at him and settled into his embrace, breaking away when Andy returned.

"James, I think I'd like to go and visit Michael before work. Can you drop me home to get my car?" she said.

"Do you think it's wise to go back to your place? Sam might still be there," he asked.

"Well, I'll call Grandma first and see who's about," she said, pulling her phone from her back pocket. Sam had indeed gone back up to London and he was not best pleased, having to wade into the pond to retrieve his keys. Her father had returned and his conference was underway again.

Okay, Stephanie decided, *after work I am going to slip in the back entrance of the guest house and find out just what my father is up to.*

* * *

James dropped Stephanie back at Wakefield House around five-thirty pm. A helicopter was parked in the field behind the house and the lights were all on in the guest house conference room. She slipped up to her bedroom to get changed and find her car keys. She wasn't sure what her father would say about her still being in the village, but she really didn't want to know, so she left the house quickly and quietly, without seeing anyone.

Stephanie drove down the long driveway and turned right onto the lane leading down into the village, and adjusted the volume on her car stereo. She began to sing along with it, not noticing the car behind her until it sped up.

Hey, she thought, disbelievingly looking in her rear vision mirror. *Back off. You're driving way too close.* She glanced at the headlights shining strongly behind her. She suddenly had a flashback to the car outside the club in London. In the dusk the one behind her now looked similar. She gasped, feeling frightened. God – was this what happened to Michael? Was she about to be run off the road too? She sped up and reached into the pocket of her jacket, retrieving her mobile phone. She rounded the bend on the narrow country lane, coming onto a straight section and slowed her car as she tried to retrieve James's number from her call list. The car behind her suddenly accelerated past her and pulled into a stop at an angle directly in front of her.

Stephanie jammed on the brakes and spun the steering wheel sharply sideways to avoid impact. Her mobile went flying out of her hands into the passenger foot well. The force of the sudden stop threw her head forward. She hit it on the steering wheel, before being thrown back in her seat. Momentarily dazed, she was aware of her door being wrenched open and a strong hand being clamped across her nose and mouth.

And then nothing.

Chapter 27

At seven-thirty pm, just as he was preparing to leave the manor and join Andy and Steph at the café, James received a text from Andy.

Andy: *Get ya hands off Steph and let her come to work.*

James: *Sadly, she's not with me. She was gonna visit Mikey on her way to the café.*

James scrolled through his mobile and found Stephanie's number and called. It rang six times and then went to voicemail. He tried again and then sent her a text asking her to call him.

Frowning, he telephoned the hospital and was put through to Mrs Morgan in Michael's room. After enquiring about Michael, whose condition hadn't changed, he asked if Stephanie was there.

"No, James. I haven't seen her today, although she was planning to visit," she replied. "Is everything okay?"

"I'm not sure," James said. "Can you get Steph to call me if you see her?"

He hung up, feeling a cold hand clutching his heart.

He called Andy. She still hadn't turned up at the café. It was now eight o'clock.

Taking a deep breath, he made a decision and called Wakefield House. Vince answered formally.

"Hello, it's James Knox, is Stephanie there, please?"

There was a brief pause.

"No, James, we haven't seen her since she left on the back of your bike this morning," Vince said, every word dripping with disapproval.

James ignored his tone and said, "I'm worried about her – she appears to be missing."

"What do you mean, missing?" Vince said.

"Well, I dropped her home around five-thirty this afternoon to pick up her car. She was going to visit her friend Michael in hospital on her way to work at the café at seven pm. But she hasn't been to either place and she isn't answering her mobile," James said.

Vince cursed on the other end of the line. "Her car is not here," he said.

"Well, if she isn't home, I'm going to start searching the road from the village to there in case she has had an accident," James said.

"We'll take it from here," Vince said and hung up.

"Whatever," James muttered down the disconnected phone line. He tapped another text to Andy.

James: *No one knows where she is. I'm going to look for her.*

Andy: *What can I do?*

James: *Stay there in case she turns up.*

Andy: *Ok. Keep me updated.*

James grabbed his leather jacket and helmet and shoved a flashlight in his pocket. He bolted down the back staircase through the kitchen and out to the garages. The house was strangely quiet. Where was everyone?

James drove his Vespa quickly to the village and turned left onto the road towards Wakefield House. He put his headlights on full and reaching into this pocket, pulled out the flashlight and switched it on. He drove slowly, weaving slightly so that his headlights covered the road and swinging the flashlight in a wide arc over the hedges that bordered the lane. After five minutes, he rounded a bend and saw flashlights ahead of him.

He pulled to a stop in front of Vince, Max and four men whom he didn't recognise. Max looked James up and down appraisingly. Remaining seated on his Vespa, James removed his helmet and held out his hand to Max.

"James Knox, sir," he said politely.

Max didn't move. He just glared at James, who lowered his hand.

"No sign of her then?" Vince asked.

James shook his head.

"I didn't know she was still seeing you." Max finally spoke, disdainfully.

"She is," James replied simply. *Keep your temper*, he told himself.

"You do know her boyfriend is back?" Max asked slyly.

"Ex-boyfriend," James corrected.

"What have you got to do with her being missing? You are the last one to see her," Max spoke accusingly.

"I wouldn't be wasting my time looking for her if I knew where she was. What do you know about her whereabouts? Are you hiding her at the house, so that she can't see me?" James was done being polite.

"It may surprise you to know, young man, that I have more important things to deal with than who my daughter is dating, regardless of how I feel about his pedigree," Max answered condescendingly.

"What? Important things like buying stolen art from my brother?" James said.

"I beg your pardon," Max said turning on him, his eyes blazing.

"Let's keep going towards the village," Vince interrupted, putting his hand on Max's shoulder. "Arguing out here isn't going to find her."

James and Max grudgingly agreed.

James swung the Vespa around and fell in beside the men, driving slowly. They all moved quietly, flashlights scanning the road and the countryside. From this direction the lane sloped gently down the valley towards the village and the fields were visible over the top of the hedgerows. As they rounded the corner, James's headlights caught on a flash of purple through a hole in a hedge on their left.

"Here," he shouted, slowing to a stop and pointing his flashlight at the hedge. He jumped off the bike, pulling it onto its stand. He remembered passing a gateway a little further on towards the village and began running towards it.

"James, wait," Vince called catching up with him. "Let's be careful here."

James looked wildly at him. Vince placed his hand on James's arm, which had the surprising effect of calming him down. He nodded and deferred to the older man, letting him go in front.

Vince signalled to the four strangers, some sort of universal military sign language. They all took up positions, scanning the road and surrounding hedges. It was then that James noticed the tell-tale bulges of weapons hidden under their jackets.

God, Steph – you'd better be okay, he thought, his stomach clenching.

Vince eased towards the gateway, quickly and quietly peeking around the edge of the hedge into the field. He turned and nodded to Max, who was at James's shoulder. They exchanged concerned glances.

Vince suddenly bent down, sweeping his flashlight along the entranceway to the farm gate. He beckoned to Max.

"Look. Fresh tyre tracks and footprints. Three different sets of footprints," he said indicating the different types of tread in the mud. He tracked his flashlight along the tyre tracks, which went through the closed gate and immediately turned left beside the hedge.

Stephanie hadn't run off the road. Her car had been purposely parked in the field behind the hedge and the gate closed again.

James's eyes widened. He couldn't contain himself any longer. He pushed past Vince and vaulted the gate. The sheep sleeping under the hedge scattered, loudly announcing their annoyance at being disturbed.

"Steph," he called, his voice catching.

"James," Vince hissed.

James ignored him and ran to her car. It was parked tightly up beside the hedge. He shone the flashlight through the driver's window. It was empty. He pulled the door open. The internal light came on. The scent of Stephanie's perfume hit him. He felt a tightening in his chest and had trouble swallowing. A half inflated airbag hung limply from the steering column.

"You're a bloody idiot," Vince said, catching up with him. "This could have been a trap."

James didn't seem to hear him. "She's not here," he said,

distraught.

Max caught up with them, along with one of the strangers. "Is she okay?"

"She's not here," James repeated helplessly.

Vince crouched down beside the open driver's door and shone his flashlight around the interior of the car. He ran his fingers over the top of the steering wheel and held them up to the light.

"Is that what I think it is?" James said, his voice coming out choked.

"Blood," Vince confirmed.

Chapter 28

"Oh, God," James said as he leant against the car. "I never should have let her drive alone, after what happened to Michael."

Vince continued his search of the interior of the car and came out with Stephanie's mobile phone in his hand.

"Six missed calls. All from you, James," Vince said, showing the phone to Max.

One of the other men circled the car.

"Sir," he called in a heavily accented voice.

Max and Vince hurried to where he was standing at the front of the car. His flashlight was focussed on the front right bumper. It was slightly dented, with black paint streaked across the shiny metal.

"I think she hit a black vehicle," he said. James looked at him, trying to place the accent.

"Is this new?" Max questioned.

"Yes. Her car didn't have a scratch on it when it was returned from the repair shop yesterday," Vince confirmed.

"Sir," another of the strangers called.

Vince and the other man ran back towards the gate.

"There is evidence of two vehicles stopping suddenly out on the lane. One on an angle in front of the other, about a hundred metres or so back up the road," the man said.

Max sighed and ran his hand through his hair. "There's nothing more we can do here tonight." He turned to James, "I think you need to come back to the house, there are a few things that we need to discuss."

He leaned over to close the door of the car. "Vince can come back and get the car in the morning."

"Hang on," James said, stopping him. He reached down in the driver's foot well and picked up the item that had caught his eye. He held it up to his flashlight. It was one of Stephanie's long silver and purple earrings. He recalled seeing them in her ears earlier in the day; she must have lost it in the accident.

"Steph's," he said simply to Max.

"I know," Max replied quietly. "I gave them to her." He closed the car door and they walked silently out of the field, closing the gate behind them. It wouldn't do for the farm manager to find that open in the morning and the stock out on the road.

On the way to Wakefield House, James called Andy.

"We found her car abandoned and hidden behind a hedge, with blood on the steering wheel. Her mobile was in it. Looks like she has been kidnapped," he said in a rush.

"No. Where are you?" Andy said, shocked.

"On my way to her place," James replied.

"Okay. I'll close the café and come as soon as I can," Andy said.

James disconnected the call and joined the men in the dining room. A map of the district was spread out on the table. Vince was speaking into a mobile phone in one corner of the room. From the conversation, it sounded like he was talking to the local police. Max crouched beside Stephanie's grandmother, who was seated on the other side of the room. He was stroking her hand and talking quietly to her. She was shaking her head in disbelief.

Vince came off the phone and walked over to James, slapping him on the shoulder. "James. Look, can you go and help Mrs Cooper to the kitchen. We are going to need coffee and sandwiches, while we co-ordinate the search." He nodded to one of the men.

Several minutes later, James returned to the dining room carrying a large tray.

".....this has to do with Knox and the painting. It's too much of a coincidence. The raid last night has alerted Knox that we are on to him. We have to move now." They stopped speaking as James came back into the room. As he set the tray down on the table, he felt all eyes in the room on him. Glancing around, he found himself surrounded.

"Take his mobile phone and keep an eye on him. It's possible that he is here spying for his family," one of the men instructed.

James held his hands in front of him and backed up towards a wall and called, "Mr Cooper. I have nothing to do with this. I care for your daughter. I would never do anything to hurt her." He took a deep breath and continued. "I know you don't trust me or my family, but you have to believe me."

Max stood and walked over to James. "What was it you mentioned earlier in the lane about me buying stolen art from your brother?" he asked.

James hesitated unsure, whether to trust Max or not. "Stephanie was investigating a piece of art work that used to hang in our library. She believed it was a van Gogh stolen before the war by the Nazis," he said.

Max's eyes narrowed. "And how exactly did she discover that? Are you sure you didn't just tell her?"

"I didn't know. To me it was just a painting that has hung in the library all my life," James said.

"How on earth would Stephanie have realised that? I am afraid your story doesn't stack up. You will have to do better than that." Max turned away.

"What he is telling you is true," a voice said from the doorway.

Everyone turned to look at Ellie Cooper who had returned from the kitchen.

"It was me who told Stephanie and James about strange goings on at Knox Manor around the outbreak of the war. James here didn't like my version of events," she said, smiling at James, who hung his head sheepishly. "But I gave Stephanie my sister's journals to read and I believe that she has continued investigating whatever it was at Knox Manor that got my sister killed all those years ago," she said.

All eyes in the room swivelled back to James.

"We think my brother Alex has also discovered the painting's provenance and is trying to sell it," he said.

There were nods and murmurs around the room.

James continued. "What is your involvement, Mr Cooper, and who are all these guys? Stephanie wasn't sure if you were working with or against Alex."

Max Cooper looked momentarily offended. "These men are from Scotland Yard's Art Theft division and from Mossad's war crimes unit. This is Detective Inspector Marks and Lt. Eli David," he said, introducing two of the men.

"We have been watching your brother for a while on suspicion of fencing stolen art, when Eli here contacted us to say they had a lead on a piece of Nazi stolen, Jewish-owned art and your brother's name came up again," DI Marks explained.

"Max has been assisting Scotland Yard for years on fraud cases, and since he lives near Knox, we pulled him in to work with us."

The seriousness of the situation suddenly hit James. "I can see why you don't trust me," he said. He paused, thinking. "So it was you guys who came to my house last night."

DI Marks nodded.

"Was it the van Gogh you were after or is there something else?" James asked.

"We are not at liberty to reveal any details at this stage," DI Marks said, eyeing James suspiciously. "Is there something else that we should be looking for?"

"Stephanie," James said, getting annoyed. "We are wasting time talking about me, when you guys need to be out there looking for her."

"That's happening as we speak, but you can help us too. Is it possible that your brother has her?" DI Marks asked, calmly.

James went to say no but paused, the word dying on his lips.

"Alex had me trying to stop Stephanie looking into our family. He said she was drawing attention to him and he had a big deal on that he didn't want jeopardised," he said eventually.

He received a number of disbelieving looks.

"Okay. I know it looks suspicious, but if he wants to keep attention off himself, surely kidnapping Steph isn't the way to do that?" James said.

"Regardless, we need to establish Stephanie's whereabouts today. Can you work with Vince?" Marks asked. James nodded as Vince beckoned to him. Together they spent the next ten minutes writing a time line on a whiteboard that had been wheeled in from the conference room.

"I spoke to her on the phone at around four-thirty" Ellie came up behind Vince and James. She reached for James's hand and gave it a squeeze. He looked at her, surprised, and smiled tentatively in return. She gave his hand a tug and pulled him to one side.

"I thought it wise, given the circumstances, not to tell Max that you spent the night here last night," she said, quietly giving him a knowing look.

James's surprise was taken to a whole other level. "How?" he asked.

Ellie smiled. "I may be old, but I see everything that goes on around here. If it's any consolation – I believe you," she said. "I trust Stephanie's judgement and she has obviously put her faith in you."

"Thanks. Remind me not to ever underestimate you," he replied.

Max Cooper's mobile phone rang loudly and the room instantly quietened. He answered it, listening carefully. DI Marks raised his eyebrows at him questioningly. Max shook his head.

"I'm in Carlswick. Family matter. No, I won't be back up to London for a few days. Can you cover until then?" Max spoke into the phone. "I'm sorry, but Stephanie's missing, so my priority is finding her. The client will have to wait," he said.

He spoke for another minute or so and ended the call frowning. "Peter, my business partner," he said by way of explanation.

Flashing lights and the sound of tyres crunching on the gravel outside signalled the arrival of the local police. Ellie showed them in. One was carrying a brick in a plastic evidence bag. Andy was right behind then and James rushed over to greet his friend. Andy introduced himself to Max and Ellie, who both knew his father and asked after him.

"Thank God you are here," James whispered to him. "I think they were about to lynch me." He quickly brought Andy up to speed.

"Mr Cooper. Has anyone contacted Anna – Stephanie was staying with her over the weekend? Maybe she's heard from her," Andy suggested.

"Good idea, Andy," Max replied. "Do you have her number?"

"I do, as it happens," he said pulling his phone out of his pocket and tapping a quick text.

DI Marks broke away from the huddle of people around the dining table.

"Okay, boys," he said. "I think we have a job for you." He pointed his finger at James. "I am going out on a limb here and trusting you. If I find that trust to be misplaced, by God – you will go sky high."

James and Andy exchanged glances. James raised his chin defiantly and straightening himself up, looked Marks directly in the eye and said, "Okay – what do you want us to do?"

James and Andy were dispatched to the manor with instructions to provide an immediate update on Alex's movements.

As they were leaving, James's mobile rang.

"Have you found her?" Michael asked in a quiet voice. "They just told me that Steph was missing."

"No. How are you feeling, mate?" James asked.

"Like someone hit me around the head with a baseball bat. I am guessing that she brought you up to speed. Have you read David's memoir?" Michael said.

"No, but Steph read some the original at the library yesterday," James told him.

"I can't remember much of what I read, I'm afraid, but he was investigating your family. There was something about the manor…" Michael trailed off.

"Don't worry – we'll find her. Text me if you think of anything else," James said.

"Okay," Michael frowned, desperately trying to grasp an elusive piece of information that stayed tantalisingly out of his reach.

Chapter 29

Stephanie woke suddenly. She flicked her eyes open and gasped. She was lying uncomfortably on her side and when she tried to move, she found that her feet were bound and her hands were tied behind her. Where was she? Some vague image teased at the edge of her memory, but she couldn't quite grasp it. She struggled to sit up, but was overcome by a wave of nausea. She flopped back down on the hard canvas bed and looked around her. She was in a dark, damp windowless room. Her memory came back in flashes – car headlights too close, forced to stop, something clamped over her nose and mouth. She shivered; she was cold and very frightened. Slowly the fog in her brain cleared.

"Hello," she called. Her voice came out as a crackle. She swallowed and licked her dry lips. She was really thirsty. "Hello," she tried again. This time her voice was a little stronger.

There was no answer. The room was partly lit by a single hanging light bulb, which gave off a dim yellowish glow. But she could only see a little way. She peered into the gloom of the far end of the room, but couldn't make out any shapes or movement.

She tried sitting up again and as the nausea hit her hard this time, she leaned over the edge of the bed and vomited onto the floor.

"Ugh," she spat, and lay back down. Her wrists behind her back were sore and each time she moved, she could feel the bonds cutting into her skin.

She took a few deep breaths as the remaining nausea subsided. *Think, Stephanie*, she urged herself.

She froze as she heard a rustling movement at the edge of the light. A soft pitter-patter sounded. *No – not rats.* She forced herself upright, fighting the next wave of nausea and stood up stamping her feet on the ground, careful to avoid the sickly puddle beside the bed.

Where am I? It looks like a storage room. She looked down at her feet. Her ankles were bound with blue plastic computer cable ties. She scanned the room. It seemed long and was really cold and smelled damp and musty. Along the wall from the foot of the bed was a heavy wooden door. It had an old fashioned round metal door knob and below that an empty key hole.

She blinked a few times. Her eyes were sore and her contact lenses felt dry. She swallowed, trying desperately to calm the panic that was rising, threatening to swamp her.

I have to get my hands free, she thought frantically. A sudden thought came to her. She looked at the bed. It was an old canvas camping bed with a thin grey blanket on one end. Stephanie sat down carefully on the edge, sliding her hands and wrists under her bottom. She kicked her feet up onto the bed and spent the next few minutes wriggling and struggling to curl her legs up and slide her hands down behind them and under her feet. Feeling her calves cramping painfully, she finally succeeded and flopped down exhausted. At least the exertion meant that she was no longer cold and her hands, although still tied, were in front of her. She lifted them to her face and rubbed at her eyes, which only made them feel worse. Her wrists were also tied with blue plastic cables. The sharp edges had cut into her skin and there were little trails of blood running down her arms.

She forced herself to sit up. Waves of nausea struck again. *What is making me sick?* she thought desperately, gulping in large breaths of air, waiting for the feeling to subside.

She looked around. Taking a deep breath she stood and shuffled toward the darkened part of the room. Blinking her eyes to adjust to the gloom, she could make out rows and rows of floor to ceiling shelves that stretched out further than she could see. She shuffled to the first shelf and reached out both hands. Realisation hit her. They weren't shelves, they were racks. She was in a wine cellar. On the edge of each row of racks were nails, some holding cards. To record the names of the wines, she supposed. She looked down the plastic ties – a nail was exactly what she needed to cut through them. Turning her body side on to the first rack, she began rubbing the plastic tie around her wrists back and forward on the edge of one of the nails. After a minute or so, the plastic made a popping sound. She rubbed harder and the tie began to fray and split. *Come on!* she urged frantically, and as she gave a final push, it snapped and her hands came free.

She leaned against the rack, feeling sick again after the exertion and gently rubbed her sore wrists. Footsteps sounded outside the door. Stricken, she bent and picked up the torn tie and a broken nail lying beside it and quickly shuffled back to the bed and lay down, putting her hands behind her back. She had just closed her eyes when the key turned in the lock and the door was flung open. Heavy footsteps entered the room.

Sensing someone looking over at her, she resisted the strong urge to open an eye and peek. Instead she strained to listen. It sounded like just one person. He smelled strongly of cigarette smoke and sweat and his breathing was slightly laboured, as though he had been running.

Obviously satisfied that she was still unconscious, the person retreated and the door closed, key turning to lock it again.

She lay quietly for another few minutes, gathering her energy and courage to get up again. She thought about her father and wondered if he knew she was missing. Her mother wouldn't, that was for certain, and probably just as well. *Toby* – her heart ached. That sparked another thought – *I wonder how long I have been here? James. He would be looking for me.* The thought gave her strength. She allowed herself a couple of minutes to think about him – the way his lips curled into a smile after he kissed her, the strength in his arms, the passion with which he played his guitar. She tried to remember the song he had written for her, but her head was too foggy to recall any of it. Her heart tightened. There had been so much anger and suspicion between them; she hadn't had a chance to tell him how she really felt. She had to get out of here and see him again.

She eased herself up, this time grateful that her arms were free to help. She pulled her feet up on the bed and started sawing at the tie around her ankles with the nail.

Finally it snapped and her feet were free. Rubbing her throbbing ankles, she left the tie on the bed in case she needed to pretend to be unconscious again and crept over to the door. She put her ear to it, listening for any sound outside. There was silence, apart from the occasional scratching sound from the wine cellar behind her. After several seconds she put her hand gingerly on the door knob. The metal was cold to her touch. Carefully she turned it. It wouldn't budge – locked. Crouching down she peered into the keyhole – there was a large key in the lock from the outside.

Stephanie groaned.

She sat back down on the edge of the bed to think. In the distance a strange thumping noise sounded. It felt like it was coming from above and below at the same time.

She took a deep breath.

Think, Stephanie!

A wine cellar as extensive as this would have to have more than one entrance – I am going to have to go down the row closest to the wall and see if I can find another door, she decided eventually. She shuddered and gathered the courage to walk into the darkness and join the rats.

Chapter 30

The manor was still very quiet when Andy and James arrived. James called out "Hi," as they walked in through the front door, but was answered only by silence. He tried Alex's study door – locked. They walked under the stairs and through the passage way to the kitchen. It was in darkness – Grace had clearly finished for the night.

James flicked his mobile phone open and called Alex again. The call went straight to voicemail – the phone was either switched off or out of range. Next he called Grace. She answered sounding sleepy.

"Sorry to disturb you – I know it's late," he said, "but you haven't seen Alex?"

"No dear, not since this morning," Grace answered. "You could ask your grandfather except he's taken a sleeping tablet, so you won't get much out of him tonight. Can I help with anything?"

"Stephanie is missing." James heard his voice catch. He quickly cleared his throat. "You haven't seen her this evening, have you?"

"No, dear," Gracie said sounding surprised. James could hear her moving in the background. "But I will come right over now."

"There's really no need, Andy's here with me," James said, but he knew she would come up from the gatehouse where she lived with her husband, anyway.

The boys checked the library. There was still an empty dusty square on the wall behind the desk where the van Gogh had hung.

James slipped down the hallway to his grandfather's room. He knocked quietly, and when there was no answer, he turned the door knob and let himself in. The old man was sound asleep. James backed quickly out of the room, so as not to disturb him.

"Let's check his study," James suggested. It wasn't locked and as the door swung open, he gasped. Along the walls were a number of empty picture hooks and the dusty outlines of where paintings had been hung. Cupboards in the room and drawers on the desk were open and several books had spilled from the bookshelves.

"Is he always this untidy or have you been burgled?" Andy asked.

"I don't know," James said slowly, "But I would really like to know where the hell Alex is – this doesn't look good, does it?" He turned to his friend uncertainly.

"No, dude, it doesn't," Andy had to concede.

They closed the door on the mess in the study and went upstairs to James's bedroom. James called Alex again. And again it went straight to voicemail. This time he left a message: *Alex can you give me a call? It's urgent.*

His next call was to DI Marks to check in. There was still no sign of Stephanie and anxiety levels were rising as time passed. The police had been methodically going through every angle of Stephanie's disappearance, although the discovery of her bloodstained car had put an extra urgency into the search. A team had been dispatched to search the area surrounding the vehicle. It appeared as if she had vanished into thin air.

James and Andy sprawled on the sofas in James's bedroom and discussed everything that had happened over the previous few days.

"I just feel so helpless," James said, jumping up and pacing the room.

"I know, dude, you and me both," Andy agreed.

"Everything keeps coming back to Alex, but it could be something else entirely. I mean, her father is reasonably wealthy, so maybe she's been kidnapped for ransom or maybe it's just some random event," James said.

"That's looking increasingly unlikely," Andy said. "Especially with Mike in hospital after a hit and run – two seemingly random events is too much of a coincidence in a small village like this."

Grace knocked on the bedroom door a short while later and came in carrying a tray laden with toasted sandwiches, slices of banana cake and a pot of tea. Despite not realising that they were hungry, James and Andy devoured the food, while updating Grace on Stephanie's disappearance. They left out their suspicions regarding Alex.

"Do you know if Grandfather has been changing things around in his study?" James asked. "It's awfully messy, which is unusual for him."

"No, dear – although Alex was in there earlier today looking for something," Grace replied frowning.

"Do you know what?" James said.

"No – but if he's made a mess I'll have a few words to say to him. You know how your grandfather likes everything to be in its place," Grace said as she gathered their plates. "Let me know as soon as you have news on Stephanie."

Shortly after she had left, the boys heard the crunch of tyres on the driveway outside. Andy jumped up and looked out James's window. It was dark outside, but the light from the downstairs windows spilled across the driveway, casting ghostly shadows. Andy saw two dark cars pull up, their headlights switching off as they came to a stop in front of the house. The driver and front seat passenger, tall, heavy set men indistinguishable in their dark clothing, leapt out as soon as the car had stopped and opened the rear doors of the vehicle to allow the backseat passengers to alight.

Andy beckoned for James to join him at the window. Four men got out of the second car. Two took up positions either side of the front entrance and two walked away from the house to the edge of the garden. The boys ducked behind the curtains out of sight as the men donned night vision goggles and scanned the house.

"What the hell is going on?" James said confused. "I don't recognise any of them from Steph's place."

Movement at the first car drew their attention. The two backseat passengers, one carrying a briefcase, were walking towards the front door. It was difficult to see in the shadowy driveway, but they were both wearing suits and from his walk one appeared older than the other who followed slightly behind, nervously looking about him.

"Come on," James whispered to Andy. "Let's see who it is." They sprinted along the passage from James's room to the top of the main staircase just in time to see Alex ushering the two suited men into his office.

"Where did he come from?" Andy asked quietly. James

shrugged, equally perplexed.

The second man turned his head slightly, looking back into the foyer, just before Alex closed the door. James gasped. It was Sam.

Chapter 31

"What the hell is Sam doing here?" James said. "He works for Steph's dad."

Two men remained just inside the front door talking quietly. They carried themselves with the alert wariness of bodyguards.

James and Andy silently edged back along the passage to James's bedroom and quietly closed the door. James called DI Marks to relay the information on their visitors. He put his phone on speaker so that Max could hear. There was a brief moment of silence when James said that one of the guys meeting with his brother was Sam Jones.

"Are you sure, James?" Max asked.

"Positive," James replied. "Is there any news on Steph?"

"No. We'll be there in fifteen minutes. Stop them if they try to leave," DI Marks instructed.

"Okay."

James had just clicked his phone off when it chimed signalling the arrival of a text message. James opened it. It was from Michael.

I remember. David says your GF smuggled Germans thru wine cellars under your house. S could be there?

He passed the phone to Andy, so he could read the text.

"Where are the wine cellars?" he asked.

"Haven't a clue – the current 'wine cellar'," James said writing air commas, "is off the kitchen in an air conditioned room. I didn't know there were any others. Although now that you mention it, Stephanie told me that she read that all of these big houses used to have tunnels which led out to the sea, relics from the old smuggling days."

"Do you know if there are any plans or drawings of the house?" Andy asked thoughtfully.

"Dunno. Let's check the library," James replied, leading the way.

The boys left the library door ajar as they searched through a row of cupboards under the bookshelves on one wall.

"Here. What are these?" Andy said, pulling out several rolls of blueprints. They began unrolling them on the desk when they heard voices coming from downstairs.

James went running from the library, leaving Andy poring over the plans.

Sam was standing in the entrance foyer looking up the staircase. Behind him Alex and the other man were shaking hands. The two security guys had taken up position, one at the front door and one bringing up the rear. Alex started leading his visitors to the door, but they didn't notice that Sam wasn't following.

"Back to get ya arse kicked again, Sammy boy," James taunted, slowly descending the stairs.

"Look, it's the gay one from the boy band," Sam scowled at him.

In the distance, James could hear the low thump of a helicopter approaching. He had to stall them.

"Find ya car keys, Sammy?" he asked.

"Piss off and die, you little bastard. She'll see you for the punk you are. And when she does I'll be there to pick up the pretty little pieces," Sam said, giving James a knowing look. James flushed an angry red, clenching his fists at his sides.

Alex cleared his throat and glaring at James, said coldly, "I see you have met my little brother. James, please go back to your room. I will deal with you later."

To his guests he said smoothly, "My apologies, gentlemen. It's been a pleasure doing business with you."

Sam smirked at James's telling off. Hearing the raised voices, Andy had come down the stairs behind James with a roll of plans in his hands.

Alex swept the front door open, ushering the older man through. The sound of cars speeding up the driveway and the flash of headlights greeted them.

"Perfect timing," Andy said softly. The noise from the helicopter was suddenly deafening as it swooped low over the house.

James leapt from the third step at Sam as Alex yelled, "Oh God, James. What. Have. You. Done?" Alex leaned forward and snatched the large art folio that the older man was carrying, and rushed back into his study, slamming the door and turning a key in the lock.

Sam went down hard, with James on top of him. They rolled around the foyer throwing punches at one another, while the older man shouted at his security, "Get into that room and stop him. He has both the money and the painting."

The security men rushed through the open doorway and started trying to force the study door open.

The headlights of at least half a dozen cars appeared around the lake, and the helicopter took another turn over the house.

Outside, one of the drivers dropped down behind the open car door, and pulling a gun took a shot at the swooping helicopter.

From the helicopter, Max Cooper surveyed the scene below. The front of the house was bathed in light from both inside and the headlights of all the vehicles in the driveway. The helicopter banked and turned at that moment, obscuring his view.

Max held onto the handrail above his head and leaned slightly out of the open door of the helicopter. Something whistled loudly past his head and hit the helicopter with a thump. They were being shot at.

"Move," the officer beside him shouted, pulling a semi-automatic rifle from beneath the seat. Max hastily undid his safety harness and slid to the middle of the bench seat, as the officer took his position in the open door and began firing on the cars immediately in front of the house. On his other side and in the front passenger seat of the helicopter the other officers were doing the same. Max sat forward and looked out of the front window. The doors of the cars were open and men with guns were taking shelter behind them and returning fire.

A police car ran off the driveway and rolled towards the lake, its tyres shot out. A man rolled from the driver's seat and lay on his stomach, weapon ready to fire. Max's thoughts drifted to Stephanie. There had been no message from her or from whoever she was with. He prayed that she hadn't somehow gotten mixed up in this. But in his heart, he didn't believe that.

He silently cursed himself for sending Stephanie to the village when he suspected what Alex Knox was up to. Although he knew that he couldn't have factored her getting involved with his younger brother into his plans.

The helicopter passed over the house and banked again for another sweep over the driveway. There was another series of thumps into the metal sides of the helicopter and the pilot came over the headset announcing that he was going to have to put it down, right now.

They landed on the grass beside the lake, behind the police cars that now lined the driveway. Max gingerly jumped onto the grass, running in a crouch position towards a line of trees until he was well away from still rotating blades of the helicopter. "Get down, sir," said an officer who had followed, covering him. Max crouched, his heart racing and breathing rapid.

All around the cracks of gunshots echoed for what seemed like an eternity, but was probably only a minute or so, until one by one they went silent.

A voice called out through the dark night, "Throw down your weapons and stand up slowly." The crash of metal hitting gravel sounded for a few more seconds. Then the sound of feet running over gravel and shouts of "Clear" as each of the security team was disarmed.

Max stayed where he was until the officer guarding him called, "It's all clear, sir." Max took a deep breath, straightened up and followed him towards the house.

Four men were lying face down in front of the house with their hands on their heads, being body searched and handcuffed. Two more sat against a car with blood on their faces and shirts.

"Paramedics on their way," said DI Marks as he stepped forward taking charge. "Secure those weapons," he ordered an officer to his right.

Max continued walking towards the house, where a man in a suit was standing by the open door with two officers holding his arms. Max's steps slowed and his mouth fell open in disbelief as he turned towards him.

"Hello, Max," said Peter Jones.

Chapter 32

When bullets had smashed two of the front windows, James and Andy had taken cover under the stairs. They didn't know (or care) what Sam had done, but once the shooting stopped, James had seen him trying to slip into his grandfather's study and had shoved him hard up against the wall and held him there. Through the open door they could see the police rounding up Peter's security team.

"It's okay, mate. The cavalry have arrived," Andy called. James stepped back letting Sam go, but the look of violence in his eye told him in no uncertain terms what would happen if he tried to escape again.

Sam stood unsteadily, wiping the blood from his nose with the back of his hand. His suit was dishevelled and tie askew. James's lip which had just healed from their last fight had opened again and blood was dripping onto his shirt. He gingerly put a hand to his ribs. He was going to be sore tomorrow.

"What are you doing with my brother?" he asked Sam.

"None of your business," Sam said.

"Actually, I'm beginning to think it might be," James said. He strode over to Alex's door and turned the handle. Locked. He shook it and banged his fist on the door.

"Alex! Open up," he shouted.

There was no answer.

He turned as Max strode into the foyer.

"Have you found her?" he asked.

James shook his head.

"Who? Not Stephanie?" Sam asked. He sat down heavily on the bottom step of the staircase.

"Yes, Stephanie. What do you know about her disappearance?" Max roughly pulled him to his feet, his voice a barely controlled growl.

"Nothing, sir," Sam said, unable to meet Max's eyes.

"Bring Peter in here," Max called through the open doorway to Vince.

Peter was frogmarched back into the foyer.

"You have a lot of questions to answer, my friend," Max said as he held up his hand in a stop motion, as Peter started to speak, "but first things first. Where. Is. My. Daughter?" he finished the sentence shouting.

Peter looked confused and a little wary. "I know nothing of Stephanie's whereabouts," he said slowly.

"Have you asked James here? The last time I saw her, she was disappearing on the back of his bike," Sam spat.

Max gave him a withering look. "A lot has happened since then," he said. He turned back to Peter and said, "I trusted you. Please don't tell me that you are involved with Alex Knox and his shady business deals?"

Peter averted his eyes.

"Dude, I've found it." Andy came bounding down the stairs carrying several large sheets of rolled paper. "These plans are from 1860 and these ones are from 1935 – both show extensive cellars and tunnels with several entrances," he said. He stopped short when he saw the foyer crowded with people. "Ah…"

"Where are the entrances – let me look." James shoved a pile of newspapers off the circular table in the centre of the foyer and helped Andy unroll the plans.

"What's this about plans and cellars?" Max asked impatiently.

James sighed and began to explain, "According to your uncle's memoirs, apparently my grandfather used the wine cellars to smuggle Germans out of Europe before and during the war. We've been talking to Michael, who read part of the memoir and he thinks that maybe whoever Alex has working for him may have Stephanie hidden in those cellars. Trouble is, I have lived here all my life and I don't know of any tunnels or cellars beneath the house," he said.

"Speaking of grandfathers – where's yours?" Max asked. "I have a few questions for him. Surely he must have heard this commotion?"

"You would think. But he's not well and takes a sleeping pill each night, so chances are he has slept through it," James replied.

Max looked long and hard at Peter, who continued to shake his head and held his hands in front of him, backing away from Max, until he ran into the solid form that was Vince.

"Were you involved with just Alex or the old man too?" Max asked.

"Just Alex, but I was of the understanding that the old man was happy to let Alex do all of the negotiating," Peter said.

"Huh – you mean Alex steamrollered him – he's old. He doesn't know what day of the week it is half the time," James hissed.

"Where is Alex now?" Max asked.

"He's locked himself in his study," James spoke up, wiping blood from his lip with the back of his hand and pointing at the closed door to Alex's study.

"Vince?" Max indicated toward the study door with his chin.

Vince rattled the door handle. Still locked.

"Marks?" Vince signalled to the detective who had just walked into the foyer. Together they shoulder-charged the door. Apart from a slight splitting sound, it didn't budge.

Vince reached into the pocket of his jacket and removed a roll of fabric. Inside were several long metal objects a little like crochet hooks. Crouching down he inserted two into the lock on the door and twisted. There was a click and the lock sprung open.

"Handy skill to have," Andy commented dryly to James.

Holding their guns aloft, Vince and Marks took up position either side of the door. Kicking it wide open, they stepped inside and swept the room with their guns pointed. The study was empty.

"Clear," Marks called.

"Clear," Vince agreed after checking behind the large leather chesterfield sofa.

"Where is he then? Gone out a window?" demanded Max.

"No. They are all locked from the inside," Marks called after checking.

Max turned to James.

"Any ideas – he can't have just vanished into thin air," Max said.

James shrugged, at a loss to explain the disappearance, as Andy called out from the foyer. "James – look at this. Does this mean a tunnel entrance?"

James jogged to Andy's side and together they studied the plans.

"Mr Cooper," James called. "Can you take a look at this?"

Max examined the plans, running his finger lightly over the parchment. "This looks like steps down here and here," he said. He pointed to the edge of an internal wall in Alex's study and also from the sitting room on the opposite side of the entrance foyer.

"Are you sure that your grandfather is not able to help us with this?" Max asked James again.

"No, sir," Grace spoke up. She had appeared at the bottom of the stairs in her dressing gown with her husband beside her. "You'll be getting nothing from him 'til morning. I've just checked and he's sleepin' like a baby," she said.

Max raised his eyebrows at James questioningly.

James nodded. "Yeah, I know it looks convenient. But it's true. This is our housekeeper Grace and her husband Ken," he added introducing them.

DI Marks and Lt David joined them in the foyer. They had been listening to the conversation and leaned over to study the plans. "Okay, then let's investigate this set of stairs," Marks said. He pointed to the ones marked on the map in Alex's study.

"Okay," said James. "But there's no doorway or anything in there that I have ever seen."

DI Marks signalled to two uniformed officers and gave them instructions on looking for a doorway or even trap door. Andy and James joined in the search. While the police officers shifted Alex's desk and lifted the rugs that were beneath it, James and Andy ran their hands along the gaps in between the bookshelves looking for a doorway.

There was nothing.

"It must have been bricked up years ago," James concluded.

Andy stood back, studying the bookshelves. He walked over and started pulling out books and stacking them on the floor. James watched him for a few seconds and then joined him. They emptied the top two shelves and stood back looking at it.

"I dunno, mate," James said. "This looks like a really solid bookcase; he wouldn't have moved it in a hurry, especially loaded with books."

"Let's try one more row," Andy suggested, reaching for a large art history volume in the centre of the shelf. There was a loud click as he started to remove it and the whole bookshelf started moving. It swung outwards and he had to leap backwards to avoid it crashing into him.

The two boys peered behind it. There, cut into the wall where the bookcase had been, was an opening and a brick staircase leading down into darkness.

Chapter 33

Stephanie took a steadying breath and edged her way along the wall into the darkness. The cold seemed to shroud her, causing goose bumps to break out along her arms, and a sweet musty smell hit her nostrils. Ahead in the gloom, she could hear little scurrying feet and she suppressed a shudder. Keeping the fingers of one hand trailing lightly against the wall, she took a few more tentative steps, desperately trying to get her eyes accustomed to the dark. *This room is much bigger than it appears.*

Suddenly, the key turned in the lock and the door flew open. She froze, her heart threatening to hammer out of her chest, as Alex strolled calmly into the room. He paused and swore as his gaze passed over the empty bed.

"Where are you, Steph? Do I have to come and find you? Is that what you want? A little game of hide and seek?" he asked mockingly. "What does the winner get?" he continued, his voice turning cold and menacing. "You won't get away and when I'm gone, no one will find you."

Stephanie looked around, terrified. There was nowhere to go, except further into the darkness. She could sense Alex stalking towards her. There was nothing for it – she had to run. She plunged into the darkness until, hands in front of her, she crashed into a wall. Turning to her left, she caught sight of row upon row of narrow shelves stretching across into the darkness. Quickly skirting along several rows, she raced down one of them, hoping that Alex hadn't seen which one she had selected. Unfortunately he had. Glancing over her shoulder, she could sense him gaining on her. A break in the shelves appeared on her right and she took it, immediately doubling back towards the far wall again. Her eyes had adapted to the gloom and this time she saw the end wall before she came to it. She quickly skipped along two rows and paused, hiding.

Alex had stopped running too.

Oh, hell, she thought, desperately listening for any sound. A scuff to her left and she started running again, back towards the light. Footsteps sounded behind or maybe they were beside her? She wasn't sure. The drum beat of her heart threatened to drown out all other sounds.

"Come on, Stephanie. You know you can't outrun me," he taunted. She halted again, but didn't reply. His voice gave her an indication of where he was – in front, somewhere. Abruptly she changed direction and tiptoed across another two rows. The cellar was vast, but the racks were empty. Weaving her way among them, she reached the final row, which was filled with wooden crates.

Maybe I could hide in one? she thought, but immediately dismissed the idea – *I would be trapped.*

Creeping slowly back towards the light, she used the crates to duck behind, every few steps.

"Well, you just make yourself comfortable down there, while I finish packing," Alex called amiably from the alcove at one end of the cellar. He set his powerful flashlight down on the floor, illuminating the rows.

Stephanie pushed herself between the crates, out of sight. *I wonder what's in all of these crates?* The crate nearest to her had been broken open. Curious, she peered inside. A skull peered sightlessly back at her.

She screamed and scrambled backwards.

"Oh, I forgot to tell you that you were sharing a room," Alex called, laughing. "They pissed me off too, you know," he added, menacingly.

They? Stephanie gulped and started running, zigzagging in and out of the shelves until she was back on the far side of the room. Terror filled her and she struggled for breath. The nausea seemed worse again and she crouched down against the wall, trying to calm herself.

Keep moving, Steph.

Creeping silently forward, she peeked through a gap in the racks and watched from the shadows as Alex lifted up a tarpaulin and pulled out a large backpack and two suitcases and placed them by the door. He crouched, sorting through a large box on the floor. *This is my chance*, she thought.

Taking a deep breath, she started running towards the open door. As she passed through the doorway, she saw Alex straighten and turn towards her, his arms outstretched.

"Come back here, you little bitch," he shouted.

She was so busy looking back over her shoulder to see where he was, that she wasn't watching where she was going.

"*Ooomph.*" Her breath was knocked out of her as she ran into a solid mass. She felt her arms trapped and looked down to see large weathered hands holding her, vice-like. Turning her frightened gaze upwards, her eyes met those of a tall, heavy set, unshaven man. He smiled, smothering her with sour breath from a mouth missing several teeth.

Terror took over. "James!" she screamed before a hand clamped over her mouth.

* * *

"Did you hear that?" James peered down into the darkness. He could have sworn that he heard Stephanie scream his name in the distance somewhere below his feet. Jeez, maybe he was hearing things now. Andy shook his head, he hadn't heard anything.

"Where are those bloody torches? Hurry up," he shouted impatiently over his shoulder.

"Grace's gone to find some," said Andy.

"Arrgh," James muttered, frustrated. "I'm sure my phone will give enough light. Come on," he said, as he pulled his phone out of his jeans pocket and switched it on by touching the screen. He quickly found the flashlight app.

"Right behind you, dude," Andy said, also pulling his phone out. Together they gingerly descended the stairs.

* * *

"Whadda ya wanna do with her?" the man said to Alex, who came running out of the room after her.

"She has caused me no end of problems, give her to me," he said. "You take care of the bags."

Alex pulled her roughly from the man. She tried unsuccessfully to bite him as his hand replaced the other man's over her mouth. He dragged her, struggling, further down the corridor. She dug her heels into the dirt floor trying to slow him down, but he was really strong. He threw her heavily into the wall, momentarily dazing her while he struggled with the rusty slide bolts on the top and bottom of a door that appeared to be cut into the brick. Stephanie briefly saw blackness at the edge of her vision and put her hand to her head feeling a trickle of blood from her temple.

Glancing back over her shoulder, she saw the big guy shake his head and disappear into the wine cellar.

"Alex," she said sweetly, straightening up and using his arm to balance.

He paused, surprised at her tone, a frown creasing his face.

Putting her other hand on his opposite shoulder, she pulled herself upright and using his arms for extra leverage, quickly raised her knee, slamming it into his groin.

"Arrgh," he gurgled, doubling over in pain. As his head lowered, Stephanie punched him hard in the jaw, sending him sprawling into the wall.

Two brothers, two days, she thought ironically, shaking her bruised hand, as she began running down the tunnel towards the light.

"Stop her," she heard Alex shout.

Heavy footsteps pounded after her, but this time she didn't make the mistake of looking back. As she rounded the corner in front of her, the tunnel abruptly ended.

Chapter 34

James and Andy crept cautiously down the steps – fifteen in all, until their feet landed on a dirt floor. The light from their phones illuminated a tunnel stretched out into the darkness in front of them. The low roof curved over them.

"What can you see?" Max called down from the study.

"Not much. It looks like a tunnel, built into the foundations. We need those torches," James called back, irritated at the delay.

"Vince is just getting some from the cars," Max said. There was a pause. "Here he is."

"Let me go first, boys – Alex is probably armed." Vince came down the steps, followed by two detectives, and handed Andy and James a torch each.

"But he's my brother….." James began. He was going to say, 'he wouldn't hurt me', but he suddenly wasn't sure that that was true. After all the beatings he had received at his hands over the years, he knew how spiteful and nasty Alex could be, especially once their father had died and there was no one around who cared enough or was able to protect him.

Vince raised his eyebrows to him and James deferred to the older man and stepped aside.

"Coming, Max?" Vince called back up the stairs.

Max shuddered, peering into the darkness, "No – I'm going to stay here while Marks and Eli question Peter and Sam. But if you find any sign of her – let me know and I'll come straight down," he said.

Vince and the two officers started moving stealthily down the tunnel with James and Andy close behind. At intervals heavy wooden doors were set into the stone walls. They stopped at the first one. The officers took up positions either side of the door with their hands holding both their guns and torches trained on the door as Vince carefully turned the knob. It swung open. Empty.

They moved slowly down the passageway, stopping and repeating the process at each doorway. Some doors opened easily, but others were so tightly shut that it was clear that they hadn't been unlocked in years. The floor of the tunnel was uneven and paved with the same red bricks as the walls and ceiling.

After about fifty metres the tunnel turned sharply to the right, leading away from under the house. As they rounded the corner they could see a dim light. Vince turned and put his finger to his lips and signalled military fashion to the two detectives who spread out, their guns raised. He held his hand in a 'stop' gesture to the boys.

The floor turned to dirt and a cold breeze gently swept through the tunnel. As they inched further along, it became clear that the light was coming from another room.

Silently creeping, they saw that the door was ajar. The officers took up a position either side and Vince entered the room, gun raised. After what seemed like an eternity to James and Andy, he called, "Clear."

They followed hard on the heels of the two officers into an enormous wine cellar. As they shone their torches to the right, it was apparent that it stretched a long way back under the house. To their left, lit by a single hanging bulb, was a small alcove with a camp bed and desk.

"Someone has been here recently," Vince said, leaning over the bed and touching something with his fingers.

"What is it?" James asked, an edge in his voice.

"Blood," Vince replied.

Andy cursed. He crouched down beside him, picking up a broken piece of plastic box tie. "Hey, what's this?"

"Not sure," Vince said, but he and the two detectives exchanged a knowing look, one of them pulling a plastic bag from his pocket and carefully placing the tie inside.

James caught the look, a feeling of dread running through him. "Steph's been here, hasn't she?" he said fearfully.

"It looks that way," Vince said as he bent down and picked up a square white cloth from the floor. He sniffed it gingerly. "Ooooh." He threw it hastily away onto the bed, for the detective to bag. "Chloroform – that's how she was subdued. And it looks like it made her ill." He nodded towards the puddle of vomit.

James shivered involuntarily. "Well, where is she then?"

The two detectives did a quick search among the rows of wine racks with their powerful flashlights.

"Vince – I think you'd better look at this," one of them called.

Vince jogged to join him at the far side of the cellar. James and Andy exchanged tense glances and then followed.

The detective was shining his flashlight into a large crate. "Here, help me get the lid off this?"

Vince handed his torch to Andy and started lifting the

broken lid of the crate. Suddenly he stopped and stepped quickly backwards. "Is that what I think it is?" he asked, horror in his voice.

The detective shook his head gravely. "And there's more than one."

James felt his mouth go dry. "Stephanie?" his voice came out in a whisper.

"Old bones," the detective answered, pulling his mobile from his pocket. "We need back up down here."

James gathered his courage and stepped forward to look in the crate, unsure that he really wanted to see discover what was inside, if the look on Vince's face was anything to go by. He tentatively held the edge and peered in. The base of the crate was covered with fabric and scattered bones. But worst of all, two skulls smiled grotesquely back at him.

"Surely Alex wouldn't do this?" he said quietly, not quite believing what he had just witnessed.

"Well, where is he then? I think we need to keep searching – he can't have gotten far with an unconscious girl," Vince said.

**

A farm truck was parked in the entrance to the tunnel. Two men stood leaning against it with their backs to her, smoking and talking in low voices.

It was a clear night, with a full moon which illuminated the landscape. Stephanie knew she had to keep moving and get out of sight. *But where, without being seen?* The sound of footsteps behind her propelled her forward and she dropped and rolled under the truck. It was cramped, dirty and smelly. *Gross.*

Alex came limping out of the tunnel.

She held her breath as his feet came to within inches of her face, inadvertently kicking dust into it. She screwed up her eyes, which watered involuntarily. She didn't dare move to rub them.

"Which way did she go?" he shouted.

"Who?" one of the men asked, pushing himself off the truck.

"The girl," Alex replied, sounding exasperated.

"Haven't seen any girls tonight, mate."

"She can't have got far. Spread out and search. Quickly," he hissed, as they hesitated. "We don't have much time." He turned and jogged back into the tunnel, the darkness immediately swallowing him.

From her prone position beneath the truck, Stephanie saw the two men slowly walk off in different directions, muttering. She crawled out, keeping the truck between her and the men. Glancing across at the tunnel entrance, afraid that Alex would reappear, she could hardly see it. It had been cleverly disguised to look like part of the hillside.

Unbelievable. Now where to hide?

She quickly made her way to a cluster of rocks and bushes to one side of the tunnel and crouched down behind them, just as the men returned from their somewhat rudimentary search.

"Girl? There's no girl here. You don't think he's losing it, do ya," one of the men said chuckling. They resumed their positions leaning against the truck.

Stephanie watched as Alex ran back out of the tunnel, a backpack slung across one shoulder and carrying a large art folio.

Her breath caught. *I hope that's not the van Gogh*, she thought.

"No sign of her?" he demanded. The waiting men shook their heads. Alex spun around slowly in a complete circle, his eyes scanning the hillside. He swore under his breath. The big guy came puffing out of the tunnel behind him, lugging two heavy suitcases which he lifted onto the flat deck of the truck

"Okay. We are out of time," Alex said, glancing at his watch. "She won't get far in the dark."

Alex and the two men climbed into the truck's cab and the big guy hoisted himself up on the back. The truck started and they began driving down the rough track towards the river.

From her hiding place, Stephanie felt a wave of relief flood through her and she let out a long shaky breath. *Jeez, that was close.*

Staying hidden, she watched the truck continue its journey down the hill. Stephanie could just make out the outlines of the hedgerows and stone walls which separated the fields. *Very different from the wire and wooden fenced paddocks of New Zealand farms*, she thought, suddenly feeling a little homesick. The river wound its way down through the valley.

She shivered in the cool night air and wrapped her arms around herself in an attempt to keep warm. Her legs began to cramp painfully. Just as she stood the truck stopped. Crouching quickly down behind the rocks again, she watched as the men got out and began unloading onto something at the river's edge. Her view was obscured by both the distance and the unfortunate position of a group of willow trees. *What are they doing?*

Suddenly a second engine roared to life and a speedboat pulled away from under the trees and raced down the river towards the coast.

Well, you had that all planned out, didn't you, Alex, she thought, standing up and stretching. *Right, I'd better work out where I am.*

She turned around and started laughing. *Of course.* There on the hill behind her loomed Knox Manor.

Chapter 35

DI Marks and Max Cooper sat across from Peter Jones in the drawing room. Two plainclothes officers stood at attention behind him.

"So you're telling me that even though you knew that as a firm we were working with Scotland Yard to follow up the leads on the missing art, you went behind my back to warn Knox?" Max was rapidly losing patience. They had been questioning Peter for half an hour and he was no closer to understanding why his trusted business partner had betrayed him.

"It's not that simple, Max," Peter began.

"I can manage complex," Max said through gritted teeth.

"We have many clients who have a penchant for exclusive art works, Max," Peter said.

"And so you thought that you would do a little side deal. What did you stand to make?" asked Max.

"No comment," Peter said quietly.

DI Marks put his hand on Max's arm, quietening him. "And the name of this client is?" he asked.

"Sorry, no can do. Attorney client privilege," Peter said sitting back.

"We'll see about that," DI Marks replied.

* * *

The boys were still reeling from the macabre discovery when a message was radioed from the house.

The girl has just turned up.

James and Andy looked at one another and raced along the tunnel and bolted up the stairs, arriving in the study at the same moment that Max walked into the room, with Stephanie leaning heavily on him.

She was a mess. Her hair was matted with blood on one side where she had a nasty gash on her temple. One cheek was shiny and bruised and her clothes were dirty and torn. James gave an involuntary gasp and rushed toward her.

She threw her arms around him.

"Thank God," James breathed, holding her close. Over his shoulder, she gave Andy a weak smile.

After a few moments, James led her to the sofa, and sat with his arms around her.

The house was a hive of activity, despite the late hour. Grace appeared in the broken doorway of the study carrying a tray of hot drinks, followed by her husband Ken, his arms full of blankets.

She put the tray on the coffee table and taking a blanket from Ken, placed it carefully around Stephanie's shoulders. "There you are, love," she murmured. James smiled gratefully at her.

"Can we get a paramedic in here?" Max called. He was hovering beside his daughter, stroking her hair, not quite believing that she had just turned up on her own.

"How did you escape? You were in the cellars, weren't you?" James asked.

Stephanie nodded. "Yeah. I got sick of waiting to be rescued, so I just had to do it myself." She gave a shaky laugh.

"Was it Alex?" James asked, quietly.

She nodded. "I'm sorry, James."

"God, no. It should be me who is sorry. I should've realised that he was capable of something like this," he replied, holding her gaze.

One of the paramedics, who had been attending to the wounded gunmen, came running. She crouched down in front of Stephanie.

"Do you want me to move?" James asked. Despite her bravado, Stephanie was leaning heavily on him.

"It's okay. I can work from here," the woman said quietly.

"Now, Stephanie, my name is Carol. Can you tell me where you hurt?" she asked.

"My head and here," Stephanie said, indicating to her ribs. "And I'm really thirsty. Could I have a glass of water, please?"

"Of course – let me look at your hand first," Carol said. The flesh across Stephanie's knuckles was completely scraped away and was oozing blood. Her sleeve rode up as she held out her hands and James noticed the deep cuts that ringed her wrists.

"Steph – how did you do that?" he asked, concern etched into his face.

"She was tied with plastic box ties," Andy explained quietly.

Stephanie nodded remembering. "I sawed them off with a nail, but they had already cut into me, I guess."

"That was clever thinking," Carol said, as she lifted some gauze from her bag and went to work cleaning and bandaging the injuries.

"James, can you hold this against that gash on her head?"

she asked, handing him a square of cloth. Stephanie winced slightly, as he applied gentle pressure.

"Sorry," he said quietly.

Stephanie sat slightly dazed, letting Carol work. She let the relief of finally being warm and safe wash over her.

"She needs to spend the night in hospital under observation," she heard Carol telling her father. "We have no idea how much chloroform she was subjected to. I would expect her to go into shock at some stage, and she will need X-rays on those ribs, she is black and blue."

"Okay – I'll talk to Marks about a police guard on her room – she is not safe until that bastard is found," he said.

"Now, young man. Let me take a look at you?" The paramedic bent over to examine James's lip.

Stephanie turned her head and looked at him properly for the first time since she had been found. His bottom lip had dried blood caked on it.

"It's fine," he waved Carol away.

"Not if you insist on kissing Stephanie and getting more blood on her it's not," Carol said sharply.

He relented and looked apologetically at Stephanie. "Sorry."

She smiled slightly. "I think I'm making more of a mess of you, than you of me," she said indicating her torn and dirty clothes. "How did you split your lip again?"

He hesitated before answering. "Ah, same as before, I'm afraid," he said sheepishly.

Stephanie shook her head and said, "I don't understand."

"I hit Sam and he hit me back," he said quietly.

"Sam?"

"Yeah – there are a couple of developments that you don't know," he said. At that moment there was a commotion outside the door and Sam rushed through followed by two uniformed police officers. His eyes settled on Stephanie.

"Thank God. Why didn't somebody tell me she'd been found?" he shouted.

James stiffened beside Stephanie and tightened his arms around her. She winced as a sharp pain shot through her. James lessened his hold. "Sorry," he murmured.

"What are you doing here?" she asked Sam, confused.

"Yeah, Sammy. Why don't you explain to Stephanie just what you are doing here?" James said, sneering.

Sam hung his head. When he looked up again, all trace of swagger was gone from his face and he looked young and uncomfortable. "Long story, but I was working with Dad and Alex," he said.

"What?" Stephanie leapt to her feet, only to find that she was hit by a wave of dizziness, causing her to sway. James caught her as she was about to lose her balance. She leaned heavily on him, but stayed standing.

"Unbelievable! You did this to me? Why?" she asked Sam.

"No. I had no idea that he had kidnapped you. If I'd known, I'd have done everything to stop him," he said, looking at her imploringly.

The look of disgust on James's face intensified. He looked like he was about ready to step forward and punch Sam again. Stephanie squeezed his hand with her good one.

"So you've just been trying to keep me out of the way?" she asked.

"Oh, Steph. It wasn't like that," Sam said, looking ashamed.

"But you were working with Alex?" she asked. "What were you doing?"

"Enough," Peter said as he was escorted into the room. "Glad to see that you are okay," he said to Stephanie. He put his hand on his son's shoulder. "I believe that we are leaving now."

Sam paused in the doorway and looked back over his shoulder at Stephanie. "Sorry," he mouthed. She nodded and looked away.

Vince came back up the stairs from the cellar at that point. He smiled kindly at Stephanie, who had sat back down heavily on the sofa still shaking her head in disbelief. Vince addressed his comments to DI Marks and Max.

"The tunnels lead out to the river. There's been activity at the entrance recently. Lots of footprints and tyre tracks and possibly a boat pulled up on the bank," he said.

"Yeah, I saw a speedboat racing down the river towards the sea, about an hour ago, I guess," Stephanie said.

"Okay. So that explains how he escaped. What about the bodies?" Max asked.

"You mean that skull?" Stephanie asked slowly. She felt James tense beside her.

Vince glanced at Stephanie and said, "Well forensics will need to look, but the bones are really old. Looks like three skeletons."

Stephanie shuddered. "Were they in that crate?"

Vince nodded.

"Ugh," she said shuddering.

"How old is really old?" James asked.

The men turned to look at him. "Hard to say, at least fifty years, if what's left of the clothing is anything to go by," Vince said.

Stephanie and James exchanged a glance.

"What?" DI Marks demanded. "If you two know anything you need to tell us."

"There were rumours about people smuggling, during the war," James spoke up first. "You'll have to ask my grandfather in the morning, but remember that he isn't always completely lucid these days."

DI Marks nodded. "Understood," he said.

Carol walked into the room again. "Okay, the ambulance is ready for you."

"Do I really have to go, Dad? I'd rather stay here," Stephanie pleaded with him.

"No, Steph, they need to run some tests and take some X-rays. James will stay with you. Won't you, James? And there will be an officer on your door at all times. I'll be up to see you later," Max said, putting his arm gently around her. "I am so glad that you are safe, my darling."

The front of the manor was littered with vehicles and lights blazed from the downstairs rooms. Stephanie and James sat silently holding hands watching the scene, as the ambulance pulled away down the driveway and past the lake.

There were still so many unanswered questions.

Chapter 36

When James arrived to collect Stephanie from the hospital on Monday evening, she was chatting to Toby on Skype. Her mother had been really concerned about her adventure, but they were all trying to downplay it for Toby's sake.

"Grandfather has asked to see you," he explained as he helped her into the car. "Are you up to going to my place now or would you rather go home? I've cleared it with your dad either way."

Stephanie smiled at him as he leaned across to pull her seatbelt carefully over her, and tilted her head up to kiss him. "Let's go and talk to him."

"Or we could just go and make out in my room," James suggested wickedly.

"Maybe we could do that after – although you will have to be gentle with me, I'm still pretty banged up." Stephanie winced as the seatbelt tightened across her. The ribs she had broken when her car was forced to stop suddenly were taped, and her face and arms were covered with cuts and bruises.

"Always," James murmured, kissing her again before closing the door and racing around to the driver's side. "Your dad is insisting that you are not left alone until Alex is found."

Stephanie rolled her eyes. "Well, I guess, if you've been assigned the task of babysitter, then it's not all bad."

James's grandfather, Charles, was waiting for them in his study. He looked a shadow of the domineering man she had encountered on previous occasions. His eyes carried a haunted look, and had dark rings under them. James helped Stephanie into a chair. Charles frowned, a look of unease at her discomfort crossing his face.

"I think I owe you some explanations, Miss Cooper," he began clearing his throat.

"Stephanie, please," she smiled at him.

"You recognised my painting – *Painter on the Road to Tarascon*. You are a clever young woman."

She nodded, unsure what to say.

"I was unable to enlist to serve in the war due to a childhood ailment. I am ashamed to say that I was unable to bear my brother Edward getting all the glory, so I decided that I would make my mark on the war in my own way.

"My old friend Karl Hoffman, who was the director at the National Gallery in Berlin, approached me before the war. He was disturbed by the number of art works that were being destroyed by the Nazis. Anything which didn't fit their criteria of what a good painting should be was considered 'degenerate' and burned. He started obtaining as many threatened pieces as he could and hiding them. But when someone became suspicious of him, he knew that his days were numbered and he came to me for help." Charles paused, his eyes distant. "My father obtained passage for him on a merchant ship to Canada, but unfortunately it was bombed and all souls on board lost."

"Oh how tragic," Stephanie said. "Sophie mentioned meeting him, in her diary."

At the mention of Sophie's name, Charles blanched.

"Ah, Sophie." He shook his head sadly. "The first time I saw you here with James, I thought for one irrational moment that you were her, you look so alike.

"She and her brother were friends with Edward and visited here on many occasions during the summer before war broke out, through to the beginning of 1940. By this time, I was working with Hoffman to smuggle as much endangered art out of Germany as we could. Unfortunately, someone got the wrong idea and thought I was collaborating with the Nazis, which drove our work even more underground. I initially had grand plans of involving the National Gallery, but the investigation put a stop to that.

"So my war efforts took a different turn. I was disillusioned and I realised that our proximity to both London and the coast meant that Carlswick was an ideal location for a clandestine black market operation. The art smuggling had given me a taste for excitement so I got involved. Very few people would suspect someone in my position of being implicated in such business. I quickly realised that we could trade in more than just food, cigarettes and booze. I started trading in people – helping those would could afford it, to escape from Europe. Payment was often in the form of paintings and jewellery and other valuables. We had a very successful little operation running for a time.

"The night your aunt died, she came to the house to talk to my mother. Apparently she and Edward were about to elope and she wanted Mother's blessing."

"Did she get it?" whispered Stephanie, a little reluctant to interrupt Charles from his reverie.

He blinked twice, returning to the present and turned his

gaze to her. "I believe so. Sophie had a big smile on her face when she walked out of the drawing room into the foyer that night, but unfortunately, my study door was open and Hoffman and I were bringing a heavy bronze statute up the hidden staircase from the cellar. Sophie, of course, recognised Hoffman and well, I don't know what she thought, but she ran.

"By the time I reached the driveway, she was driving away at speed. I followed in my car only to see her take the corner to the village too fast. Her car skidded on the wet road and slammed into the old oak tree. By the time I got to her it was too late. She was dead."

Stephanie gasped and put her hand over her mouth.

"I didn't run her off the road as David accused, but she was running from me. And like the coward that I was, I left her there for someone else to find the next morning. I didn't think the family would survive another scandal so soon after the last one. Please forgive my cowardice," he pleaded, as tears started rolling down his cheeks. He put his head in his hands.

Stephanie stood and moved gingerly around the desk, putting her arms gently across his shaking shoulders.

"Sshh, it's okay. You've had to live with this your whole life. Of course, I forgive you. It was an accident, a tragic accident," she said, glancing at James who had sat forward in his chair and was staring at his hands, his jaw clenched.

"So where do you think Alex is now, Grandfather?" James voice was cold.

Stephanie frowned at him.

The old man looked up and wiped his eyes on a handkerchief and patted Stephanie's hand. "I have no idea," he replied. "James, don't think too badly of me. Over the years, as the horror of what went on in Nazi Germany came out, I repatriated as many pieces anonymously to survivors and their descendants as I could. But many families I simply couldn't find. Unbeknown to me, Alex found out what I was doing and saw an opportunity to make money through his vast network of antiques clients. He sold several smaller pieces that I didn't realise were missing and then had gotten greedy and decided to sell the van Gogh, despite my fervent protests. The Painter, you see, is special to me. It was the last piece that Hoffman brought to me."

Epilogue

S till digesting everything that James's grandfather had told them, Stephanie and James drove back into Carlswick, stopping at the café. Stephanie scanned the room, her eyes resting on Michael sitting at one end of a sofa talking with Anna, who was perched on Andy's knee at the other end.

"Steph," Anna squealed and jumped up. Stephanie grinned and tentatively returned Anna's hug.

"Ribs," she mumbled, reminding Anna of her injuries.

Michael eased himself up slowly.

"Hi," he said shyly.

"Michael – I'm so glad you are alright. I feel so bad that I got you involved with this," Stephanie said.

"S'okay," he mumbled, embarrassed. She put her arm around him and hugged him to her carefully. He blushed bright red.

"Steady on there, Michael. You know what I'm like where Steph is concerned," James called from the counter, where he was ordering coffee.

They all laughed as Stephanie and Michael helped each other to sit on the sofa.

"I think we should just sit back and enjoy letting the 'rock god' wait on us," she stage whispered to him.

"Heard that," James called.

Stephanie looked around the café. Dave, Liam and Jack were setting up in the corner. Groups of teenagers were beginning to congregate. It was a typical summer's night. She sighed contentedly at the normality of it all.

Max's involvement had finally become clear. A Jewish group had engaged his firm to prosecute a European businessman who was trying to sell stolen art on the black market, several years earlier. Their success had drawn the attention of Scotland Yard's art theft division, who, after realising that Max Cooper's family home was in Carlswick, had shared a long-held suspicion regarding the legitimacy of Alex Knox's business dealings.

Stephanie's photo was the only tangible evidence of the painting.

"This painting was believed to have been destroyed when the Allies bombed Berlin in 1944," DI Marks had explained to her. "This is such an important piece with historical significance that you have rediscovered. I am hugely impressed with your research skills."

Ellie Cooper had spent the week pronouncing to anyone who would listen that she had been right about that family all along.

Peter and Sam were still being questioned by Scotland Yard, with various charges pending, although it was clear that neither of them had anything to do with Stephanie's kidnapping. That appeared to be solely the work of Alex and his unknown accomplices. Peter's motive, it seemed, was greed.

Alex had disappeared off the face of the earth with a number of extremely valuable items in his possession, including the van Gogh, whose frame was found smashed in the cellar. James and his grandfather had catalogued what they believed was missing from the house, including more paintings, some rare books, small sculptures and jewellery.

Grace came forward with her mother's wartime diary, which detailed the sad story of the Jewish family who made it out of Germany only to die in the cellars of Knox Manor, despite her and Charles's best efforts to nurse them. Unsure what to do with bodies, amidst the continued fallout from the collaboration investigation, they had sealed them in one of the old storage rooms off the wine cellars.

James placed Stephanie's coffee on the low table beside the sofa. She smiled warmly at him. "Thanks. Hey, I was just thinking. Has anyone seen Victoria? She might know something of Alex's whereabouts," she said.

"No one has seen her for several days," said Andy. "Although according to her mother, she will be back in the village on Friday."

"That's great – because she might let something slip about Alex. She doesn't know we saw them together, James," said Stephanie, sitting forward on the sofa.

James hesitated for a moment. "Actually, she does know," he said.

Stephanie raised her eyebrows.

James looked uncomfortable and studied his feet for a moment. "Um, that night that we saw them, I went back to the house and confronted them both," he said.

"Oh." Stephanie nodded slowly.

Anna glanced between them in the uneasy silence that followed. "Okay," she said brightly to Andy, jumping up from his knee and pulling him to his feet. "Get up there and play for me."

James looked into Stephanie's eyes with raised eyebrows, concern etched into his features. *We okay?* he seemed to be asking silently. She held his gaze and smiled at him. The intimacy was too much for Michael, who cleared his throat and shuffled uncomfortably. James leaned down and kissed Stephanie on the lips. "I'm watching you," he teased Michael, before sauntering over to where the rest of the band was waiting for him.

Stephanie sat back in her seat and let the music wash over her, stolen art and runaway thieves far from her mind.

Halfway through the second song, her mobile phone chimed with an incoming message. She picked it up off the coffee table and flicked it open. The sender was unknown, but the message very clear;

Don't get too cosy with my little brother – this isn't over.

Acknowledgements

My eternal thanks and *aroha* to my husband Craig, and my sons Jude, Zak and Scott. This book wouldn't have happened without your support and encouragement.

Love and thanks to my parents, Jack and the late Irene, who instilled in me my love of books. I miss you every day, Mum.

My gratitude goes to the Writer's Workshop UK, for their editorial support, particularly to Philip Womack for his helpful suggestions. Huge thanks to Julia Gibbs for proof reading and to Jessica Bell for the amazing cover.

Thanks to my wonderful friends for their encouragement and all those essential coffee breaks.

And finally, a big thank-you to you, my readers. I know many of you are enjoying the exploits of Stephanie, James and their friends, just as much as I am enjoying writing them! If you would like further information about me or my books you can check out my website at www.slbeaumont.com or join my Reader's Group to be kept up to date about up-coming book launches and exclusive giveaways and competitions.

A Note from the Author

Did you enjoy this book?

Please consider leaving a review on Amazon. As a writer, it's critically important to get reviews.

Why?

You probably consider reviews when making a decision whether to try a new author – I know I do. Reviews also help indie authors like me gain exposure for their work and get advertising opportunities.

So if you enjoyed the book, and would like to help spread the word, I'd be so grateful if you could leave a review (as short or as long as you like) on the site where you purchased it and don't forget to tell your friends.

Thank you so much!

SL